SANTA MONICA PUBLIC LIBRARY

I SMP 00 2446518 F

D0398335

SANTA MONICA PUBLIC LIBRARY

APR − − 2015

LINCOLN'S BODYGUARD

LINCOLN'S BODYGUARD

A NOVEL

TJ TURNER

Oceanview Publishing
Longboat Key, Florida

Copyright © 2015 by TJ Turner

FIRST EDITION

All rights reserved. No part of this book may be reproduced in any form
or by any electronic or mechanical means, including information storage
and retrieval systems, without permission in writing from the publisher,
except by a reviewer who may quote brief passages in a review.

This book is a work of fiction. Names, characters, businesses, organizations,
places, and incidents either are the products of the author's imagination or
are used fictitiously. Any resemblance to actual events, businesses, locales,
or persons, living or dead, is entirely coincidental.

ISBN: 978-1-60809-143-0

Published in the United States of America by Oceanview Publishing
Longboat Key, Florida

www.oceanviewpub.com

10 9 8 7 6 5 4 3 1

PRINTED IN THE UNITED STATES OF AMERICA

*To Nancy and the three little people (Cheyan, Jia, Sierra)
who share our lives. And to Uncle Fred.*

ACKNOWLEDGMENTS

Writing may be a solitary act, but no writer can go it alone. There is no way I can adequately thank everyone who has inspired, pushed, cajoled, or sometimes kicked me forward to see Lincoln's Bodyguard in print, but I will at least try. This list is by no means exhaustive, and I am humbled by the realization that telling Joseph and Molly's story was truly such a community effort.

First, I must thank my beautiful wife. Nancy taunted me into writing my first novel, not realizing the many nights she would go to bed without me as I stayed up at my keyboard. My children—Cheyan, Jia, and Sierra (Boo)— who all think it's normal for Daddy to spend so much time at the computer. To my parents, Connie and Jim, and my brothers Nick and Erik, who suffered through those early drafts and meandering storylines. I also have to thank Gwyn Sundell for reading many, many drafts, and Basil Blank for testing out the final version. Then there are the readers of the Yellow Springs Wine Sipping Club With a Book Problem who pulled no punches: Jen Clark (and Jason Clark who came for the wine), Karla Horvath, Kathleen Galarza, Eden Matteson, Nan Meekin, Melissa Tinker and Betty Tinker.

The Antioch Writer's Workshop and the Bill Baker Award got me started on this writing career. Thank you Sharon Short, Becky Morean, Lee Huntington, and Wendy Hart-Beckman for helping me fine-tune the story, and Jane Baker and family for establishing the award named after her husband. I also have Col. (ret.) Vic Brown, Carol Callicotte, Jim Satterfield, and Peter Hogenkamp to thank for lending their perspective, as well as Bill Phillips, who pushed me toward writing this story. Thanks also to Maddee James for a fantastic website in an age where authors and social media are impossible to separate.

My amazing literary agent Elizabeth Kracht (Kimberley Cameron & Associates) is the kind of agent who is in it for the long haul with all her writers, honing their craft while she guides their careers. I will be forever indebted to Liz for the guidance and all her hard work. Lincoln's Bodyguard would never have wound up in front of Liz if not for Mary Moore, who read that early draft and believed in the story. Finally, I have to thank Pat and Bob Gussin at Oceanview Publishing for taking a chance on a debut author!

LINCOLN'S BODYGUARD

I expect to maintain this contest until successful, or till I die, or am conquered, or my term expires, or Congress or the country forsakes me.

—Abraham Lincoln

PROLOGUE

Death creeps quietly behind a man. This lesson I learned early in life and, on that April night, the Old Man learned it too. The audience below strained in their seats, desperate to glimpse the President. A single actor held center stage—his monologue bringing laughter, rising till it filled the theatre. The gas lamps issued a constant hiss, luring me toward sleep. And the Old Man reached out to hold his wife's hand, then let go.

As I stood along the back wall, obscured in flickering shadows against dark wallpaper, a noise reached me—the Old Man's messenger talking to someone outside. The far door opened behind us, then closed. Footsteps followed down the short corridor of the vestibule. I readied myself. No need for a pistol at this range. I pulled my knife from its sheath.

I waited as he opened the inner door and closed it, making no sound. He moved past me, placing each foot with deliberate purpose to keep the flooring silent, confirming his motive. Even with his dark suit and felt hat I recognized him, his movement graceful and confident. He was a famous actor, the Hamlet of our day. I had seen him onstage before, other nights when I stood watch behind the Old Man in this theatre. He paused, watching the play over the Old Man's head, like a man standing at a cliff gathering courage to jump.

I should have leapt—cut him down before he had the chance to strike. But I hesitated. When more laughter erupted from below, he drew a pistol in one hand, a knife in the other.

As he lunged I jolted to action. From my position I had the advantage. Grabbing his shoulder, I spun him toward me. With my free hand I gripped his gun while my knife tore through soft tissue, deflecting off bone. I drew him near, locked in a dance. For a moment our eyes met. He had accounted for everything except this. Twisting my blade, I stripped the pistol from his hand.

His eyes lost their focus—dying men see another world.

The audience below knew nothing until he shifted his weight in a final act to reach the President. I guided him past the Old Man, throwing him over the balcony. A spur on his heel caught, snagging a flag decorating the State Box. He tumbled and crashed onto the stage, ripping the Stars and Stripes down on top of him. The play stopped, a collective gasp rose from the audience, and actors scrambled offstage. The Old Man leapt to his feet. I faced him, the pistol in one hand. My other hand still gripped my knife, blood dripping from the blade to the floor.

Death stalked the Old Man in the theatre that night. But sometimes, even Death has to wait.

CHAPTER ONE

I approached the White House slowly, my first time back in seven years. I left after saving the Old Man, after things changed. Washington looked as before, but the feel of the place had shifted. No one loitered or met the gaze of fellow citizens on the street. A cold city—scared. There were rumors of attacks in the heart of the Capital, of daring rebel assaults in broad daylight, meant to terrorize. The papers never reported them, but the rumors circulated, passed by word of mouth until truth and myth were intertwined but unreconciled.

As the sun reached higher the fog dissolved around the White House. The building took shape, a gray mass against the pure white of the mist. Something deep nagged that I should ask admittance and let the walls of the palace shield me.

I took the letter from my breast pocket. My fingers traced the outline of my name.

Feb. 22, 1872

Joseph,

I know much time has passed unspoken between us, but there is something important to discuss. Please, I need you.

—A. Lincoln

Please. The word pleaded through the letter. Maybe I assigned it gravity beyond its intent. *Please.* I tucked the paper back into my breast pocket.

Once inside, my fingers tingled, anticipation mixed with fear. Two soldiers led me down the corridors I knew so well. An air lingered about the place, a scent—musty with the taste of history and power, like the building itself sweat it from the walls. My shoes found the well-worn path, the slight indentation down the middle of the carpet from decades of wear. We walked past closed door-ways, behind which my mind could paint every turn in vivid detail. With my eyes shut I could walk to the Old Man's study, take my post along the back wall, and blend into the dark green wallpaper. I was home.

One of the soldiers showed me inside the great wood door. The room was empty. Two windows laid claim to the far wall, spanning from floor to ceiling. The first framed the Washington Monument. It remained partially complete, the sun blinding off the bleached white stone. During the War, maps plastered these walls, obscuring the wallpaper as they tracked battles and the movement of armies. At times they covered the windows. With-out the maps the place felt empty, but the walls knew the truth.

I walked to the middle of the room, something I rarely did in my earlier days when I preferred a solid structure at my back. The fire hissed, a few pops betraying overly wet wood placed into the flame. A table stood in front of the fireplace, and I ran my fin-gertips over the edge. It hadn't budged in years, the carpet under it more plush and vividly green than elsewhere.

A map covered the wood tabletop, its corners curled from repeated rolling. It showed the South, the land from Richmond and below. Even though the generals had surrendered their swords, the fighting raged on. The War wouldn't give up. Though no longer the boil of '63, she simmered, nine years later. She still claimed lives, and would until the day she died. The Confederates had disbanded their armies to mold themselves into an efficient enemy—small networks of rebels who attacked and then dis-solved into society. Fighting ghosts. Small *x*'s dotted the roads in all directions.

Ambush sites.

"How are you, Joseph?"

I never heard him coming, one of the things I hated about this carpet. Anything could creep quietly behind you.

"I'm fine, Mr. Lamon."

Ward Hill Lamon, the President's right hand. He had always despised me. His body language betrayed him. I had worked for Allan Pinkerton, the famed detective and forerunner of military intelligence, while Ward Hill Lamon was the President's best friend, advisor, and confidant. They competed for the Old Man's loyalties.

"I see the President's note found you. Mr. Pinkerton told us to expect you today."

I played over his intonation in my head, searching his choice of words. He stood more bent, though he still cut an imposing figure. His suit spoke of wealth and power. How a man composes himself and how he dresses tells an immense amount about his status, both real and self-imagined. In this, Lamon had grown more powerful than last we met.

"Will Mr. Pinkerton be joining us?" I asked.

"Not today. We need to discuss matters of great sensitivity, and discretion will be the priority. There are things he doesn't need to know. Do you understand?"

I lied and nodded. Another political chess match.

"Do you know why you're here, Joseph?"

"I received the President's letter. That's all I know."

"When the President arrives, we'll explain the situation. He insisted on having you. It's only proper we wait for him. I'll go check on things."

He turned to leave but then stopped. "Joseph, I don't want to leave you with the wrong impression about Mr. Pinkerton. Someone is reporting to the enemy—a fox in the henhouse, as the President would say. I have long suspected it to be among Pinkerton's people. These things happen, but what we will discuss cannot be compromised. The very life of our nation depends on that."

"My loyalty belongs to the President alone," I answered.

Lamon considered my reply. "Very well. I will not mention it again. If the President trusts you, that will suffice." This time he turned and left. When the door closed, I stood alone.

I turned to the little marks that littered the map in front of me, filling the roadways from Richmond all the way south. Parts of Louisiana and lower Mississippi had a line drawn across them. The country remained divided, the result of a failed surrender. When General Joe Johnston walked from the negotiation table years ago, the Old Man had called it the greatest treason. It surpassed even General Lee or Benedict Arnold. Other rebel leaders followed. Eighty thousand men burned their uniforms and returned to their farms. They melted back into the fabric of the South. But they kept their guns and the country knew no closure.

As I studied the map a younger man entered the room, resplendent in a three-piece suit fashioned from a shimmering cloth. Behind him the Old Man filled the doorframe, pausing to get a good look at me before he walked across the room with the aid of a cane.

"Joseph," he held out a hand after switching the cane. "How we both have changed. I'm afraid that in beauty, neither of us has any more to claim, my friend."

His hand felt frail, the bones barely covered by the tissue paper masquerading as skin. Tall and thin, he towered above me still. I felt like a child. The cane in his hand forced him to stoop—too short for his height. His suit hung loosely, indicating weight lost. His knee-length jacket appeared hollow, his neck gaunt inside the white collar and bow tie. But time had weathered his face the most. The lines were deep and furrowed, as if recently plowed. His beard had grayed, and his hairline retreated. It had only been seven years, but the office had drained him, pulling his very essence from the shell of his suit.

"It has been too long." He motioned for me to sit at the table with him as the younger man circled the room and stood along the back wall, like I had done for years. Lamon entered the room and closed the door behind him. He joined us at the table.

"How is your mother?" The Old Man asked.

The question caught me by surprise, amazed at how far her influence spread. In retirement she had become famous, articles published on her exploits, the newspapers using her story to blot out the little marks on the map.

"She is fine, sir, the last I checked. I haven't seen her in a while."

"She was here once, did you know?"

"No." In my mind some worlds were never meant to mix.

"Many of the conductors came, your mother, Harriet Tubman, a few others who risked so much. I hosted a ceremony and a banquet. Several years back now. She told me a few good stories about you. To think, the things you withheld in our time together."

The event would have been bald-faced propaganda arranged by Lamon to mask the sour reports from down South. My mother would cringe if she heard herself called a distraction.

"I hope we find time to catch up, Joseph. But my schedule is worse than ever, and I am sure you are wondering why you are here." The Old Man nodded toward Lamon.

"As you might suspect, Joseph," Lamon began, "the rebellion has grown." He flattened a curled edge of the map. "Some say we are losing. A fight like this is ugly, and even with our best efforts, we have been unable to rid ourselves of it.

"But we have a rare opportunity. A senior member of the resistance wants to end the fighting. The information he has would be devastating for the rebels. We could break them—push the fight out of this stalemate." Lamon swept his hand across the map.

I looked to the President. He held one hand across his chest while the other rubbed his beard.

"Who?" I asked.

Lamon looked to the Old Man before answering. "Norris."

"Colonel Norris?"

The weight of the name caught me off guard. It made me nauseated. I slouched, grateful for my chair, letting it hold my weight. Colonel William Norris had been the head of the Confederate Secret Service during the War, Pinkerton's nemesis. The end of the organized fighting accelerated his rise as leader of a decentralized yet effective resistance. I tried to kill him once and damn near succeeded. His name appeared last on my list—a roster of the men who left my wife for dead and took my daughter to avenge their failed attempt to kill the Old Man.

"He grows tired of the fight," Lamon answered. "I believe his letters and the promises of his envoy to be sincere. He sees the error of this conflict—that nothing will improve until we close this final chapter and move forward."

I looked at the Old Man. He was lost in thought.

"So what do you want from me?"

"He requested you," Lamon's voice was flat.

"Norris did? Why? Last time you sent me to bring back his body," I said.

Lamon provided the list that I had worked from.

"There's symbolism for him. You killed Booth, and Norris planned the attempt on the President. He says he will trust only you."

"Maybe he means to kill me?"

A smile flickered on Lamon's face before he suppressed it. "He's gone to a lot of trouble to convince us he wants to come in. Do you suppose you're so important?"

"No," I lied. But that was exactly what I thought. Years ago I had made a deal with Norris—a deal to spare my daughter. Unable to do what he asked, he would want me dead for my failings. "Even if I agree, how am I to find him?"

"He provided meeting instructions. You will take Baxter with you," Lamon said.

"Baxter?"

Lamon motioned to the young man standing along the wall. "Mr. Winston Baxter, the President's security advisor."

The suggestion surprised me. I glanced at the man in the shiny suit standing against the bookcase. He was almost ten years my junior and far too confident for his age. Proximity to power can have that effect. The light material of his suit shimmered, the cloth likely from Europe. Polished leather boots extended under the pleats in his trousers, and his slicked-back hair lent an oily appearance.

"I work by myself." I turned toward the Old Man.

"Absolutely not," Lamon answered. "You have a history with Colonel Norris, and we cannot run the risk of that past getting in the way of what needs to be done. You'll forgive me, but the stakes are too high to trust this matter to you alone. You'll take Baxter. He knows the particulars of finding Norris. There is no room for compromise on this."

"Why would I take someone of such little..." I paused, trying to find a word that would somehow diminish Baxter and Lamon alike, "...experience."

Lamon smiled. "You and Baxter are quite alike. He is young, but not green. You will find him a hard customer, with more starch than one his age should lay claim to."

Baxter stood motionless along the bookshelf—a complacent look on his face. A partner would make killing Norris that much harder.

"And if I say no?"

The Old Man reached out and placed his hand on my arm. "Please, Joseph. This is my chance to end this. I had so long planned to leave after my second term, like Washington himself, or Jefferson. But I promised I would not step down until the country was whole. I came in with this mess, and I will see it done right. I fear that with my stubborn disposition and with Congress refusing to impose limits on the office, I may never leave unless something helps us end this war."

I avoided his eyes. They would remind me of my dying wife as I held her, and of Aurora, the little girl stolen from me and, if still alive, old enough that I might not recognize her.

"Fine."

"Good," Lamon said. "You will leave tomorrow morning. Baxter will guide you to the meeting, and then you'll both escort Colonel Norris to Washington. If there are no issues, we'll have his sword this time next week."

"Thank you, Joseph," the Old Man said.

Lamon stood and placed a hand on my shoulder. "We need Norris *alive*." His voice lingered on that last word. "That's why Baxter goes with you tomorrow."

I nodded, though I would never let Norris speak of our arrangement to save my daughter. Lamon headed toward the door, leaving me with the Old Man, who struggled to rise. I helped him to his feet.

"It is so good to see you, Joseph. I'm afraid I have a cabinet meeting. But you will stay the night." The Old Man looked to the door and Lamon. Baxter held it open, not looking in our direction. When they were out of earshot, the Old Man lowered his voice. "We will visit later. There is another purpose for my letter."

CHAPTER TWO

Baxter escorted me to my old bedroom. It was redecorated as a guest room. Hot water filled a bathtub in the corner, and I stripped, anxious to wash days of travel from my body. The heat penetrated to my core. I fell asleep, only waking when the water cooled beyond comfort. A set of fresh clothes hung in the small closet, nothing extravagant like Baxter's suit, but better than what I had relied on to get me to Washington. I changed and fell back on the bed, slipping into a deep sleep. I didn't wake until late in the afternoon.

When I stirred, I found a tray perched on the bedside table with a half-filled bottle of whiskey and a glass—Pinkerton's whiskey. Lamon had excluded him from the meeting, but he knew how to look after me. He also meant the bottle as a message. Sooner or later I would have to face him. After Lamon had handed me the list with Norris' name, Pinkerton had counseled a more subtle path. But with my daughter gone and my wife dead, his influence proved of no avail. Revenge robbed my sanity. He would be upset with me still, so it would be best to visit when he least expected it, especially since they had taken my weapons when I entered the White House. I filled the glass and downed my first drink. It had been hours since my last, and my hands were beginning to shake.

To pass the time I unpacked my bag, filling my flask from Pinkerton's bottle to ensure a supply for the road. I refilled the glass and packed a second set of clean clothes. Putting the bag away I pulled out a small black velvet pouch, the only possession other than my knife that I cared about. Living light made life easier. In a hurry, I had little to leave behind. Even as the years passed, I hadn't collected many possessions—or friends. Habits were hard to break.

I dragged a chair to the one small window and pulled at the strings of the velvet bag. I rarely opened it, only in those sparing moments I wished to remember Aurora. Releasing the drawstring, I upended the bag into my hand. A silver necklace fell out—the evening sunlight caught the polished edges. A small pendant dangled on the chain, a tiny and amazingly detailed eagle's feather. My stepfather had been a silversmith, an incredible artisan. He tried teaching me his craft, but my hands were better for coarser tools, like a Bowie knife. He was a progressive man who took in a pregnant Indian woman, and after I was born, he molded me with his fiery dinner table orations. He preached extreme abolitionist views that he kept none too hidden. They would eventually account for his death. But he drilled me on my lessons every day and ensured my education was second to none across the Kansas plains. He intended me to return as a great chief to my mother's people. How wrong he had predicted my destiny.

The feather nearly floated in my palm, as if it might catch the draft from the fireplace and take flight. I never had that kind of skill, to make something of such fine beauty. If I could, the world would be a different place. I struggled to hold it still as the whiskey had yet to drown the shakes. At one time the feather had a twin, a pair of earrings made for my mother—a reminder of her Miami Indian ancestors. With the birth of my daughter, my mother split them up, one for my wife and one for the baby. I only recovered the one around my wife's neck.

Muffled voices filled the hallway outside and then a soft knock rapped against the door. I put the necklace back in its bag, and the bag in my pocket. Even after so long, I tried never to think about it. *Please*—the last word my wife had said to me as I held her, the memory of her face lost to me. Little wonder I didn't resist the Old Man's letter.

I started across the room when the door opened and the Old Man stepped in. He glanced down the hallway before closing the door behind him. Things had changed. The king had to slink about his castle.

"I'm sorry to barge in, Joseph."

I stood and motioned him to the chair by the window. "It's not a problem, sir." I offered my poured drink. "I have only one glass."

"Oh, no. It does not sit well with me."

He sat and rested his cane between his legs—both hands clutched the curved handle. The War rode heavy on him.

The Old Man broke the silence after looking around the room. "Sometimes I feel a visitor in my own house, like I came for a dinner party, and they never asked me to leave." He laughed while staring at the floor.

"It's time for that quiet cabin you always talked about—woods nearby, a stream to fish in, birds in the spring."

"I'm afraid even those good dreams leave me to my solitude." He paused, his stare piercing and unbroken. "Sometimes I believe I would accept the bad ones, if only for the company."

During the War, the Old Man had strange and disturbing dreams of his death. He saw them as a message—from the Great Spirit perhaps—showing his eventual demise and the reason for it. His was to be the last death in our War—a noble sacrifice to end the nation's suffering. By saving him, I had stolen his place in history.

"Joseph, I know there are plenty of things we should talk about, but I asked you here because you are the only person I can trust." He sounded unsure of himself.

"I came to help."

The Old Man nodded. "That's why it has to be you. This business with Norris is not why I wrote to you. I used it merely as a decoy to bring you here."

"Lamon knows nothing of this?"

"No, and he must not. Do you understand?"

"No, I don't. But I have no love for Lamon."

The Old Man stood and turned to the window. "This job is not what it once was. The lines were clear when the armies faced one another. But now there is no righteous path. I have been south on many occasions, trying to broker a lasting peace. It always shatters. Stronger forces than I benefit from the fight. I'm afraid this will never end."

"But Lamon thinks Norris' surrender will finish the rebels."

He turned toward me. "There is so little I am certain of anymore. But I am convinced that Colonel Norris does not intend to surrender. But that is not why I wrote you. My request is personal."

"Sir, I would do anything."

"I know that, Joseph." He leaned on his cane as he once again labored to sit in the chair. "I never thought I would still be here. I had hoped the War would die with me, that I could at least see the country through it. Now this job is so lonely, almost a sentence to endure. After you left and Mary passed from the fever, I had no company. There is Lamon, but he has charted a course that will tear this nation apart, and I am mostly powerless but to watch it unfold. This War has been so evil, Joseph. It takes good men and turns them wicked— all the fighting, the death. Lamon was a good man, but I fear what he has become."

"The Draft," I whispered.

The Old Man's eyes narrowed, then relaxed. I had touched upon something deep.

"I lay no claim to that idea. I detest it." His words were flat. He understood the extent of Lamon's twisted logic. The Draft started during the War to swell the Union ranks with fresh soldiers. As the fighting subsided, the Draft Board adapted. The states below the Mason-Dixon Line were desperate for reconstruction, but needed skilled labor. Congress passed a modernization act, part charity, part reconstruction, and ultimately part retribution. Children of Confederates were shipped north to work the factories. The more important the Confederate family, the more children the Draft took. At first, it was just the older children, but the factories were ever hungry, and children as young as five had small fingers to work the textile looms. They were supposed to learn a new trade and bring those skills home when they returned. But they never returned.

"I can't stop it, Joseph. Congress overrides anything I veto. I can't save everyone. And if I step aside, I fear what will happen. Lamon has powerful backers. It takes all I have left to keep them in check. I am a prisoner of circumstance."

An uncomfortable silence filled the space between us. Finally, he spoke again.

"There is a young woman, Joseph. I need you to bring her to me, deliver her safely."

"Who is she, sir?"

The Old Man looked to his shoes as if they held the answer. "She is no one, and yet, she is everything. I did not intend it to happen. I see her but a week a year..." He turned away, twisting in the chair. "I do fear what you'll think of me."

I pictured Aurora in her blue dress. "I am no one to judge."

"She is much younger than I, younger even than you." A seriousness descended over him. The War had extracted his dry wit, his last line of defense against the ever-increasing demands of a nation.

"It's not entirely what you think. This woman, she is...," he stopped to think. "I have only one son left. Robert is bright and ambitious, but we are very distant. The boy so loved his mother. They were infinitely closer. But this girl, she feels like...," he paused, "she is family."

"Where do I find her?"

"At a resort, the same place we have the Peace Summit each year. The island south of Savannah."

I had left long before the summits began—yearly meetings designed to heal the wounds of the nation. The President met with Southerners who had no power to influence the rebels. They were propaganda, set in a beautiful playground for rich Northern industrialists, many of whom built winter retreats among the old-growth oaks covered in Spanish moss.

The Old Man handed me a piece of paper. I unfolded it. He had neatly printed each letter of her name—*Annice*.

"This is her?"

He nodded.

"Her last name?"

"She's part of the staff, Joseph. She doesn't use her last name. It came from the plantation where she was born."

I let it sink in—the reason for secrecy, why the Old Man had revealed this to no one else. The man who freed a nation could not bridge the social canyon separating colored from white. A colored mistress would be a scandal beyond all proportions, and if the truth were discovered while she still lived in the Deep South, her life would be forfeit.

"And Lamon doesn't know?"

The Old Man shook his head. "I am not ashamed, Joseph. But you realize what this would mean."

"Yes, sir. Washington won't be much safer. What will you do with her?"

He exhaled deeply. It hadn't entered his consideration, at least not fully. "I don't know, Joseph. I could send her north, where she will be safe. And free. Maybe Canada. I can't imagine what the rebels would do to her if she was discovered."

"And Colonel Norris?" I asked. I had no intentions of doing anything to Norris other than running him through.

He ran a hand over his forehead. "Even if he intended to surrender, I am certain Lamon would not accept it. Other politics are at work, and I am not privy to it all. Despite the office and all the trappings, I do not hold influence as I once did. I can't continue this struggle with Lamon and the masters he serves knowing that Annice is trapped. And if they find out about her, they will use her against me. I can trust no one else. What I ask of you is selfish, but I need this, Joseph. *Please.*"

My task had become more difficult. It would be hard enough to escape Baxter and the South after killing Norris, but it would be impossible if laden with this girl. I had to choose—my revenge, or the Old Man's forgiveness.

"If no one knows about her, I might put her in greater danger," I said. "You've thought of this, sir? Getting her out might be what kills her."

The Old Man shook his head. "If I could leave her to my dreams and, by so doing, she could live her days safely, then I would never have asked you here. It is more complicated than this, Joseph." He paused. "She is expecting, and her child is mine."

CHAPTER THREE

Please. It made sense now. Everyone else would have an agenda when they found this girl. The Old Man needed me. But if I were to head south, I would need more help. I had only one place to turn—Pinkerton.

I escaped the palace that night without difficulty, slipping through the underground tunnels below the White House. Their state of disrepair told me that no one had used them in a long time. Pinkerton's insistence on constant repetitions through these dark passages years ago without candle or lamp proved invaluable, and I arrived on street level certain I had avoided detection. The dim gaslights made the façade of the executive mansion more majestic, suggesting its two stories extended toward the heavens. My eyes traced the stars above, searching out Polaris—my constant guide north those many years on the Underground Railroad. The end of the Big Dipper—or *Drinking Gourd* as all runaways called it—pointed to the North Star.

Without my knife and pistol I had only my fists for defense. I took a drink from my flask to keep them steady. The crisp night air and the cobblestones were a relief. Curfew had set, but I knew the city well. During the War, Pinkerton had made me memorize the streets—even establish an escape network in every neighborhood, places I could flee with the Old Man if it ever came to that. An Underground Railroad for the Presidency, ready and waiting if by chance the Confederates broke through the ramparts. Despite the years, that knowledge served me well as I slipped past the checkpoints.

Pinkerton made his home in a nondescript brick building undistinguished from every other house on the street, protecting him and the secrets he collected. At the front of the house a few gas lamps illuminated arcs of light into the street. A man sat in a small central park. He pretended to sleep, slouched on a bench.

But he scanned the buildings with regularity—a front lookout. I tried the back, sticking to the shadows.

Another guard stood at a rear door down a narrow alley. Pulling my flask from my jacket, I poured some of the whiskey on the front of my clothes. I stumbled down the alley in the manner of a happy drunk. The guard watched my approach, his right hand dropping to his side. He unlooped the hammer of his pistol, the first step in freeing the weapon from its holster. I shuffled, stopping at the side of the house to let my trousers loose and piss on the corner.

"Hey, out of here!"

He came down the steps, and I spun to face him, my pants still down, piss spraying. He stepped back to miss the arc. I made sure not to get him wet—I didn't want him throwing the first punch.

"You bastard." He minded his distance while I finished, his eyes averted, uncomfortable at my nakedness.

"Just a minute," I slurred. I fumbled with my trousers, making a struggle of the top button with the flask in my hand. "Hold this."

He took the flask from me, grabbing hold of it with his pistol hand. I finished buttoning my trousers.

"Thanks, partner."

As he handed back the flask, I grabbed his wrist, pulling him toward and past me. I reached down and pulled his pistol. One hard blow with the butt of the weapon and he slumped into the alley. I pulled him up and sat him in the corner by the stairs. Then I unloaded the gun, placing the cartridges into my pocket. I tucked the pistol into the front of my shirt.

A pair of wooden storm cellar doors was built into Pinkerton's house beyond the back stairs. Pinkerton kept a staircase hidden behind a false wall that ran from his upstairs study all the way to the cellar—his route of desperation. But for those who knew of its existence it could be the weakest link in the armor. I crept down the cellar stairs, fumbling in the dark. It took me a moment to recall how to find the door concealing his escape route. The door creaked as I pushed enough to pass through, and the dust in the air told me he hadn't practiced his escape in some time.

I felt my way up the staircase. It hugged the outside wall of the house, barely wide enough for my shoulders. Occasionally, a thread of light slipped through some small crack in an interior wall, but, otherwise, darkness filled the stairwell. I climbed to the second floor, careful to test each stair before it bore my full weight. At the top I stood on a small, two-step landing with a cast iron lever set into the wall. The cold from the metal sunk into my hand when I grasped the lever. I pulled, hoping the latch behind the office bookshelf would release without commotion.

As the lever clicked the door popped open. I pushed, swinging the shelf into the room. Light flowed down the stairs, flickering from a lamp on the desk. I stuck my head through the opening—empty. I pushed the bookcase wide enough to step from behind it.

"Far enough!"

The Scottish accent had waned over the years, but some things never fade. The bookshelf had blocked my view of him until I stepped from its cover. He wore a red velvet smoking jacket tied around his middle, and his hand clutched a small derringer.

"You're late." He kept the gun leveled at me. "And you clomp worse than a horse on a wood bridge, Joseph. I thought Indians were light of foot."

"You sent me all that whiskey. And I'm only half-Indian."

He waved the gun at the bookshelf. "Close that damn thing."

I stepped into the room and pushed the bookcase shut.

"I was beginning to think you wouldn't show," he said.

"You knew I'd come. Were you sitting there waiting?"

"No. I didn't expect you this late, and I rather thought you'd knock like anyone else. Have a seat." He pointed toward a small, leather-bound chair, the desk between us.

As I went for the chair, Pinkerton stepped too close. His

breath stunk of whiskey. I turned and grabbed the derringer from his hand. With my other hand I pulled the pistol from my waistline. I cocked the hammer and pressed the gun to his forehead.

"Sit." I forced him into his chair. "What do you know about Norris?"

"Nothing."

"Don't play games. I'm in no mood to be trifled with." I kept the barrel pressed to his flesh to conceal the empty chambers. "What is Lamon planning for Colonel Norris?"

"I know nothing of Lamon's plans." His voice remained flat.

"You lie."

I pulled the trigger and the hammer slammed forward. A hollow metallic click echoed from the far wall. Pinkerton cringed— his eyes squinted shut. Then they popped open with rage. He started to push up out of the chair.

"Goddamn it, Joseph."

I cocked the hammer, the cylinder indexed to the next round, and I pushed the barrel back to his head.

"The next one's loaded. Now tell me."

"I don't know what the hell you're talking about. Get that thing out of my face." Enraged, Pinkerton swatted at the pistol, but not before I pulled the trigger. Again the room filled with the sound of the metal hammer falling on an empty cylinder. He slumped.

"Bastard!"

He rose out of the chair, but I pushed him down. I cocked the hammer once more, but then thought better of it. I tossed the pistol onto the desk between us.

"It's not even loaded, is it, Joseph?"

"No, but this one is." I pulled his derringer from my pocket and put it at his head.

He started laughing. "That one's not, either."

I hefted the gun in my hand, calibrating it against some known standard tucked in my head. I dropped it on the desk beside the other one and sat back in the chair across from his desk.

"Well, aren't we a pair?" he started. "So what's this business about Lamon?" He reached across his desk and unstopped a whiskey bottle, identical to the one he had sent me. He poured two glasses and slid one across the desk.

"They want to bring in Colonel Norris. Lamon claimed they received letters from him. He wants to end the fight."

Pinkerton shook his head. "Don't believe it. Norris has been killing off my detectives man by man."

"How?"

"He sends some insufferable ghost of a man who taunts my every turn. And Lamon uses my losses to his advantage. I'm expelled from the White House."

"Norris is killing off your people?"

Pinkerton stood. He looked at me as if asking permission. I waved my hand. From a chain around his neck, he produced a key and used it to open the middle drawer of a wood cabinet from which he took out a brown paper folder. From the folder he produced a piece of black paper folded in the shape of a small animal.

"The Black Fox."

I took the paper from him. The folds were perfect.

"He leaves these behind. Goddamn ghost." He upended the folder and dozens of little black foxes poured onto the table. "He killed one of my detectives here in Washington last week. He'll come for you, too, I'd wager."

"Why would he care about me? I don't work for you anymore."

Pinkerton laughed. "I can think of plenty of reasons. You killed Booth, or did you forget? The whole of the South would love to see you strung up. And then, in that little killing spree of yours to find your daughter, you almost had Colonel Norris himself. No one else made it that close."

"That was almost ten years ago," I said.

My Bowie had set across Norris' neck when he told me my daughter still lived. Norris played my hopes, and though he offered no proof, I let him live in exchange for Aurora's life. *What father could do less?* The price for her release was much higher. He sent me back to Washington to finish where Booth had failed—Aurora's freedom for the Old Man's life. The bodyguard would become assassin. I couldn't do it.

"And this Black Fox works for Norris?" I asked. Pinkerton nodded, offering nothing more.

"You don't know who he is?" I turned the little paper fox in my hand.

"No," Pinkerton muttered. "It's like watching a jigsaw puzzle dissolve in front of me. And I think the bastard enjoys it, taking his time and savoring every insult he hurls at me."

"Lamon says he can find Norris. He's sending Winston Baxter with me to bring him back."

"I don't know what to tell you, Joseph. I've been barred from the White House. Lamon's sun is rising, and mine setting. His agents outnumber mine. Before long, I'll be obsolete."

"I find it hard to foresee the day when you're dislodged from power."

"Things are different, the President is different, and the War is different. No one saw the rebels lasting, dragging the fight on for so damn long. Lamon has all the power now. He eclipses even the President, trapping him like a canary in that gilded cage."

"The President still blames me, doesn't he?" I asked.

Pinkerton didn't answer at first, picking his words carefully.

"He never blamed you, Joseph. He wanted to be remembered like Jefferson. I know he had some fanciful notion about it, those damn dreams of his. I even tried having the wallpaper at Ford's Theatre changed, you know, those awful dark red flowers. He said that wallpaper was in those dreams. But he wouldn't let me. He doesn't go there much, but when he does, I think he hopes it's his last night."

"They were leaves," I said.

"How's that?"

"The wallpaper. They were leaves, not flowers." I had stood against that wall so many times, examining every detail of the theatre.

"Same thing, Joseph. Either way, he can't last much longer," Pinkerton continued. "One term in that office drains a man, but he's in his third. Congress has yet to set term limits like they promised years ago. Lamon won't let them. And the rebels are worse than ever. There are rumblings of a new secession in the West. Federal troops abandoned Memphis last year—too much violence. This country will soon be three unless things change."

Was it my fault? The Draft, Aurora, my wife—all fixed had I heeded the Old Man's dreams. If I had allowed him to die that night there might have been peace, as the South exacted its revenge.

"He should leave." I pictured his cabin deep in the woods.

"Would you? Just walk away?"

"Yes, I would."

"I forgot who I'm talking to," Pinkerton muttered. "It's not so simple for him. I never saw a man so depressed after you saved him. It was worse than after his son died. You weren't here, Joseph. He believed those dreams—that if he died the War would end. Each report from the front lines, each death he heard about, he took personally, like it was his fault for living. But slowly he rededicated himself to killing this damn bitch of a War. That's how he made it through, with the promise of a nation made whole. He *is* the office, Joseph. I don't think he knows anymore where *it* ends and *he* begins. There are things he needs to see finished, and as long as his name appears on the ballot, he'll be elected. The Barons will see to that. It won't change until the South can vote again."

"Barons?"

Pinkerton laughed, a soft sound that filled the air between us. He lowered his voice as he glanced toward the door behind me. "I forget how long you've been gone, Joseph. Captains of industry—steel, oil, guns, textiles, and the railroad. They are the real power, even more than Congress. They established a council to forward their agenda, and you'll never guess who they appointed chairman."

I had no idea.

"Lamon," Pinkerton said. "Every congressman is in their pocket through bribery or blackmail. There's nothing they can't pass as law—even without the President's signature, most times. It's a new world, Joseph. While this rebellion lasts, only the North rules the land, and the Barons are at the top. They extended the Draft—cheap labor to counter the rising labor unions. It's not about modernization. Lamon's true design is to fan the fires of rebellion while the Barons reap the rewards. They break the unions with the children of the South."

Pinkerton paused to finish his drink, holding the glass between the fingertips of both hands.

"You know the Underground Railroad is working again?" Pinkerton grew serious.

"Why? To what purpose?"

"Children. It flows in reverse, heading south and carrying home the spoils of the Draft. Your mother is helping."

"My mother?"

Pinkerton nodded. "She is still a conductor, just like before—one of the best."

It made sense. The Railroad could work in both directions. It had delivered colored folks from slavery—now it freed the children of their former masters.

"You have to save Norris, Joseph. Lamon doesn't want him brought in alive. Norris' surrender would signal the end of the War, and Lamon needs the rebellion to continue."

"Why?"

"The Barons need their labor." Pinkerton leaned forward. "It makes perfect sense, doesn't it? Norris has enough information to crush the resistance. He knows where they live, who the lieutenants are. Without their middlemen, the rebellion will halt and fail. Lamon wants a simmering conflict. This War of ours is an exacting mistress, but she's Lamon's mistress. She keeps the Draft in place and cheap labor moving. It's about money, Joseph. The Barons want the gulf to widen between North and South. Ending the rebellion only narrows the gap, making the Draft unnecessary. If Norris truly wants to surrender, then Lamon wants him dead."

It was twisted. And I was the bait to lure Norris from his hole.

"Why would Norris ask for me? Lamon didn't make that up just to drag me to Washington."

"He has some game planned," Pinkerton continued. "I don't know what he wants, but you have to save him. Beat Baxter to Norris and bring him to me. That's the only way to end this miserable War. It's the only way to save the President from himself."

"Norris killed my wife...and my daughter. I'm not bringing him back, I'm burying him where I find him." My teeth were clenched to keep me from filling the room with my rage.

Pinkerton pulled me closer. "She's not dead, Joseph. Aurora is alive. If you kill Norris, we may never find her. You still have a daughter out there."

The room spun, a sure sign the whiskey was wearing off.

"I know Norris. He didn't keep her alive. I never told you..." I didn't finish the thought.

"I know why Norris sent you back all those years ago, Joseph. I know he meant for you to kill the President, to finish what he had started. But I also know he made good on his end of it. Listen to me," Pinkerton said, "she's alive. Norris still has her. You must stop Baxter and bring Norris in. We can find her."

I sat with my head in my hands. And I still had to fulfill my promise to the Old Man. I couldn't tell Pinkerton about that. *How would I bring back his mistress and save Aurora?* My stomach turned.

"What do I do?" I asked. "Just tell me what to do."

"Get rid of Baxter as soon as you can. Beat him to Norris."

"But Baxter is the only one who knows where the meeting is."

His voice suddenly sharpened. "You can't trust Baxter. Lamon wants you dead. Sending Baxter is sure proof of it."

"I think I can handle a mere boy."

"He's young, but he's no boy. He's worse than the Black Fox, worse than..." Pinkerton didn't finish his thought.

"Worse than *me*?"

"No," Pinkerton said, but it wasn't convincing. "He's not what you think, Joseph. He's a tracker. The slave catchers of yesterday. They bring back today's runaways, track the children who run from the factories."

"And why should that concern me? He can track children. I can handle Winston Baxter."

"He's killed more than you, Joseph. Lamon doesn't want Norris brought in alive. He means to kill you both. You need to save him."

A steel bridle tugged my head against my will. I had planned to kill Norris, and now Pinkerton expected me to save him.

"Baxter may know where to meet Norris," Pinkerton continued, "but Norris is too clever to walk in blind. You can't follow Baxter. You'll have to find another way."

"I barely found Norris last time, and now you think I can do it without Baxter? He knows the time and location. I have nothing."

"I have another way, Joseph. I have someone tracking Norris. She can get you close."

For a second the hope lit again. "Who?"

"Go to Richmond, understand? I'll tell you where to find her."

"Find who?" I asked. The soothing tone in his voice worried me.

"Molly. She knows where Norris is."

Molly. It seemed I would never escape my sins.

"No." I was forceful. I sat upright in the chair and walked to the window facing the street below. Pinkerton's guard still sat on the bench in front of the house. "I can't see her."

"You have to. There's no other way. She can get you to Norris, not to mention, she lowers your profile. With Baxter you'll be easy to spot. But Norris won't expect you to come from a different direction, and he won't expect a woman. You'll find her at a saloon on the outskirts of Richmond, *The Wild West Rogues*."

"Sounds like a brothel."

"It is," Pinkerton admitted. "She's the madam. If you want Aurora, you have to save Norris. And Molly is the key."

My choices narrowed. I looked to the night sky. Clouds obscured the *Drinking Gourd* and the North Star. I willed them to part, but they remained stubborn. After so many years, I faced the same dilemma—the Old Man for my daughter. It trapped me still.

"I need to go." I started toward the hidden staircase.

"Bring him back, Joseph. And be careful." Pinkerton handed me the polished pistol on the desk. "Take this."

I shook my head. "I don't want it. If the patrols catch me with a pistol, they'll shoot me on sight. Besides, if the Black Fox comes for you, you'll need it more than I."

"That beast means not to kill me. It's mean-spirited sport—watching my people die. There are worse things than death."

"Take care anyway," I answered as I slipped down the hidden stairs.

Once outside I hugged the shadows and rounded the front of the house. Curiously, the guard at the front had left, the bench where he sat empty. At the far end of the street a large black crow perched on top of a corner gaslight. I had never seen a bird like that at night. I waited to see if he would take wing, and, if so, in which direction. My mother would have called it an omen from the Great Spirit, sent to deliver a message. She would have waited for the bird to fly. I had a vague notion that if it lofted and went left—left of heaven—it signaled a harbinger of death. It stretched its wings, but then settled, content to cock its head.

I walked in that direction, taking care not to move too fast and scare him to flight. Maybe the Great Spirit had sent him as a guide, to help me choose a path. When I stood an arm's length from the lamppost, the crow cocked his head and stared at me with one eye. I froze. He was a huge bird.

We stayed like that for several moments, man and beast sizing one another. I searched for the message in it. My mother's people were too far removed to help me decipher it. In an instant he stretched his wings and dove off the lamppost. I ducked to avoid being struck. Turning to watch, I lost him against the sky—pitch black melting into the night.

I reached out to steady myself against the lamppost. My fingers held the rough wrought iron, but something along the top ledge near the lamp caught my eye—a little piece of paper, nearly blending with the post. With every second the passing wind threatened to blow it away. I plucked it to safety, holding it in my hand. Every fold was perfect and delicate—a little black fox.

CHAPTER FOUR

The Black Fox. None of Pinkerton's detectives were on the street. I spun around. My right hand dropped to my side where my knife would have been.

Nothing.

I backed a step off the lamppost, the seconds flittering away and my heart racing to propel me from the corner. Again, I searched the street—nothing. I didn't want to head back to Pinkerton's. If I were the Black Fox, I would lie in wait down that back alley. My right hand began to shake as fear seeped in. Ten years ago I would have been steady. Time had hollowed the warrior in me.

I ran, and with each footstep I regained my senses. Nothing pursued me. I slowed my run to a jog, then a brisk walk, in order to hear over the sound my boots made on the cobbled streets.

I headed in the general direction of the White House, hugging the shadows to avoid the patrols. The soldiers would shoot first, assuming they had found a rebel. I searched my memory for a place to hide. It would be smarter not to make it back until after the curfew lifted in the morning. If the Black Fox hunted me, he might also be near the White House. And since the boarding houses wouldn't take guests this time of night, I had few options.

Then the perfect place occurred to me. When I watched over the Old Man, there were only a few locations we would go in the city. But he never missed his theatre nights if he could help it— every Thursday. I knew all the theatres, and once inside, I would be alone. Ford's Theatre was closest.

I reached the alley behind the great brick building. It took longer than I had hoped to pick the lock on the rear door, but I entered the darkened theatre and closed the door behind me. Making my way backstage, the building made muffled noises, the settling of floors and the scurrying of little feet in faraway corners. My eyes adjusted to the dark, straining against the depths. I didn't want to cross the open stage, so I followed the back walls and crept toward the stairs at stage left. Before I descended into the general audience seating, I stopped to listen. Only distant noises reached me—nothing to cause concern.

At the top of the theatre the doors were unlocked, and I pushed on the nearest pair to slip into the lobby. I stopped and waited—still nothing. I made my way to the curved staircase at the far end of the lobby and then up the stairs. My nerves frayed, climbing ever higher into perfect darkness without the means to protect myself. Normally, I would have led with my knife. On the second floor, I entered the theatre again, this time at the balcony level. I made my way along the dress circle, down the long stairs to the door guarding the State Box.

I pushed the door open and stepped into the small vestibule. A second door guarded the far end of the short hall, behind it the place where I had saved the Old Man. I left the outer door open to hear anything coming, and then I slipped into the box past that inner door. The dark red wallpaper still lined the room, covered in ornate little maple leaves.

I sat in the presidential chair and listened to the theatre—the ideal place to wait out the curfew, to stay out of reach of the blue uniforms prowling the streets looking for rebels. After the War began, I had filled that role once too. My military career was short, punctuated with long days building defenses to cocoon the city, and long nights pulling patrols through the streets. Pinkerton's men were numerous and poorly vetted in those days. During my last night in uniform, I laid out seven of them in a brawl. They were drunk, not ready for the fight—easy pickings. But my commander viewed it differently. He saw an Indian who assaulted white men. Even with half my creation at the hands of a white man, I still counted as Indian. He elevated the incident until I landed in front of General McClellan. Pinkerton sat next to the general when I reported the next day. He wanted to see who had taken out his men with such ease. They had exaggerated the story to cover up their drunken incompetence, telling a tale of ten men as opponents.

McClellan questioned me for a minute before letting Pinkerton have a turn. They weren't interested in the infraction of the previous night, at least not for punitive action. Pinkerton wanted to know how I had walked out of a tavern scuffle with seven of his best detectives. I told him they could have another try, drunk or sober, but the outcome would be the same. He liked my arrogance, and he had a plan for a man like me.

The President needed protection, someone who could follow him day to day and protect with the scrutiny of a circling raptor. Inside a day's time, I had gone from building the outermost protection—ditches and artillery ramparts—to being the very last wall, the last layer of security. And my skin proved an advantage—not colored and not white. I was invisible. Most took me for a servant, someone in the background of high society. They didn't pay it credence that an Indian would be a bodyguard, overlooking me even when I stood next to them.

Under Pinkerton's employ I met my wife, and, as luck would have it, Molly. My mother would appreciate my current situation. Everything connected like a great circle—my past, the future. She would call it intervention by the Great Spirit. If I believed as she did, the Spirit brought me here for a reason.

I breathed deep, smelling the theatre. It was musty. The faint fragrance of actor's sweat permeated the stale air. In my hand I still clutched the little black fox. Without light to examine it my fingers ran over the edges, feeling the precision of the folds. It required patience to get details so perfect. I wondered what manner of beast had created it. Perhaps the crow that leapt off the gas lamp, transforming into a man in black. My mother told stories like that, men who changed shape and took animal form. Hunting rabbits and squirrels, I worried one would assume the figure of a man before I shot, or after I had killed it.

I put the paper fox in my pocket and took out my flask. With the running I needed more—my hands trembled from the effort and only the whiskey would calm them. As I took a swig, the top of the flask slipped through my fingers and fell to the floor. The noise echoed throughout the theatre followed by the silence. It rushed to fill the space again, like water after the splash from a pebble.

I sat for ten minutes, maybe twenty. Breathing deep, I savored the smell. The little things are what I forgot. This theatre had so long haunted my sleep, yet, when I closed my eyes, it was only the blur of a place—like how I couldn't picture Aurora's face. I would never forget the blood, the stickiness after my wife had passed and I laid her on the floor. Or the faces of the men I killed trying to get Aurora back, small details like scars on their cheeks and uneven mustaches. No matter how I tried, my daughter's face always escaped my memory. She had been so small when they took her, barely reaching my waist, and now she would be tall—coming of age in a few short years. If Pinkerton was right, and she lived, she would never recognize me.

Sleep tugged at me, so I lay down on the long seat against the far wall. It held comfort enough to pass the night. But, as I closed my eyes, the door at the back of the dress circle creaked. The first stair groaned with the weight of a man—then the next. I stood, timing my rise as he came closer. I stepped toward the outer door and peered out, but the dark was impossible to penetrate. It left me only one means of escape, over the edge and onto the stage, just how I had sent Booth to his death.

I waited, counting another step, and another. I peered into the darkness below me, trying to remember how far the jump would be. With every step he took, my chances for escape died. At the next creak in the floor I hurled myself over the edge, lifting both feet off the ground and sailing into the void. I hit the stage harder than I had expected. Though I regained my feet, I stumbled, falling backwards, landing hard on my back facing the balcony. He rushed up the last stairs, and then a figure stood in the balcony—more the impression of a man.

I ran toward the back door. Behind me, his weight landed

on the stage, more gracefully than I had managed. I made toward the door, but the hard soles of my boots slipped, surrendering valuable ground. I managed to reach the back door, but even with my hand upon the latch I had lost. A rush of air fell on my back, and a hand pulled my shoulder. His grip tore into my flesh, gaining purchase on my jacket and ripping me from the door. I made out nothing but the form of a man. A fist plunged through the darkness, the blow landing roughly across the top of my head. It stung, but left me intact. Then a distinct sound filled the dark— a knife clearing leather. I lashed out before he had the chance to use it. My fist found something hard, though he made no noise with the impact, no grunt to signal that I had hurt him.

I flung the door open, but stumbled in the alley and landed on my knees. The whiskey slowed my senses, delayed my balance. My hands felt slow, my reflexes muffled, as if wrapped in a wet blanket.

I struggled to my feet as he landed behind me, pulling me upright with an arm locked around my neck. I still hadn't seen a face to know if I fought man or beast. I tugged to loosen the grip, trying to throw him over my shoulder. I couldn't, but I fought to keep him off center, to keep him unbalanced before he could use his knife.

And then as quickly as it started, it ended. He shoved me to the ground, and I fell on my hands and knees again. When I swung around there was nothing. He had vanished. I searched through the open doorway of the theatre. Footsteps echoed across the wooden stage and voices reached me from the alley. Soldiers ran down the narrow passage, their boots making a racket against the cobblestone. I started to pick myself up, but a gunshot split the night. The bullet skipped off the alley by my head, kicking little chips of stone and dirt into my eyes. Instinctively, I reached for my face, but before I looked up, I was crushed by the weight of several men.

CHAPTER FIVE

I woke early the next morning with Baxter standing outside my cell. The soldiers had taken me to the naval stockade, stripped most of my clothes, and questioned me far past exhaustion. I spent the remainder of the night on a stone slab that passed for a cot. The cold seeped into my back and allowed for little sleep. Baxter signed for my release and escorted me from the stockade. He was disappointed to see me.

"I urged Mr. Lamon to reconsider your involvement in this matter," Baxter said as we left the Navy Yard. "But despite last night, he still insisted."

I said nothing. It seemed to confirm what I most feared. They intended to kill me.

When we reached the train station, Baxter released my weapons, the ones the guards had taken when I first arrived at the White House the day before. Cold, dark eyes pierced through me, but he reached into his bag and brought out my Bowie.

"The knife that killed John Wilkes Booth." He tugged on the handle to see the blade. For a moment it resisted before it broke free in a fluid movement, causing it to sing as it cleared the leather. Rust gathered in spots along the worn steel, a sign of my complacency.

"I'd appreciate it if you let it be." It was the only possession I had from my mother. She gave it to me before I enlisted, though I had carried it often when guiding runaways north.

He plunged the knife back into the sheath and handed it to me, keeping hold of the handle. He meant it as a sign, passing the knife blade first. I said nothing and took my knife, tucking it into my trousers where my belt would hold the sheath in place.

Baxter reached into his bag and brought out my derringer.

"And I see you kept Booth's gun." He studied the pistol in his hand. "A memento?"

"It kills just fine."

It was a crude weapon, meant for a man's head at close range. It nearly succeeded that night with the Old Man. I used it sparingly, despising the fact that it required no skill. There was no denying the sense of irony when it became the last thing a Confederate agent saw—like the man with the uneven mustache. I tucked it into the small of my back.

* * *

Once on the train, Baxter and I sat across from one another as it pulled away from the station. His stare remained cold, his face incapable of hiding disdain. I had once valued my youth over experience. His expression hardened as I brought out my flask. It didn't bother me. Over the years I had learned to distrust those who didn't drink—my ghost killer. Men without the need of it, even from time to time, lacked the experience I would trust.

I fought sleep for the first hour as silence became a wall between us. The soothing vibration from the tracks lulled my eyes closed, especially with my late night. But heading south left me uneasy and kept my nerves on edge. Before the Great War my mother and I had used Ohio as a refuge after guiding runaways north. Crossing the river and moving out of the southern states always brought relief—away from the reach of the slave catchers.

My mother and I fled Bloody Kansas after seeing my stepfather murdered. We stumbled onto the system of safe houses that moved a sweeping tide of color north, past the Mason-Dixon Line to safety—the Underground Railroad. We weren't colored, but we found ourselves escaping the South as if we were. Outsiders set our place by the company we kept. Among slaves we were colored, but alongside whites we were something else—a civilized savage and her half-breed son. The other half of my conception had been at the hands of a white man I knew nothing about.

Our first refuge came after crossing the Ohio River, a few days of rest and sunlight after traveling for weeks under the watchful moon, making our way north guided by the *Drinking*

Gourd. By the time we crossed the river my mother had changed. We had started scared, looking over our shoulders, planning only for the next day. But in the exodus she had found a purpose. Her mother had trained her as a healer, in the folk sense. Traditional knowledge passed from generation to generation before European medicine landed on the continent. Those skills were in demand along the Underground Railroad, where seeking medical attention was impossible.

And now I headed south to once more guide someone to freedom. The dreary landscape of winter passed through the window as the train jolted, pulling me from my drowsiness. The tracks became rougher and louder. Baxter read a newspaper, making a production to look my way every few minutes. Finally he folded the paper, set it on the bench, and tested the silence.

"I know Mr. Lamon insisted on your presence, but this is my responsibility. Do you understand? We do this my way."

Baxter was as flat as paper—as yet a child when the War ended, and everything about him revealed an attempt to overcompensate. His generation had grown up on the legends of heroes and envied those of us who had been through it. In truth, I would eagerly change places, if for nothing more than trading painful memories for peaceful nights.

"You're too young to have your own way. One look at you tells me you don't know what the hell you're doing."

His suit was darker than the day before but was still made from elegant fabric, an obvious show of wealth. It shimmered. My clothes were plain, the way I liked. I preferred to blend in, to be forgettable. My invisibility had always served me well. But Baxter announced his presence—arrogance or stupidity. His polished pistols strutted from their perch on his hips, and he made an obvious display of them.

"I've had plenty of trips south. Long before I worked for the President, I made a damn good living hunting runaways."

"Don't make me out foolish. I know what you did. You hunted children."

He leaned forward, one hand dropping to the butt of a pistol. His voice rose barely above a hiss, more snake than man.

"You believe the rebels want to give up their children? No, sir. I brought their children back north, but it was far more dangerous than that." His eyes were dark, and I sensed real hatred. Pinkerton had told the truth—Baxter was cold to the core.

"How much would you get for a child?"

He leaned back. "That depends. If they walked, I got forty a head. I could deliver seven or eight a month."

He crossed one leg over the other knee. Both of his arms stretched across the back of the seat. If he was honest, he had made a small fortune. It didn't make sense. The factories paid a steep price for a child they only paid a few dollars a month. But if it broke organized labor, the intangibles outweighed Baxter's fee.

"And if you had to carry them?" I asked.

Baxter smiled. "That's where I made real money. You see, I could bring in a dozen at a time. Sometimes more."

"Did you bind and gag them in the back of a wagon? Stack them like cordwood?"

Baxter reached inside his jacket and removed a small velvet bag from a pocket. "I put them in here."

I looked at the bag. "Children?"

"Thumbs."

I had no idea what he meant.

"When they arrive up north, the factories take ink impressions of all their fingers. They give them papers and record their names. So if I couldn't bring one back, I just used the thumbs. You need a set to get paid. Early on, some trackers accepted bribes and would deliver only one thumb, claiming the child had died. But no one wants to live with both thumbs missing."

The whiskey rose in my stomach. Baxter wasn't a man. I had killed plenty in my time, but not like him.

"Only ten dollars for thumbs," he said. He pocketed the velvet bag and placed a hand on his pistol. "A dozen makes it worth the trip, and you don't have to feed them."

I thought of the velvet bag in my pocket—the silver eagle's feather, how it hung around Aurora's neck.

We sat like that for a minute, maybe longer. His smile taunted me, dared me to sweep back my jacket and unsheathe the Bowie. I played it out in my mind. I would have to trap his arm, and pull my knife. I could do it, leaving him cut from navel to neck, drowning in a pool of his own blood.

I looked away, bringing us back from the edge. He laughed, and his hand relaxed from his gun.

"Mr. Lamon told me about you. Your methods are old. When I track, I prefer it slow. My prey die tired, there's less fight in them that way. They beg for it, so tired they are from the running. We'll find Norris, even if we have to catch him on his hands and knees crawling in the other direction."

"I need air." I couldn't look at him.

Through the rough jostling of the train, I stood and walked to the end of the passenger car. I opened the door and stepped into the small area before the next coach. My hands held the cold steel railing, and, for a moment, I thought I would vomit watching the ground pass in a blur. The door to the next car opened, and a conductor stepped out. He steadied himself on the railing in front of me.

"Sir, you're supposed to be inside at your seat. I need to check tickets."

"Just a minute. I'm feeling sick."

He said nothing as he entered the coach, leaving me alone. I watched him through the window, working his way down the aisle. Baxter handed him a ticket, his back facing me.

I pulled the door open to return to my seat when the conductor took Baxter's newspaper off the bench. It was a subtle motion, far too subtle—practiced almost. Baxter said nothing. He continued to face forward and away from me. Surely he saw. The conductor continued down the aisle, the newspaper tucked under one arm. He punched ticket after ticket. At the end of the car, he left the newspaper next to another passenger. Again, it seemed practiced. The passenger waited a moment, and just as casually slid the paper across the seat and began to open it, as if it had always been there.

I strained to see through the window. After the chase the previous night, I had been attentive when we entered the train, searching the faces and noting everyone. But this man sat at the far end of the car, his back toward mine. He may have sat down after me, or had found his way into my coach when I had nearly fallen asleep earlier. Another mistake I would never have made in my youth. As much as I didn't want to admit it, the whiskey didn't help.

The man leafed through the paper, a black duster jacket and blond hair just teasing his shoulders. Under a hat it would barely show—a black hat. *The Black Fox.*

It made sense. He worked for Lamon, not Norris. That was why he killed off Pinkerton's men—another move in their chess match. My fingers tingled the way they would when I closed in on someone. The sensation of discovery overpowered my fear. I wished Pinkerton could share in it, the piece of the puzzle he hadn't known last night. The Black Fox was killing his men for Lamon. And it meant Pinkerton was right. I had to beat Baxter to Norris.

I waited a moment longer. Baxter stretched out, and the Black Fox put the paper down. He must have received whatever message Baxter left for him. I couldn't go back inside the car. That would be suicide with both Baxter and this assassin waiting.

I opened the far door and walked through the next coach, then through the next, all the way to the end of the train until I reached the caboose. I found it locked. So I pulled myself onto the roof and walked across, dropping down at the far end and making the caboose a barrier to the danger behind. The rails sped by below in a blur of wood on gravel. I would leave my bag. It contained nothing worthwhile besides the whiskey, and I still had a small flask. Long ago I had learned to keep everything valuable on my person. And the abandoned bag would serve as a distraction to Baxter. Eventually, he would come looking, but it would buy time. For the hunted, time counted as precious.

When the train slowed to swing around a corner, I clung to the ladder and lowered myself off the edge. Timing my jump, I landed hard. I rolled to a stop down a slight incline. The train disappeared down the tracks, and, when out of sight, I dared to stand and brush off the dirt. I took stock of my surroundings. The next town would be a walk, but I had a plan and a sense of what needed doing. More importantly, I knew friend from foe. I would still need to choose between the Old Man and the chance to find Aurora, but that would come later. For now, I needed an ally, and the closest lived down the tracks in Richmond.

CHAPTER SIX

I never told Molly why I had left. I never wrote her so much as a note. Our affair was short and furious, starting a few months after I saved the Old Man. My marriage had long been fallow—a relationship of passion, not love. For my wife—the daughter of a southern Senator and the sister of a Confederate cavalry officer—a half-breed Indian who protected a northern president held destructive appeal. But after that night in the theatre, my wife distanced herself. In her eyes my luster faded when her father cut her off. My marriage died with her allowance. I spent more time at the White House, and more time close to Molly. While Pinkerton used me as defense, Molly served as offense—a spy. She worked the political and diplomatic circles, extracting details and deceptions with ease. Most powerful men think nothing of the women at their arm or in their bed. She hid behind her femininity just as I cloaked myself with my skin color. We circled each other for months, denying the inevitable.

Molly didn't know that I blamed myself, even blamed her. If I hadn't moved into the White House to be with her, I would have been home when they came. They were after *me*, taking my wife and daughter only as consolation for an opportunity missed. *How could I ever look at Molly again without seeing how far I failed?* It was easier to flee with my list in hand than to face her and admit my shortcomings.

* * *

A light drizzle soaked Richmond. The rain rolled off my jacket as I walked through the moist air into the late afternoon. I had stopped a few times to ask for directions along the way. The train would have brought me straight through Richmond, but when I jumped from the caboose, we were still an hour away. Everyone I asked knew *The Wild West Rogues*. When I arrived, I saw why.

The War had destroyed Richmond. Not with the fighting,

but in the hasty retreat Jefferson Davis sounded from his capital. He had ordered the city burned, denying sanctuary to the Union troops who advanced from Petersburg. Ruin still reigned supreme, while rebuilding the wreckage only inched along, partly as a symbol. Until the South relented and abandoned the simmering rebellion, the former Confederate capital would remain in rubble. An influx of construction had restored the surrounding area, and the rail yards were operating at nearly full capacity through the abandoned wreckage.

Mud mixed with rain and flowed down the street. The rest of the settlement took after a Western rail stop or prairie-trading town. Large wood boardwalks covered both sides of Main Street, and false-front façades extolled the virtues waiting inside. Debauchery and sin ruled—casinos, saloons, boarding houses, and, of course, brothels.

I stood in front of *The Wild West Rogues.* The building stood out, more paint on the trim, the windows cleaned, and the brass doorknobs polished until they shone. A porch ran the length of the building, and wood doors with ornate, etched glass decorated the front. The side windows were blocked with bright plaid curtains, and dashes of lively piano music escaped to where I stood.

On the porch I shook the water off, damp all over. When I stepped inside I felt underdressed. The bottom floor held a saloon, with a grand wood bar and several bartenders behind the counter. Little round tables filled the rest of the floor, most with drunken patrons. This was not a working-class bar, or, if it was, it tried for a more upscale clientele. The conversations rose into an incoherent babble, mixing with the smoke congealing about the ceiling. The barmaids wore low-cut dresses with high hemlines, dark stockings, and satin accents. Their high heels struck a staccato chord as they walked. Two sets of stairs at either end of the room ascended to a long balcony area, where several doors disappeared into the far upstairs wall. My imagination fell far short of what happened behind them.

Only a few patrons looked up when I entered. I scanned the

faces, searching out Molly. I didn't see her. The barkeeps were young, busy filling the trays of the barmaids who did double duty, earning more money behind those closed doors after alcohol had loosened the grip on hard-earned cash. Supplying two vices proved better than one.

I ordered whiskey at the bar and then sat at one of the tables by the staircase to wait. I took off my hat but left my coat on as I warmed. When I checked the progress of my drink, I noticed a well-dressed man taking stock of me with no pretense of subtlety. He didn't look away when I met his stare. A black bowler hat topped his head, and he leaned sideways against the bar as if he owned it. A gold chain strung across the front of his suit, disappearing into a small side pocket. He leaned back with both elbows perched upon the wooden bar. As he did, his jacket fell away, revealing a tin star on his left breast and a pair of pistols mounted cross draw on his hips. The mount of his guns told me that he had never drawn down on a man. Dime-store novels had that effect. Everyone thought they could be the sheriff through bluster and bravado.

When my hostess placed her tray upon the bar, the man with the tin star grabbed the glass from her and headed in my direction. I let my jacket fall open. Leaning back, I pressed my right forearm against the butt of my knife, trying not to be obvious.

"You must have missed our sign." He pointed to a plaque hanging between the two great mirrors that backstopped the bar. *No Firearms.*

"I saw it. I've got no guns." I didn't count the derringer as a firearm. With a gun that small he wouldn't know I had it. "I just want something to drink, some food."

He stared, taking a sip from the glass in his hand—my drink. "I saw you when you came in. You think I started this job yesterday, boy? On your right side."

I inhaled and held it. Then slowly I reached for my knife. "You must mean this." I pulled the Bowie from its sheath.

His hands dropped across his waist for the butt of a pistol. He let go when he saw the blade.

"Why, I declare, an Arkansas toothpick. Just like an Indian. Or are you a half-breed?"

"I don't want no trouble, just dinner."

"Get up, boy," he ordered as he took a step back. His hand rested on his pistol again as the eyes in the room fell upon us. The music from the piano softened, then slowed. I rose from my seat, gripping the handle of my knife while letting the tip balance on the surface of the table. We stood staring at each other while the rest of the room waited. A fight would be entertainment.

The staircase creaked behind me, and a woman's voice probed the tension. Subtle tones from her father's Irish accent mixed with a slight Southern drawl. I didn't need to see her to recognize it. Many a man had fallen, bewitched with a mere few words.

"Now, Sheriff, go back to the bar and enjoy another drink. Joseph is an old friend."

I didn't divert my attention from the sheriff, and, in truth, I didn't want to see her yet.

"I've got this handled, Molly," he said. "I'm about to show your friend to the door."

Molly finished coming down the stairs and passed between us. "Why, Sheriff, you don't have a thing handled. He won this fight the moment he walked through those doors. I've seen him work that knife. He'll drop you before you pull those six-guns of yours. Even with a hundred paces and a Henry rifle, I'd wager against you. You'd best go get another drink and let me handle him."

The sheriff didn't break eye contact, even when Molly approached and rested a hand on his shoulder. Her other hand motioned to the bar. A girl brought a tray with two glasses and a bottle of whiskey. It looked like Pinkerton's brand.

She leaned close to the sheriff, whispering loud enough to be overheard. "I wouldn't steer you wrong. There's no winning in this for you, other than drinking at the bar. He's killed scores of men who played at sheriff."

For the first time, he took his attention off me. His hand pulled off his gun ever so slightly. "If he's your friend, Molly. I don't want any trouble, is all. I don't like no Indians walking around with as much as a pocketknife."

Molly took the bottle and glasses in one hand. She placed a hand on my face to direct my stare into her eyes. I had forgotten how deep blue they were, how they contrasted against her dark hair—more auburn than red. Her touch upon my cheek lingered after her hand slipped away.

"Come, Joseph. We can get reacquainted better upstairs."

I sheathed the knife while still staring at the sheriff and followed Molly up the stairs. At the top along the balcony, I looked to the floor below. The music flowed again, the chatter building to match the smoke. But the sheriff remained fixed, watching me leave, drinking from my glass. Molly opened a door along the hallway and led me to a large suite with a front sitting room. The din below faded as she closed the door behind us.

"Joseph," she said, more sigh than anything. She drew me near as if to kiss me, one hand on my chest with a loose grip on my jacket. Then she pulled back, her right hand falling hard against my cheek.

My hand felt the rising welt along my left side. "What would you have me say?"

"That you were safe. You were always free to leave."

"I'm sorry." I couldn't look at her, so I turned to the room. The trappings were ornate, and warm. Deep red wallpaper covered the walls. A large bedroom peered through another door. I didn't look at it. She was the madam, not a simple whore, but it still tethered my imagination. I didn't need to know what happened there. "You don't seem surprised to see me."

Molly crossed the room to a small table. A pair of suitcases stood on the floor beside it. They were leather with polished brass buckles, no doubt expensive.

"Pinkerton said you were coming."

"I should have known. Did he tell you why?"

She turned. Her beauty had grown despite the lines that deepened over the years, eclipsing my memory of her.

"You're looking for Norris."

"You know where he is?"

She placed the bottle of whiskey and the glasses on her table, pouring both half-full. I sat facing her in a plush cloth chair with a high round back. She crossed the room to hand me my share of the whiskey.

"More or less," she answered.

"Tell me how to find him and I'll leave you be. Pinkerton thought you were tracking him."

"I am. That's what this place is for."

"Tracking Norris?"

"The rebels." She walked to the door and motioned for me to follow her as she opened it. We paused in the doorway. From our vantage we overlooked the bar and those standing at it. "We created this place, made it a safe haven for them. They launch their attacks up north—kill soldiers, plant bombs—then they descend through Richmond on their way south. Meanwhile, my girls collect everything they can—snippets of information, names, places, addresses."

"We?"

"It's Pinkerton's place. I run the business, train the girls, and send him reports." She motioned toward the bar. "See the man at the bar, in the gray? The young one?"

He swirled a drink in one hand while talking to a barmaid, a pistol loosely concealed under his jacket.

"He's a regular, transports explosives. Tomorrow night he'll be arrested in a boarding house a day's ride from here. That is if he goes without a fight, otherwise it'll be a pine box. Pinkerton's detectives are waiting. You see, we track the important ones, the middlemen, and dispose of them when needed. It slows the attacks."

Her perfume was the same she wore years ago. A hand reached up and felt my beard.

"You should shave." She turned and brushed past me, closing the door behind her.

I followed her back to the sitting table. "Please, I just need to find Norris." If I trusted anyone, I wanted it to be Molly. But time changes things in ways that are hard to predict or see. "He has Aurora."

"Your daughter?"

I nodded. I had killed so many trying to get her back.

"How do you know?"

"He told me, when last I caught him."

"Seven years ago? That's why you didn't kill him? What did he want from you?" She sat at the small table as she deciphered my dilemma.

"He'd release her if I let him go," I paused, "and if I went back and killed the Old—" I caught myself, "—the President." Molly hated it when I called him the *Old Man*. She never understood what my mother had taught, the amount of respect elders held in her Miami Indian tradition.

"I didn't know. That's why you never came back?"

I nodded. Maybe she saw my shame.

"I thought it was your wife."

"No. It was always Aurora. I wanted her back."

My marriage had been a poor means to cover the growing bump at my wife's belly—Aurora. I worked through Lamon's list, the names of Norris' men who had taken her. Aurora was the one good thing from my marriage, and I was desperate to get her back. I wouldn't have killed to avenge my wife. In a manner, my wife's death provided a way out, a means to relieve the guilt over my affair with Molly. This was shameful to admit, but Aurora was innocent, and she was mine.

"You're sure he still has her? It's been years."

"Pinkerton thinks so. Norris is my best chance. Lamon means to kill him, and I need to stop it."

"I already packed." She pointed to the suitcases. "I have a buggy downstairs, and there's a bag for you in the other room. I figured you'd need new clothes."

"You're planning on coming?"

She smiled, but said nothing.

"I can't ask you to go. This is my problem, I need to fix it."

Molly picked up her suitcases. "You're not asking. Pinkerton did. He doesn't trust what you'll do when you finally find Norris. I'm along to make certain you don't kill him."

She stepped close and put a hand on my chest, then let it fall to my stomach.

"By the looks of things, you've let yourself go a bit. You'll need me." She removed her hand and turned to her luggage.

Another chaperone. First it was Baxter, and now Molly. But it felt good to have a partner. And for the first time since I lost Aurora, she might be within my grasp. I would deal with my dilemma about the Old Man later, allowing myself the dream of hope. Aurora was three when they took her. She would be a young woman soon. I ached at the thought.

Would she remember me?

CHAPTER SEVEN

We rode late into the night. Molly had a two-seat buggy, a fancy cabriolet painted black with ornate gold trim. It handled well, but pitched something awful with the ill-maintained road. Heavy wagons passing through the area coupled with soggy winter weather created deep ruts, and the buggy jolted whenever we hit one. The roughness of the road held one appeal, enforcing my precarious grasp on consciousness. We crossed the Union lines outside of Petersburg, a city now famous for horrendous trench warfare. General Grant wore down his opposition here, surrounding the city and cutting the ties to Richmond through a web of earthen trenches that became cemeteries.

Between the late hour of our travel and the bite of the wet cold, we saw no one upon the road that night. At times we passed small cabins or houses tucked off the roadway. Smoke and sparks billowed from the chimneys, creating thoughts of warmth that were hard to shake, especially as my fingers numbed upon the reins. But we pressed on. By the time we pulled into a small town called Belfield, I was sure I would expire from exhaustion. We crossed the Meherrin River on a wagon bridge and reached Hicksford on the southern shore.

We were still in Virginia, but Molly chose this as our first stop. She could board the horses and find us passage on one of the many army trains that rumbled south along the old Confederate supply line. Commercial trains were still inconsistent in the South. Passengers were robbed, tracks removed overnight for their steel, or the trains failed to show. But the army logistics network made for the height of efficiency. Regular departure times and heavily armed trains created a black market in transportation. It garnered the train crews a decent second salary, as they charged twice the going rate.

We arrived far after midnight, and Molly directed me to

a boarding house she knew. A small bed claimed most of the space in our room. She handed me a pillow and a blanket and pointed to the floor—just as well. I placed my feet flush to the door, a simple alarm in case of surprise. No one had tracked us, but Molly's suitcases alone spoke of wealth, and in the South, wealth meant Northerner. This could buy us plenty of trouble. I put the Bowie on my stomach, one hand on the handle, the other on the sheath. Anyone coming through the door would startle me awake, and find the business end of my knife awaiting their entrance.

Molly turned off the oil lamp and the dark fell over us. We didn't speak. I let the sounds of the house envelop me, trying for a few hours of sleep. My whiskey was wearing off, and we hadn't brought another supply for the trip. Every time I closed my eyes, the suffocating darkness of Ford's Theatre fell over me—how the Black Fox had stalked me. My grip tightened then loosened on the Bowie. Despite the fatigue my mind fought sleep, enhancing sounds in the dark that made me flinch.

The clanging of church bells bolted me awake. I had managed a light sleep and missed the sun rise, but otherwise my rest was poor. Hicksford had only one small church, and the bell rang incessantly, not the typical call to worship. I laid on the floor, my knife beside me.

"What's going on?"

"I don't know," Molly answered. "They started ringing, but I don't see anything outside."

Molly dressed, and, as much as I wished to turn and watch, I waited. With the daylight, I would know so much more when I looked into her eyes to see what the years had done. When she finished, I moved to my own bag to get fresh clothes, trying to catch glimpses of her without seeming obvious.

"We should get downstairs to see what the commotion is, and I need breakfast. Then we can check on the train schedule. I know the stationmaster. He comes up on furlough and spends a week straight in Richmond. He's fond of some of the girls."

I wanted to ask which girls, but I feared the answer. Molly's red hair and subtle southern mannerisms could drive men insane. I reminded myself that she was Pinkerton's spymaster, his madam—not a simple girl he would whore out for information. Still, that thought brought little comfort.

"We can leave the bags for now," she said. Nothing in her voice betrayed her feelings. I found it hard to reconcile the woman before me with the old Molly, the playfulness that had lured me to her.

The church bells stopped. Silence rushed to fill the void. It left me uneasy as I went to the window to look. The road lay empty, not a soul in sight.

"I have everything I need." Molly opened the door to the room and walked out. She didn't wait for me to escort her.

Outside, spring had broken winter's grip. There were still months ahead until summer, but every mile south softened the edges of the bitter weather. We made our way to the main street and headed for the train depot on the far side of town. Stores lining the dirt road were broken and adrift, with little regard to outward appearance. Their shelves were bare while their doors stood propped off their hinges. The windows were broken and boarded for lack of glass. Even the boardwalk was ill-repaired, missing planks that had broken and were never fixed. This War still had her hands firmly around the throat of the South. The strangle of occupation and rebellion crushed the guilty and innocent alike.

Hicksford suffered for its pivotal role in the defense of the Confederate capital. Late in the War, the Union tried to cut the rail lines at the town in an effort to starve out both Petersburg and Richmond. Confederate cavalry spared the destruction, and federal troops didn't march through its dirt street until well after the South had fallen. The occupying troops had since erected a magnificent courthouse of polished granite and a train station at the far end of town, establishing a depot for transferring troops and supplies south, while cotton and children flowed north.

At the courthouse we discovered the meaning of the church bells. I hadn't expected to come face to face with the Draft, not in the way it happened in Hicksford—Selection Day. The courthouse steps were bare, but a small crowd had assembled in front of the building. A squad of Union troops assembled to one side, their rifles and brass shone in the early morning sun. At the top of the steps a well-dressed man stood behind a table that held a tarnished tin can. He wore the gold star of the Draft Board on his chest. From the murmurs in the crowd, this appeared to be a special Draft—revenge for attacks along the Union rail lines. The factories would claim two more children from their parents, punishment for cotton delays to the textile industry.

Children filled the area before the steps, roped off and separated by soldiers who kept everyone else at bay. Bayonets were fixed to their rifles. There weren't many children, perhaps twenty. They ranged from four or five years to near sixteen. Each held a bag in one hand, or a suitcase at their feet. Their clothes were worn thin, patched in places. Some had no shoes. The crowd strained. Adults peered into the flock of children. The youngest looked bewildered, and the older ones in shock.

It was hard to believe most of them would be of much use. I had seen the factories up north in my youth, awful places where conditions cut lives short on a regular basis. Poor northern families, mostly immigrants from Ireland and other parts of Europe, sent their children to earn an additional meager income. But these children could be working the fields, tending to the crops and animals, revitalizing a devastated homeland. The Draft was punishment, nothing more.

The man at the table unrolled a large paper scroll. He read the authorization under law for the Draft. The crowd blocked some of his words from reaching us. He spoke of the benevolence, the sacrifice. He told the parents in front of him that their children would return prosperous, leading the South to a new era. The town should be proud of those chosen today, he said. Every man and woman with a child in the center knew he lied.

He reached into the can and pulled out a piece of paper. People surged forward until the soldiers pushed them back. He took his time unfolding it, as if revealing a prize. Timing the tension perfectly, he read the name to himself before announcing it to the crowd. He enjoyed it—pure torture. When they heard the name, the crowd gasped. A woman sobbed. Soldiers escorted her to the rope line where she clung to a small boy. His eyes watered at the sight of his mother. A moment later they pulled him away, a soldier at either arm. The woman shrieked and another soldier dragged her through the dirt after she collapsed.

The man reached into the can again—the town owed another name. I searched the faces of the children, in a sick fashion wondering who would be next—*an older child*? That might be best, someone more able to cope with the separation, and who might escape when the time came.

It was a girl this time. She appeared younger than the boy before her. The crowd reacted the same, a collective sigh of grief, mixed with relief by those who would keep their children for another month, or year—no one knew. That was the punishment. At any time, their most precious possessions could be ripped from them.

The crowd made room for the mother. The little girl clutched her dress. It made me sick. She was no older than Aurora had been—no factory could use her. She wore a blue dress, worn though it was, her Sunday best to meet the new strangers up north. A hollow screech rose as the mother unleashed her pain upon the crowd. I had been in that place. When Aurora was taken, I turned the rage into murder.

But then a different noise met us. It crashed over the din of voices, building sharp and distinct, angry in its intensity. *A rebel yell.* During the War, it was a sound that brought fear into the heart of soldiers—part animal instinct, part murderous rage. The man on the steps recognized it too. For a second, fear lingered on his face.

The soldiers pushed forward—another yell started, and another. Molly gripped my arm and pulled me toward the rail station. The soldiers were in disorder, confused about the response of the crowd. Several men stood at the back. They were rougher than the rest—wild—their clothes marked with the dirt from a long road behind them. One held a revolver low in his hand.

The first shot came from the town—an old Sharps rifle. I knew the sound. Deadly accurate despite the old design. The crowd fell silent. Soldiers near the steps crouched and began searching distant windows for the shooter. No one noticed that the man on the steps fell. Perfect shot placement stamped a red dot on his forehead, marking the bullet's entrance. He crashed forward and tumbled down the stairs. A woman shrieked, and, like a herd of spooked cattle, the crowd dispersed, surging in all directions. The men with the revolvers pushed through, intent on reaching their targets. They fired indiscriminately at their enemy.

The soldiers near the ropes fell first, cut down in the opening volley. As the public thinned, the soldiers near the courthouse organized. A trickle of fire broke from them. Two of the rough men fell—then a woman. She had nothing to do with the fight other than she blocked the path of some errant bullet. From the town behind us more rifles responded, cutting down the soldiers near the steps. They were in the open with no cover.

Molly pulled me to the train station, plowing her way through the swarms of people. Her determined grip held my hand tight, as the surge of humanity threatened to tear us apart. She held fast and found a way through, only stopping when we reached the stone pillars of the station. We had left the buggy in the town stable, and to get it we'd have to cross the open ground between the soldiers and their attackers. Our best option fell to the train. The steam engine began to chug. It would leave immediately, not wanting to get caught in the crossfire.

Our clothing turned from liability to asset. We were better dressed than most in town—better dressed than Southerners. The occupation and embargo had left them in tatters. The soldiers at the train station waved us through. When we reached the platform, the train had started and a conductor reached out and pulled Molly on board. I grabbed the side railing while running beside the coach. I heaved myself up behind her.

We were in the last railcar. Through the side windows we saw the soldiers fall or cower behind their fallen comrades looking for cover. The rebels overwhelmed them, not with numbers, but through surprise. Sporadic gunfire popped, and the remaining soldiers fell back to the courthouse. Bodies adorned the steps. Most wore blue uniforms. A blue dress lay mixed in with the dead, tiny and motionless. She was facedown, a puddle of red underneath her.

A massive explosion rocked the courthouse. It shook the windows in the train. Debris fell upon the car, pelting the metal roof with a sound like hail. A window cracked from the blast, and the car swayed in response to the pressure. It robbed my breath as it washed over us.

"My God...," the conductor said. He stared in disbelief.

This was no mere uprising. The bombing was planned. Coordination like this took experience. We had seen the rebellion up close—rough men with revolvers, sharpshooters from a distance, every one of them disappearing into the crowd, invisible. They hid in plain sight.

"Watch him, will you?" The conductor said. "The guards ran for the shooting when it started." He pointed toward a little boy in the back, the only other person in the coach—the first boy chosen from the Draft. The conductor walked through the door at the front of the car, toward the engine.

The boy sat balled into a seat and tightly pressed against the far window. As I walked toward him he shook, but I picked him up and headed toward the back door. We were in the last railcar and the train pulled no caboose. I held the boy firmly though I had little need to, he clutched tight.

"You're getting off this train, understand?" I said. The train gained speed with each passing second.

"Don't throw me, mister."

"I'll find somewhere soft and swing you down."

"No!" He clutched tighter.

I tore his hands off my shirt and gripped him about the upper arms. Looking straight into his eyes, I pulled him close.

"Look," I turned him toward the side of the train where his town fast disappeared. "That's the last time you'll see home unless you get off."

I peered around the corner of the car and found what I needed, a gentle slope falling away from the tracks. His body stiffened as I held him over the rails, and his hand reached and clutched mine as I dropped him down the incline. He rolled down the slight hill, and I tossed his bag out the door. Behind me the conductor yelled as he ran down the aisle.

"Where is he?" Anger filled his voice.

"He jumped. Just ran and jumped off the end."

"Jumped?" The man looked frantic. He walked toward me, trying to make it past to see down the tracks. My right hand pulled back, and I pummeled his face with all my strength. He fell to the aisle in between the seats. I knelt over him and struck him about the head. His hands clutched his face as he moaned. My fist fell several more times until the blood poured from his nose, bloodying my fists a deep crimson—like the pool under the little girl on the stone steps.

"Joseph!" Molly screamed at me.

I stopped with my fist reared back and my other hand pulling the man forward by his shirt. She took a step back from me when I looked up. I let go of the conductor's shirt, and his head fell to the floor. He moaned underneath me.

Molly stared. I couldn't tell what she was thinking, and I didn't care. Rage welled inside me. A blue dress—that was all I saw. I let the man wiggle trying to get away, and then I reached down with both hands and pulled him to his feet by his shirt. I dragged him to the end of the car and heaved him onto the metal railing. My right foot planted square on his back, and he fell forward, off the end of the train. Alone and injured in rebel territory, I had as good as killed him.

I walked inside the railcar. Violence came so easily, especially when mixed with rage. It scared me, how fast it turned on, and how little I cared. Molly stepped back as I approached. The anger still contorted my face.

She reached out to touch my arm when the first window broke—the report of a gun followed. Then another. The bullet cracked in the air as it flew through the coach. I pushed Molly to the floor and fell on top of her. The firing intensified into steady popping. Then an enormous lurch pushed us both along the floor—another explosion. The smell of black powder and dust mixed to fill the railcar. The train bucked skyward. Leaving the tracks, it crashed to its side. The concussive force of the blast shook through my body, a massive pressure upon my chest. The explosion overpowered my hearing, and broken glass mixed with dirt showered the car.

When I regained my senses I found myself pinned on my side. Molly lay a few feet away, motionless. Dust hazed my vision. I tried to crawl over to her, but my body fought every command. No use. I reached out and held her arm, trying to shake her awake. She didn't move. The coach rested on its side.

Outside, men closed in on us. Their voices reached me as I yelled for help. But my voice came out raspy and wouldn't carry far. I tried again as I heard glass break with someone climbing inside.

I recognized the first one to reach me, one of the rough men with revolvers from the courthouse steps. He held an old Henry rifle and squatted down to my level. He showed no sign of helping.

"Where's the boy?"

I pointed out the back of the car. "I got him off the train." Each breath hurt. "Back along the tracks, he's safe."

The man looked puzzled. "You got him off?"

I nodded in response. He stood and looked at me.

"Well then, welcome to Dixie."

He raised his rifle, and then crashed the stock down on my head.

CHAPTER EIGHT

I lost track of time, drifting between consciousness and dreaming until one blended with the other. When awake, a dank cloth covered my head, keeping me in darkness. It smelled foul, like rotting onions. My wrists were bound tight behind my back, cheap burlap twine cut into my flesh. They hurt every time I moved. Both the derringer and my Bowie were gone, and I had no sign of Molly. The one time I called out for her, someone struck me about the head again. It brought tears to my eyes, as the blow fell where the rifle had struck earlier.

When next I woke I was sitting. From the sound it was a large room, but the cloth still covered my head.

"You can leave now." Someone stood in front of me.

A door at my back opened and closed. For a minute, silence took over. I began to believe I might be alone, but subtle signs of another person gave him away—slight movements in a chair, the floor creaking under the weight.

"It's been a long time, Joseph."

I strained at my wrists, but they were still bound. His footsteps circled around me, and then the bag yanked free from my head. Sunlight poured through a window behind a large wood desk, and I lowered my head, trying to shield my eyes.

"I wondered when you might arrive," Colonel Norris said.

Time had worn on him from last we met, but he still kept himself immaculate. He had a fresh gray suit near the equal of Baxter's in appearance. His beard had whitened, though still close-cropped and well-groomed, and his hair had lost all color. Despite his age, his composure held dignity and power.

"Where's Molly?"

"Ms. Harris is fine. A few bruises, but, otherwise, without a scratch from me." Even his accent remained impeccable, the very essence of a Southern gentleman—nothing rushed, every word and sentence rehearsed before he released it upon the world.

He continued his full circle of the room to once again sit behind his desk. Questions poured through my mind. *Where is Aurora? How did I get here? Where was Baxter?* But I let the silence grow. This would be a chess match, and I had no position to demand answers.

I looked to the desk in front of us. The contents of my pockets were neatly arraigned across its top—a handful of Union notes, a derringer, my black velvet bag with the silver chain and eagle feather, the small black fox, and my Bowie.

"You've had an interesting trip."

Norris reached over the desk and picked up the little black fox. He turned it over in his hands, his fingers probing the meticulous folds. "I trained him, you know. The best I ever saw. During the War, he led a unit that stopped the Union from crossing the river at Hicksford."

"If he were that good, I wouldn't be here now." I fought to keep my voice clear of emotion.

"That's not true at all, Joseph. You were always meant to arrive here. I sent my man to guarantee it."

"The Black Fox works for you?" I stared at the little paper black fox.

"He does, indeed. I had him personally deliver my letters to Mr. Lamon and Mr. Lincoln. He was to bring you to me under the pretense of surrender. I expected that a man as despicable in his character as Mr. Lamon might try to have you killed. So I sent my man along."

"That's how Baxter knew where to find you," I thought aloud—something didn't sit right. "Why did your man attack me?" My shoulder was still bruised where he had grabbed me in Ford's Theatre.

"This man?" He held up the little paper fox.

I nodded, remembering the black fox I had found on the lamppost outside Pinkerton's house.

"You are mistaken," he replied. "My man had explicit instructions to deliver you safely. Any action on his part was designed to that end."

I studied his face, hoping his expression might give me some read on his true intentions. I found nothing to decipher, though his voice waivered ever so slightly.

"Enough of this. Why do you think I asked you here?"

Breaking eye contact, I looked to the desk. My Bowie sat within reach, but as I tested the bindings on my wrists, they would not budge no matter how I pulled. I averted my eyes as I answered.

"Because the President is still alive."

He sat quiet for a moment. "Well, that is a good guess, but it would be wrong, Joseph. You did fail me. But failure is a funny thing. You and I want one thing today, but tomorrow, we may desire something altogether different. And to complicate matters, what we desired yesterday might preclude obtaining what we need today. We are, I believe, at such a juncture."

"How do you mean?"

He stood, composing himself as a professor would for a lecture. "When last we met, I desired nothing more than the destruction of the President. I wanted to see him dead. My cause was lost, but it needed some small victory for the South to emerge from our Great War with a measure of dignity."

He walked to the window and looked out.

"I spent a great deal of care and planning on the operation with Mr. Booth. But you stole that from me." He remained calm, but his eyes were piercing and intent.

"You killed my wife and took my daughter." I pulled against the bindings until my wrists burned. The pain overwhelmed the anger.

We were both quiet a moment. "I did indeed," he admitted. "But don't expect an apology. If not for you, I would right now be enjoying my grandson. Peace rested on Booth's success. Instead, I am an old man and I am still at the fight. You took as much from me as I did from you. Think of how many died because of your actions that night."

The rage coursed through me, though even with it, there was no breaking my restraint.

"That was my job." I stared at the black velvet bag on the desk. "She had nothing to do with it. Where is she?"

"Aurora is well, Joseph. I might even consider letting you see her, although I do not expect her to know you now."

"But she's alive?" I couldn't picture her. She would be ten, though always my little girl.

Norris nodded. "I am not a monster, Joseph."

"You killed her mother."

Norris sat in his chair. "An unfortunate affair. Your wife fought. The man who killed her proved too vigorous in his response. We buried him as soon as we crossed into Virginia and I no longer had need of him. I did not intend her to die."

"Why should I believe you?"

"I admit my anger, Joseph, but it was not blind rage. I needed another way to get to the President, and you were my plan. You could get close, and no one would suspect it. Not to mention the irony. The bodyguard becomes the assassin. Now that would be a symbol!" He paused. "But if your daughter died, I lost all leverage. She is worth more alive—even now." Nothing in his body language indicated deception.

"What do you want from me? Why did you ask for me?"

Norris stood and walked back to the window. "You and I have the same enemy, Joseph."

I looked to my Bowie sitting on the desk. "I can think of only one person I intend to kill." Again, I twisted the twine binding my wrists.

"Would you be so shortsighted? That is why you remain tied until you come to your senses. Lamon knows I have your daughter, and he will suspect that I will use that fact against you. He is also smart enough to realize that I intend not to surrender, that I have another purpose for you. He never wanted you to make it this far. He meant to kill us both."

"So you want me to handle Lamon, then?"

Norris sat back behind his desk. "Although I would not be opposed to such a thing," he said, "my ambitions are greater than one man. There is one thing I want, Joseph, and only you can deliver it."

"What?" I imagined nothing that I could do except to kill Lamon.

"Peace." Norris leaned back in his chair. "I want peace."

"What?"

"No more fighting. The South needs to recover."

"I was just in Hicksford. That didn't look like peace." I pictured the little girl lying on the courthouse steps, her blood trickling down the stone stairs and pooling on the ground.

"Precisely. My grip over the rebellion is slipping. I do not wield influence as I once did. There is a younger generation taking over. They were young when the occupation started, and now they have known nothing except suffering. They are brutal, and at times, independent. I did not order the attack in Hicksford. Incidents like that will happen again, and the violence will deepen. Seven years I have fought this occupation. I led men, planted bombs, and planned ambushes. Nothing has improved. We are worse now than at the end of the War. More soldiers pour into our towns every day. We watch as our crops travel north, our plantations are distributed to the Negros, and our buildings crumble around us. The North gets rich as we sink deeper and deeper. And then, they steal our children for their factories. Even you must understand that. I need to regain control so I can negotiate the hostilities to an end. I want peace. It is the only way to improve our lot."

I leaned as far forward as the chair and my bound wrists would permit. "You want to consolidate power. You have no intention of ending anything. This is just another part of your game."

For a moment the anger welled in his face, and his eyes narrowed as he glared at me. He reached for a photograph on his desk. He spun it around and placed it in front of me.

"That is my grandson," he said.

I looked at the photograph. A young boy sat on a parlor chair that was far too large for him. His legs stuck straight out, the backs of his knees unable to reach the end of the cushion as he sat all the way back. He looked uncomfortable and stiff in his formal clothes.

"He is my only grandchild. My son died a year ago, leading an ambush on a Union troop column. I have no other heir, Joseph."

"So you want peace for him?" It sounded too sentimental for a man who spent most of his life fighting and killing—for the man who had taken my daughter.

Norris looked at me and then down at his desk. "If that is what it takes. You see, Joseph, my grandson is gone. Seven months ago, they pulled his name from a tin can, and I wasn't even there to say good-bye. They didn't know he was my family, or he would have been taken long ago. I kept him sheltered for so long, hidden away where Mr. Lamon's Draft would never find him. But in a moment of indulgence, his mother brought him to town. It was unlucky that federal troops were there. They took the boy and in the struggle killed his mother." Norris stood, resting both hands on his desk. He stared at me, leaning closer and lowering his voice. "I want him back."

Peace? Could the Draft coax it from the rebellion? I didn't want it to be true. That would serve only to validate the practice, even intensify or expand it. As Norris reached for the photograph, his eyes lingered on the boy. Children are the foundation of every land. The Draft cut deep to what we all held most sacred.

Norris played with a ring on his little finger—a woman's ring, a few diamonds embedded along its circumference. He saw me looking at it.

"My wife's wedding ring. She died after my son. I blame a broken heart, made worse after they took our grandson."

"I think you overestimate what I can do. I am just one man."

Norris took his time in placing the photograph on his desk, arranging it exactly as before.

"It is fallacy to believe all men are equal, Joseph. Some lives touch their world more than a thousand men could ever hope. Take our Great War as example. We flung armies at one another. Each soldier was just a man, but sometimes one would rise up and control the fate of an entire battle. The men who pull their flag from the ground and run headlong into their enemy. Who knows why God wills it so? You and I are such men. We were meant to control the fate of our world far beyond the influence of an ordinary soul. You did more damage to the Southern cause than all the armies that came before you."

"My job was to damage your cause."

"And now I offer you the chance to help me fix it. I know you won't do it for me. But you will for Aurora."

"What would you have me do? Last time you sent me back as an assassin."

Norris stood and grasped my Bowie by its handle. He drew the knife from the sheath. Looking at the blade, he circled behind me again. I faced forward, not wanting to turn and watch. I had never feared my own knife before. It had a wicked history. Many men had died on its steel, including its maker—the white man who forced himself upon my mother. She killed him with it immediately afterward, as soon as he loosened his grip. It was a wonder she loved me, having lived through my creation.

"Can we agree that for now our common interests align, Joseph? You want your daughter back, I want my grandson."

"For now, I agree."

He grabbed my wrist. The cold steel of the blade poised on the twine binding my arms together.

"I will cut you loose, and we can discuss matters as equals, you and I. Understand? But if you fight, I will find another way. And I will not be lenient on your daughter."

I nodded and pulled my wrists as far as they would go to avoid the blade. With a quick tug, the Bowie severed the twine. My wrists were free. Norris walked back to his desk, keeping a close watch on me. I rubbed the welts from my skin. The twine had cut deep, drawing blood in a few places. As he pulled out his chair and sat, Norris held the Bowie, spinning the blade and examining it closer.

"If you want your daughter back, you must first help me retrieve my grandson."

"I wouldn't know where to begin. Once they head north, I don't know where they go."

"But your mother does. She helps them escape—helps shelter them south. I have written her, asking for her help. I do not expect her to take my plea seriously. I expect you to intervene on my behalf, plead my case to her. She has the contacts to find and retrieve him."

"I'll go see her."

"There's not time. You can write her a letter. I will have it delivered. I have other plans for you before you have your daughter back."

"What plans?" Yet again he would ask the impossible, forcing me into another losing proposition.

"I know why you were sent," Norris said.

"To bring you back."

"No." He shook his head. "I know the other reason—the President's mistress. You will get her for me."

I said nothing, fighting so my face revealed none of my shock. Not even Molly knew.

"Do not provoke me, Joseph. Now is not the time to play dumb. All you have to do is get her and bring her north, just like the President requested."

"Why?"

"It's very easy, actually. I don't want to kill the President. Not now. That would be shortsighted, and would only serve to turn him into a folk hero. And then there would be more pain and suffering for my people. He is not what he once was, but he is still a mighty symbol, even if he is a puppet for the truly powerful. A pregnant mistress—a Negro mistress—will be an embarrassment from which the North will not likely recover. He will resign, and his industrial backers will distance themselves. The Vice President does not get on well with Lamon, and he hates the Barons. I have already seen to it that the Draft ends with the next president. We need only to change the guard."

Once again, choosing between the Old Man and Aurora would hold me hostage. But this time no one had to die.

"I have already predicted the fall of the President," Norris continued. "Once he steps down, I will have the backing of the rebel commanders to negotiate on their behalf. The Draft fuels the fire of our rebellion. Once it dies, there will be peace."

"Why me? You could go get her."

"I could," Norris said. "But my claims of her association with the President would be dismissed, written off as a ploy to undermine the Union. Your voice is the only one that will carry weight on such a matter. You have already proved yourself in the President's service. If you say that she is his mistress, the people will believe."

It was a political solution, more elegant than the emotions that would carry the day with an assassination.

"If I do what you say, there are conditions. You give me Molly, I need her. Together we will get the girl north how I see fit. And you free my daughter, regardless if the President resigns."

"I can accept those—"

"I'm not done. If the President steps down, you guarantee his safety. No one touches him, no assassination."

"Anything else?"

"Yes. When the time comes, I kill Lamon."

"I accept. You have my word as a gentleman. I will give you the names of my reporters, the ones I have in Baltimore. You deliver the girl, and they will break the story. In the meantime, I have a present."

He stood and walked around his desk, opening the door behind me. For a moment, he talked to someone in the hall. A minute or two passed, then two guards entered the room dragging a third man between them, bloodied and beaten. They dropped him on the floor at my feet. I wouldn't have recognized the face so bruised and swollen, but I knew the suit, torn beyond any repair. The material still shimmered in the light. Norris handed me my Bowie.

"I was going to dispose of him myself, but since you are here, you can have him."

I held the knife in my hand, the blade balanced above my index finger. The tip danced effortlessly in the air as I moved my wrist. I squatted down and pulled Baxter's head by his hair. He was still conscious. When he saw me he laughed, a delusional sound like a madman. They had either tortured him past breaking, or he was more twisted than I had realized. I pushed the blade under his chin, the edge resting on his throat. It required such little pressure. He would split open and bleed out on the floor. But I had no stomach for it. I would kill Lamon, and that would be it.

I pulled Baxter close, the knife still against his neck. Barely above a whisper, I spoke in his ear. "Tell Mr. Lamon I'm coming. When I'm through here, I'm going to kill him." I let his hair slide out of my hand. His forehead hit the floor. He offered a small whimper, then fell silent.

"Let him go."

"He would be better dead. He intended to kill us both. If he lives, he will warn Lamon."

"You and I have done enough killing, haven't we? And I want Lamon to know I'm coming. It will be torture until I arrive."

Norris smiled. "I'm glad I did not kill you, Joseph. You are the right man for this job. To think—Lincoln's bodyguard will be the man to rescue the South."

CHAPTER NINE

Norris arranged for a train headed south from Charlotte. It was a federal train, but money fueled the black market, not ideals. No one asked us for paperwork. No one asked for anything. We transferred trains in Columbia, South Carolina, and then passed several hours waiting for the tracks to clear. Attacks along the lines were common—rebel units barricaded the rails as blackmail. The train crews paid the ransom requests to clear the route, in essence funding the rebellion. But with enough money, everyone won. We arrived late in Savannah and chose a boarding house to pass the night. Norris recommended a place, a rebel safe house. He would monitor our progress, and I saw no purpose to obscure it from him, at least not for the immediate time.

The boarding house needed repairs, but I took comfort in its plain appearance. I would rather be cloaked in anonymity. I lay on the floor as Molly took the bed, once again with my feet to the door as an alarm. We had passed most of the day in silence. Not counting the time we spent in Richmond that first night together, we hadn't talked. The next morning had been at Hicksford, landing us in Norris' hands. When they took us they bound her hands and feet. Nothing upset her worse than being tied up. It had happened once before with some fat senator that Pinkerton had sent her to blackmail. Ever since then, she hated it when anyone tied her hands.

To make it worse, I hadn't told her about the Old Man's mistress. She took that as a betrayal—I had another agenda I had kept hidden. The few words I did get from her were short. She fumed, her face nearly matching the color of her hair. When we did speak, she barely looked in my direction. I had forgotten about her temper.

She blew out the oil lamp at the bedside, letting the darkness envelop both of us. In a way it was comforting. I wanted the day to pass, to get us closer to finding the Old Man's mistress and heading north. As the minutes passed I drifted toward sleep.

"You should have told me." Molly caught me by surprise. I thought she slept.

"I didn't know who to trust." The flooring beneath me creaked as I leaned up on my side. "I planned to find Norris and then go get the girl. I didn't know how I would do both. And I didn't figure on you being along."

"Well, I am along." Her words were clipped. "As soon as I came, you should have told me."

"I wasn't going to bring you—" I stopped. No good would come from arguing. In truth, I had no idea how I would juggle it all. It no longer mattered.

"We should turn around, or at least tell Pinkerton. Bringing Norris back was the plan. Nothing more. He doesn't even know about this girl," she said.

"No," I snapped. Her mood wore on me. "No one else needs to know until we figure out what to do. Pinkerton wants the end of the War. He wanted to get it from Norris, and he will. Just not the way he thought. This girl is the answer to both problems. We get her and, after that, we let Pinkerton know."

She fumbled at the bedside table before striking a match. In the dim light she lifted the lens of the oil lamp and lit the wick, keeping the light low.

"I'll telegram Pinkerton in the morning." She was defiant, looking for a fight.

"I'd have no trouble tying you to that bed and leaving you."

She picked up a china cup from the bedside stand and hurled it at me. I raised my hand in time to deflect it from my face. It smashed off the wall next to the door.

"Try leaving me," she screamed. She grabbed the matching china saucer and held it ready to throw.

I pushed up onto my elbows and began to kneel when she flung the saucer. It struck me above my left eye. The surge of pain fueled my anger. I rose to my knees and reached for the end of the bed to pull myself up. Her hand darted to the bedside table where she grabbed her pistol. She cocked the hammer and pulled the gun to her lap. Her eyes glanced to my hand. I stopped. I held my Bowie, still sheathed, but my knuckles were white in their grip. I threw the knife to the ground. It skidded across the floor.

"Damn it." I grabbed hold of the pistol barrel. As I pulled, Molly resisted. I grabbed higher on the weapon, my hand closing around the cylinder. Molly jerked the trigger and the hammer snapped forward. It caught the web of my hand. The pain filled me with rage. I pulled the pistol from her hand and tossed it aside. If it hadn't been for the placement of my hand, the gun would have fired. Grabbing her leg, I pulled her across the bed.

"I didn't mean..." She didn't finish the thought.

I eased my grip on her thigh, her skin as soft as I remembered. In an instant, we were at the White House again—as it had been—as if the years hadn't passed. I focused on her eyes and her body eased beneath me. She pulled the blankets free between us and tore at my clothes. I drew her toward me. She arched her body as I lifted her nightgown over her head. I brought my lips to her neck and breathed deep of her perfume, running my hands along the sides of her body. She wrapped her arms and legs tight around me and pulled me into her. My mind receded in an upward spiral as her body shuddered and she whispered, "Don't leave me, Joseph."

We were quiet for a time. I reached out to hold her and feel the softness of her body again. I listened to her breathe.

"I would have helped you find Aurora."

"That was seven years ago."

"You never asked."

"I couldn't. I did things to find her...things I couldn't ask from you."

"I never even knew where you went."

We were quiet for a few moments. I let the sounds of the boarding house settle around us, wondering if we had woken anyone. Surely we had. Slowly, I reached across her for the flask of whiskey that Norris sent with us. Fumbling along the nightstand, I found it. I undid the lid and took a sip.

"I'm asking now. Norris will let her go if we deliver the President's mistress. But I need you. Will you come with me?"

She said nothing, but her hands found mine as she took the flask from me. After a long pull she handed it back. The smell of whiskey filled the space between us.

"If we find this girl, it will ruin the President. You've thought of that?" she asked.

"He asked for her. I've never seen him like this—she's something to live for. He wanted to die before," I said.

As close as we were years ago, we never talked about our jobs. I never told her about the Old Man, and she never told me what she did behind closed doors. I could guess, but I didn't want to know.

"What do you mean?" she asked.

"He believed he would have to die for the War to end. He dreamt about it. When I was alone with him, he would tell me. It was an obsession."

"You never told me that."

"I didn't think much on it at the time. What was I supposed to do, let him die?" I stayed quiet for a moment. "We spoke little after that night."

The bed creaked as Molly shifted. "That's not fair, Joseph. You did what you had to."

"Maybe. But if I had let Booth kill him, I would have Aurora now. And I wouldn't have dragged you into all this. That little girl in Hicksford would be alive. Norris would have his grandson."

If I had listened to Norris when he sent me back to Washington, the same might be true. But I couldn't tell Molly that part.

"And you think revealing the President's mistress will somehow set it right?"

"Norris can end the Draft if the President resigns," I said. "That has to count for something. With that, he can end the fighting. Can you think of a better way?"

"Even if it ruins the President?"

"The President asked me to get this girl. Norris was supposed to be a distraction, a way to shake free of Baxter." We were quiet for a moment. "She's pregnant."

Molly said nothing.

"Lamon will find out," I continued. "The President needs a way out, as bad as he did back then—worse. He won't step down, so something needs to force his hand, to take the decision from him. I'm going to bring her back. I'll understand if you won't come."

"No." Anger filled her voice again. "I told Pinkerton I would watch you. I don't just leave." She meant that last comment to sting. I deserved it. I reached for her hand, but she pulled it back. The anger faded. "I didn't have to come," she said. "Pinkerton asked, but he gave me a choice. I want to be here."

"Why?"

"I needed to see you. I knew you would be back, though I didn't think it would take so long. I wanted to know what might have been."

She reached for my hand. I grasped it, letting her fingers intertwine with mine.

"I need to tell you about the resort." I dreaded getting up in the morning, making our way to the island, and finding the girl. "Norris arranged for a reservation in your name. Security is tight with the rebels so close. Most of the industrialists travel by boat from the North. We'll take the ferry across, so that might already arouse suspicion. And then there's the constable."

"What about him?"

"It's Red Billings."

"Do you think he'll remember you?" she asked.

"I don't know. It's been a long time. The real question is, will he recognize you?"

"He never paid me much attention. I can't recall if I ever talked with him. But he might if we're face to face."

"We need a story. Something he'll believe, or something that will take him long enough to check out so we can disappear before he has the chance."

"How about the truth?" Molly baited me.

"I'm serious—we'd never leave the island."

"If he recognizes me, there's only one explanation. He knew what I did for Pinkerton. I am on the island to entertain. Rich men in Washington are the same as rich men anywhere. They all have their needs."

It was a cover story, but all good covers contained an element of truth. Even worse, they had to be believable to the point of carrying out if that were the only option.

"I guess that would work." I couldn't look in her direction as I answered.

"The best option is not to get caught." The edge in her voice returned.

I didn't answer.

"Is there anything else you need to tell me? Anything else you thought it better I didn't know?"

"I keep thinking about something Norris said."

"What?"

"Do you think she'll remember me?"

"Aurora?"

I didn't answer. I already knew, and I certainly didn't need Molly's response.

"No."

CHAPTER TEN

I scanned the dock for our contact, but no one appeared interested in us. Norris provided enough cash that we were able to rent a buggy for the remainder of the journey. It took most of the day, but once in Brunswick, we had no trouble finding the entrance to the wharf and ferry launch. They were off the main road along the coast.

As I unloaded the luggage I caught sight of a man to one side. He stared in our direction. I had noticed him, but I hadn't thought anything of it—a colored man. I rather expected Norris to shy away from former slaves. But everyone has their price. Norris supplemented his meager salary several times over to buy loyalty. More than likely, the man knew nothing about working for Norris or the rebels. Nonetheless, it embarrassed me that I had paid him no attention. Of all people, I should have been better than that. Even to my eyes he had been invisible.

He approached us, a worn blue cap in his hand. I nodded him forward.

"Is the buggy made in Savannah, sir?" His voice cracked. It was the phrase he had been told to repeat as a means of introduction.

"No, I believe Atlanta."

"Mista Beck?" He looked like he might run at any moment.

"I am Mrs. Beck," Molly answered. "This is my man Joseph." She adopted a rigid posture, the type of woman expected in a place like Jekyll Island. With it, she relegated me from her equal to her servant.

"I'm sorry, ma'am. I was told your husband would be with you." He glanced at me, his eyes darting back to Molly. "I'm William. I will help you to the island."

"Thank you, William. Please show Joseph where to take the luggage."

I walked with him to the back of the carriage to finish unloading the bags. He watched me like a beaten dog. Fear has a certain feel, and William reeked of it. Placing the final bag on the ground, I turned toward him.

"What is it?"

He shook his head and took a half-step back. "Nothin', sir."

He made me nervous. Either he was new to this kind of work or we were falling prey to a trap. I looked around the front of the carriage. We were on a long cargo area leading toward a wood pier. The smell of the salt marsh washed over us. Gulls floated on the wind above. At the end a small steam ferry bobbed in the channel that shielded the island from the mainland. Security men looked through the stacks of luggage, occasionally searching a passenger as they boarded the boat. The guards wore identical gray uniforms—their polished buckles sparkled in the sun. From a distance they looked professional.

I stepped behind the buggy where no one could see. My hand reached back, and I pulled the Bowie free. The blade caught the late afternoon sun. Then I pulled the sheath out. I re-holstered the blade, making a production of it so our new friend would see. I stepped closer.

"Are you sure there's nothing you need to tell me?"

He stared toward the ground. "The sheriff is a wicked man. If they catch you, they'll kill me. He whipped a boy for taking food from the kitchen last week. Made us all watch."

"The constable?"

William nodded.

"They call him Red?"

William nodded again, keeping his eyes on his feet.

"Why are you helping us, William?" I made sure to use his name. I wanted him to feel that I knew him—that I owned him. It was degrading, especially to a former slave, but I needed to know what we were walking into. He didn't answer.

"Look at me," I ordered. My voice held cold and steady. When he looked up I continued. "Why are you helping me?"

He stared at the knife in my hand. "My wife. You have my wife, sir."

Norris had bought William without cash. "What do you mean?"

"That man, sir, the one who came yesterday and told me to be here, he's the one who took my wife."

"Who came, William? What did he look like?"

"A white man, sir. Younger than you."

It wasn't Norris. He would leave the dangerous work of creating new assets like William to someone far lower in the organization. But the tactics were his.

"They have something of mine, too." I didn't elaborate. William didn't need to know, although in truth, it seemed we had much in common.

"Your wife?" He had found someone who could share in his misery. Even his face lifted.

"No, but not far off. These men are evil, William. You're not alone, and it's not your fault." I transferred the Bowie to my left hand and stepped forward to hold his shoulder. Slow sobs rose, but he fought and they subsided.

"Could you ask on her?"

"I will try, but I'm like you. I do what they say. That's the best way to get her back, you understand?"

He nodded.

"All right, help me get the luggage to the pier. Do they search everyone?"

"They search the men. I can't say I remember them looking at the ladies."

Once again, having Molly along provided a crucial advantage. I left William at the back of the carriage and walked back to Molly. She sat inside the buggy, readying herself to be escorted to the pier.

"Are we ready?" Her tone remained prim and cold.

"Not yet. Can you take these? You'll have to carry them on your person. They're searching the bags, but not the women."

Molly accepted my knife. As I slid the derringer out from underneath my coat, she placed the knife high on the inside of her thigh, caught in her garter. I stole a glimpse—her skin fair and soft. For a moment, it brought me back to the night before and to the White House—the smell of fresh linen. She caught me looking.

The guards accepted the luggage and started their search. Molly had extra bags. Norris supplied them. They were filled with exquisite clothes, befitting a woman of stature who planned an extended stay. We would leave them, further obscuring our departure when the time came.

The guards opened each bag and gave a quick look through their contents, the search completely inadequate. It would have been easy to conceal my weapons between the clothes. William and I walked back to get Molly. His feet shuffled against the ground. The soles of his shoes had worn into an uneven tread.

"You live on the island, William?"

"No, sir. I work here on the docks and live over yonder." He pointed to a grouping of shanty-like sheds, maybe a quarter mile away. They were patched together from scrap lumber; some looked like driftwood poorly sawn and tacked on top of one another. Fishing boats and poorly maintained nets stood next to the shacks.

"They don't let too many workers stay on the island, sir. My wife worked there, in the kitchen. Was a good job. Sometimes she brought leftovers on the weekend. That cooking over there is good eating, sir."

"Is the ferry the only way on or off the island?"

"No, sir. There's a dock on the north side. It's for the big boats coming from the sea."

"But that's it? Only two ways off?"

"Unless you won't mind wading them marshes."

"You can get all the way across the channel?"

William shook his head. "No, sir. But we pull in small fishing boats close to shore along DuBignon Creek that cuts through them marshes. You'd have to wade through the muck an' all."

"Where?"

William pointed north of the dock. "That's where the best spots are. They don't let us fish in the channel no more, but some of us still go out under the moon to catch breakfast."

"Will you be fishing tonight?"

"I might, sir. You want me to catch you something?"

"I was thinking of having you row out to get us. Can you be out an hour or two before dawn?"

"That's when we go," William said.

"If we need it, I'll signal you from the shore. Will you see a lantern?"

"Long as there ain't no fog out."

I reached into my pocket and felt the wad of money. Norris gave it to us. Without taking them from my pocket I peeled two off the stack. William was already leveraged with his missing wife, but a little cash would serve us well if it kept him on our side.

"Here." I handed him the money, a half year's salary or better for a man like William. "I don't plan on staying long. You be out there tonight, and the night after if we don't see you. Understand?"

Any longer than that meant things had gone wrong, and we would never leave the island. His eyes fixed at the bills while his stare lingered for a second before stuffing them in his pocket.

"And I'll be sure to ask about your wife."

"Thank you, sir," he said. "I..." He stopped. For a moment I feared the sobbing might come back, but he held it together.

"Just be out there tonight, and if you can, have this carriage ready to go."

I helped Molly step down onto the dock. We would leave the carriage as the ferry didn't have room. William took charge of the horses, steering the buggy toward a stable along the road.

As we walked toward the pier, I told Molly of the plan, at least the backup escape route. She listened without appearing to pay me any attention. She could change roles so easily, adapt to any situation.

Before boarding the small ferry, the guards searched me.

They left Molly alone, especially after she fussed over their attempt to look in her small handbag. Her clothes spoke of wealth and distinction, and the guards in gray didn't want to upset a rich patron. They searched me twice, going over each pocket. It made up for letting Molly walk ahead without so much as a simple frisk.

A small gathering of passengers stood near the bow, some well-dressed. It gave us extra cover. We weren't the only ones arriving by ferry. I stood next to Molly, leaning over the railing to gauge the depth of the water. I wasn't a strong swimmer. My childhood summers were spent corralling a sea of humanity north, not swimming in the creeks like other boys my age.

The little boat rocked as they started the steam engine, pushing us toward the island. We rode into the open water, through a channel cut in the salt marshes that lined both the shore and island alike. The smell of salt permeated the breeze, and I breathed deep.

"I love that smell," Molly whispered.

The glare of the sun forced me to hold a hand to my eyes when I looked to her. Beyond the island lay an open expanse of water, spilling out into the ocean. I was grateful the island was in sight of the mainland.

"I better not have to swim, Joseph."

"It doesn't look that deep." I struggled to see anything through the black water. It was well over our heads.

"I can tolerate much, but a soaked dress is my limit."

"Maybe we can find her before the ferry returns at the end of the day. I promise, I'll find a way. We won't swim."

"I'll meet you at the stables, then?"

"Be careful, Molly."

She turned to me, still keeping her distance to avoid suspicion from the others on the boat. I played the role of servant, not equal.

"You're not the only one who is good at his job, Joseph."

"I'm not saying that. I feel responsible, I asked you to come."

"I wanted you to ask. I'll find her and I'll meet you at the stables."

The ride across the channel lasted only a few minutes. It took longer to board the boat. When we docked on the island there were more men in gray uniforms waiting to meet the boat. My heart quickened. A single man stood among the guards, dressed in a dark suit with a leather gun belt and a gold star pinned to his chest. I lowered my head, averting my eyes. Molly stood next to me, but before I warned her, she started toward the ramp leading off the boat. I watched helpless as she crossed, setting foot on the pier right in front of Red Billings. There was a moment, a flash on Red's face that told me he recognized her. A small smile formed, and he stepped toward her. But Molly beat him to it.

"Why, Mr. Billings. I heard you were here, and I so hoped we would run into one another." She used her most refined southern accent.

It caught Red off guard. She chose the direct method, confronting him on his own ground—daring, but smart.

"Ms.—" Red struggled to come up with a name. Certainly, he had scanned the passenger manifest, and he wouldn't have recognized her cover.

"It's Mrs. Beck, of course. We met in Washington, I believe at one of Mr. Lamon's social occasions."

"Of course. Are you traveling alone, or is your husband with you?"

Molly flashed a smile as she leaned toward Red in a suggestive manner. One of her gloved hands reached for his arm, and she drew him in as an escort, turning him from the boat.

"I'm afraid my husband, such as he is, will be somewhat delayed. I trust I can find good company until he makes his appearance." Molly began walking Red toward a carriage at the end of the pier. "You will join me for a refreshment once I get settled? I'm sure we have much catching up to do."

Twice, Red turned to look back at the boat. Both times Molly clutched his arm tighter and kept him steered toward the carriage. He offered a hand to help her into the seat, and then settled next to her, motioning for the driver to start for the clubhouse. I busied myself gathering Molly's luggage and getting it hauled to a waiting wagon. As I had hoped, Red spent no time scrutinizing the help.

Once Molly and Red were out of sight, I set off to get a fix on the island. Being alone unsettled me. So much was out of my hands. We were close, yet I could do nothing. With any luck, we would be on our way north before dawn, but the wait would be torture. Molly had left with both my derringer and my Bowie. I longed for the weight of the blade tucked in behind my hip.

I pulled out Norris' flask and took a long drink. It would have to last the day, and I had finished half the whiskey on the buggy ride. It wasn't as good as Pinkerton's, burning a bit on the way down, but it was likely the best that the bootleggers had managed to sneak into the South. It quieted the shakes. I might need every drop to make it off the island, particularly if I needed to be steady. After this trip it was time to stop the drink. I swore it to the Great Spirit.

The late afternoon sun bothered my eyes as I finally located the stables. There were a few servants around, a pair of women looking after children, and some men maintaining the grounds. They were all colored, their condition little improved since the day of liberation. I stepped inside the stable and adjusted to the dim light, standing just inside the barn-like doors. The clubhouse framed in the doorway—a beautiful building, the trappings of the north and spoils of war created amazing luxury in the heart of the rebellion. The very existence of this club, the infusion of such rich and powerful men, served as a symbol. The building was power, a reminder to the rebels across the channel of who held it and who didn't.

A few men worked the horses, but they paid me little attention—either too white to confront or I blended in as one of the servants. They went about their business of cleaning the stables and brushing the horses. I walked through the building to the far side, the polished end of the stable facing the clubhouse. Everything on this island was a façade. The portion of the stable facing the guests held fresh paint and trim, the illusion of luxury, while the servants lived out of sight.

I approached one of the horses, a dark brown mare. She seemed extra spooked. Intensity filled her stare. I spoke to her, coaxing her forward until I could reach over the gate and stroke along her head. Her hoof dragged along the floor, still nervous, but she calmed as I focused on her.

With a stomp on the stable floor she started, backing away from me. He had come from behind with my attention drawn to the horse. I had let my guard down.

"Joseph Foster."

Slowly I turned, keeping my hands in plain sight. He had one man with him, holding a short-barreled double shotgun while he kept out of the line of fire, approaching as close as he dared.

"Red."

"Put these on," he said, tossing a pair of irons in my direction. They were attached with a short chain, not long enough to get around a man's neck. The metal made a dull clank as it landed on the wood floor of the stable.

I hesitated, staring at the irons. There was little I could do. I had nothing, no Bowie, no derringer. It wouldn't have mattered anyway. That shotgun couldn't miss from this distance. I leaned over and picked up the irons.

"Go ahead, put them on."

He waited until each of the locks clicked shut. The cold of the metal bit against my wrists, and I had no way to keep them loose enough to slip out.

"I never thought I'd see you again," Red said. He was one of the Pinkerton detectives I had tangled with in the streets of Washington—one of the drunken men I had fought that night on patrol, my last night in uniform.

My mind raced. *What happened to Molly?* She was nowhere in sight. Red had her somewhere. He must have seen through our story or forced the truth from her. He would believe little from me, and I had no idea what Molly might have revealed, so I played the only idea I had.

"Mr. Lamon sent me."

"That so? Why would he send you?"

I struggled to keep my cool. I desperately wanted to charge him, to choke him with the chains. But it would be better to talk my way out.

"To check on you. He's worried you don't have a full grip on the situation here." Red's face contorted slightly and his eyes narrowed for just a second. He had failed once before, and Lamon might just check on him.

"We'll see. I already sent a telegram."

I struggled to keep any alarm from my expression. If Baxter had managed to return, or at least to send a message north, then Lamon would know I meant to come for him. Any telegram back to Red would mean my death.

Red turned to the man holding the shotgun. "Take him to the stockade. I'll deal with him after I see to that whore he brought with him."

CHAPTER ELEVEN

Wood lined the walls of the cell, thick and dark with moisture while the heavy air tasted stale. A small window with an iron grating let in the last remnants of the dying daylight. Night would fall soon. I waited for my eyes to adjust, then walked to the window. I tugged at the bars. They held my weight, even as I pulled with all my body against them. My irons clanked against the bars. Nothing moved, not even a perceptible amount. Panting from my labors, I leaned my head against the bars and fought for the sweet cool air from outside.

Molly could handle Red, though her prospects would be much improved if she knew he had discovered our deception. I walked to the door and tried the other window there. It was as solid as the first. The cell was a separate building across a court-yard from the constable's office, and there was no jailer in sight. They were confident of their cage. Even the door hinges were on the outside. I ran my fingers over the seam the door made with the wall, the workmanship taunted me. The cell held solid.

My eyes strained against the dark. A small bench sat in the far corner of the cell. It had a hole in the top, not wide enough for a man to pass through. The stagnant smell of urine and feces rose from the depths. With one whiff I pulled back. Holding my breath, I placed an ear into the void and listened. A small trickle of water babbled from below. I went to the window on the far wall to see along the outside of the cell. A clay pipe stuck out, emptying the latrine into a creek that flowed down the hillside. It might be large enough for a man to squeeze through if I pried the pipe out of the way.

I pulled at the lid of the latrine, but nails held it fast. I even tried catching the chain between my wrists on one corner and pulling up. The wood gave a little, but I feared my wrists would break before it tore free. I scanned the room. On the same far wall two sets of irons hung toward the floor anchored near shoulder height. I grabbed hold of the nearest set and yanked. They were bolted tight, but the wood moved. I stopped and gained a better grip on the shackles. The rough iron scale told me no one had used them in a long time.

Gripping a length of chain in both hands and placing a foot upon the wall, I held with my arms and pushed with my leg. Then I put both feet up and pulled. A cracking noise filled the cell. I flew backwards and landed hard on my back. The chains piled on top of me. They were free.

I crossed to the door and did my best to look outside. Night had truly descended, but I was certain no one watched the cell—no one heard the crash, and no one would hear what I planned to do. I gathered the chain in the middle, with the iron shackles at either end. At the latrine I swung the cuffs hard against the top of the bench. I hit it again and again. The collision of metal on wood echoed through the wretched pit below as if I was beating a primitive drum.

On the fifth or sixth strike the wood splintered. Then it shattered, revealing a large gap in the latrine cover. I let the chains drop to the floor and I pulled at the remnants of the lid. They pried off with ease as soon as I had a handhold. I could stick my whole head into the void below. No light entered or escaped—black as roof tar.

I lowered myself into the latrine, trying not to land hard in the muck below. But even as I eased down I couldn't touch the bottom with my arms extended. I had to let go. Landing in nearly two feet of rancid slop, the stench battered my senses. I fought the urge to vomit, especially as my boots leaked and soaked my feet with the simmering waste.

My hands felt along the fieldstone wall. It took a minute of searching to find the entrance to the clay pipe. The slop half-submerged it and I slipped twice, falling face forward in the soupy mix. My hands found the bottom of the latrine and my fingers dug into the mud.

I forced the pipe loose, and kicked free the rocks that held it anchored to the wall. That created a gap just large enough to squeeze through. With a little writhing I made it into the night—free. Sucking in the sweet night air I purged the smell of the latrine from my nostrils. I fought the urge to vomit again as my sense of smell returned. I reeked, but I had little time to think on it, or clean up. Immediately I headed toward the guesthouse, hoping to find a rear entrance and then Molly.

The gaslights were lit, pushing the night back into the shadows. As I neared the building I kept to the large willow trees. Spanish moss covered their branches, hanging like clothes left to dry. They cast haunting shadows through the light from the gas lamps, perfect cover close to the guesthouse. At the back of the building I spotted Red. I slipped in with the shadows. He stood by an entrance with the door open, speaking to someone. With one hand he leaned back into the doorway and pulled her out by the arm. She fought his grip, but he overpowered her—Molly.

The man with the shotgun emerged from the door behind her, and Red led them both down a crushed gravel path. I hugged along the trees and began to follow. Red pulled Molly's arm every few steps. She responded stiffly, but complied. The upper part of her dress hung loose, obviously torn, and a large welt formed on her left cheek. Her lip looked split. A trickle of dried blood hung down her chin.

I followed them, staying in the dark, stepping like my mother. She could move like a cat stalking prey. Red led Molly north, to the shoreline. I searched the air for any sign of a shifting wind, which would send the smell of my clothes down wind. But the night blew in from the salt marshes, carrying my stench in the opposite direction. It mixed with the smell of the sea. The only thing to give me away was the rising moon, still bright and low in the sky.

The path came to a slight bend, with a great tree blocking my view. I stayed off the gravel and in the knee-high grass. Creeping toward the path I knelt in a patch of stones and selected two round river rocks. They were placed as decoration and white-washed at the base of the tree, but at the size of my fist they made perfect weapons. One I would throw and the other could bash in a head. I started to close the distance when the sound of horses forced me to dive behind the tree. They approached fast, and there were many of them. I pressed my stomach to the ground. The horses stopped in front of Red and Molly, six in total, each with one of the gray uniformed men.

"He broke through the cell, sir," one of the horsemen called to Red. "Made it out the latrine."

The horses were in a frenzy, reading the body language of their riders. They circled, and tossed to either side. The lead rider kept a tight hold of his reins, but still had to force his horse to face Red every few moments.

"Fools. Get the dogs. Head north and set up on the beach. That's the only way he can get off." He tugged Molly into sight. "This bitch says they have a boat waiting. Shoot him when he's in the water. I don't want him back here, understand?"

The lead rider directed his horse north and kicked with the stirrups. The others followed and their heavy gallop faded as the humid air muffled the sound. Red jerked Molly's arm again, bringing it high so she had to stand on her toes.

"Lamon will be happy with Joseph dead. But you, I get to keep." With his free hand he grabbed her jaw, squeezing her face until she looked at him. "A little opium will calm your fight. I'll leave you in my quarters for a month before I whore you out to the guests. They will love the red hair. I may even turn some money. Now show me where they are!"

He jerked Molly forward, headed toward the docks. I stalked again, waiting for another chance. But the trees became less frequent as we approached the water's edge. The lack of cover forced me to hang farther back, with only the grass as means to hide. Red led them north past the dock and along the shore. They headed toward the marshes, where we were supposed to wade into the swamp and signal William out on the fishing boat. I held the chain tight between my wrists so it wouldn't rattle and ruin any chance of surprise.

Over the open ground I began to close in, kneeling to obscure my silhouette whenever Red stopped. We approached a cluster of trees along the water's edge, a hundred feet or so along the shore. Red kept his voice low and turned to the man with the shotgun. He gave some kind of instructions, and the man headed inland, sweeping around the trees from the far end. Red continued with Molly. He pulled his pistol and cocked the weapon. Someone stood in the stand of trees.

I followed the man with the shotgun. He walked alone, making a terrible racket in the tall grass. I approached without fear, covering the last few feet without much care for staying quiet. He swung around at the last moment, smelling my stench as I neared. I caught the barrel of the shotgun in one hand as I tossed a rock toward him. I didn't throw it hard, but gentle as if passing a ball. Instinctively he reached for the rock, loosening his grip on the gun. I pulled on the barrel and the shotgun came loose. Swinging the gun with all my might, I broke the wood stock against his head. It sounded like a cane hitting a rug on a clothesline. He collapsed at my feet.

I knelt down and felt in the man's pockets. I recovered the flask and wad of bills Norris had provided while I searched for the keys to my irons. I found them in a vest pocket, and quietly slipped out of the shackles. It felt good to be free, but I spent no time tending to the welts on my wrists. I picked up the shotgun.

The grass muffled my approach as I converged on the stand of trees. I walked quietly through it. Two figures huddled in the shadows at the base of the larger trunk, a woman and her child. Red burst forward into the clearing. He held his pistol in one hand as he flung Molly toward the figures.

"So you thought you'd leave? You thought it would be so simple to walk out on me?" His voice raised, pure anger spilled out. He lifted his free hand and struck the woman across her face. She fell to one side, sheltering the child at her feet.

"Get up." Red demanded. He pulled on Molly to keep her close.

With his attention turned toward the woman, I approached from behind. I gripped the broken shotgun stock like a pistol and leveled the gun at Red's back. Standing upwind the putrid odor ruined my approach. Red turned and pulled Molly close. One hand clutched her about the waist while the other pushed the pistol against her head.

"And now we have everyone," he said. Then he yelled. "Miller, over here."

He adjusted his position as he scanned in the direction where I had emerged from the night. "Miller!" His voice had more urgency, and he tucked himself deeper behind Molly for cover.

I let him take another probing glance into the dark—long enough to punctuate his growing fear. I raised the shotgun.

"Recognize this?"

He stared at the gun and then me.

"Makes no difference." But his voice betrayed him. He pushed his pistol farther under Molly's jawline. She squirmed from the barrel as best she could, but one pull of the trigger would kill her right in front of me.

"Let her go, and you walk away." I kept my voice level, trying my best not to look at Molly. The fright on her face would unnerve me, and if I saw the bruises and her split lip I would lose control. But I had a worse problem. I had been several hours without a drop of liquor, and the first signs of it showed in my hands.

"That doesn't sound like much of a deal." Red scanned the horizon to the north of the island.

Time was crucial. Red's men were bound to arrive with the dogs, especially as I would be easy to track. Red kept his head half-tucked behind Molly—cover from the shotgun. But then she caught my eye. Without moving her head she glanced down to her left hand. She held my knife, the blade pressed against the length of her arm, tucked away and out of sight.

I stepped a half foot to my left, distracting Red to give Molly the opportunity to act. Red tightened his grip and swung Molly to cover the angle I had created. Suddenly, she let go of her weight. Her legs came out from underneath her. The hand holding the knife plunged the blade into Red's thigh. He pulled the trigger, but the bullet went over her head and into the trees. The shotgun kicked hard in my hand, flinging the barrel up over my head with the recoil. Wood splinters from the broken stock dug into my palm, but I didn't take my eyes from Red. I hit him in the right shoulder and upper chest. The buckshot spun him around, and he reeled backwards, his pistol sailing off into the dark.

I regained control over the shotgun and stepped forward to stand above him. I cocked the second hammer and put light pressure on the trigger. Red lay on the ground looking up at me.

"Are you okay?" I asked Molly without taking my eyes from Red.

She said nothing. Her hand held the bloody blade, and she stared at me towering above Red. He spit blood, his teeth stained and his right arm mangled. For a moment, I held the barrel on him, feeling the trigger weight against my finger. He was badly wounded, but he might live. I de-cocked the shotgun, saving what ammunition we had. Red presented no threat, but we had to get moving. The sound of the shot might be heard at the north beach. I released my grip from the shotgun and reached out to examine Molly's face.

"Don't...," her voice trailed off as she turned her head from me. Her dress fell off her shoulders, torn, bruises developed along her arm.

"We've got to go," I said. "The others will come soon."

I took my knife from Molly's hand. She shook. At first she didn't want to let go. Behind Molly, the two figures sat huddled by the tree. The girl tucked her face deep into her mother, burying it in the woman's dress. Even in the dim moonlight a fierce look preyed upon the mother. As she stood the bump at her stomach told me we had found the right woman—five years my junior.

She appeared four or five months with child. She walked over to examine Red, leaving her daughter to stare at me and Molly. The little girl had long features and a gangly gait. There was no mistaking it.

"It's *his* daughter," Molly said quietly.

"She told you?"

Molly nodded.

"Does he know?"

"No. The girl doesn't either. It's the only way she would be safe."

"What's her name?" I asked.

"Emeline."

"Does anyone else know?"

Molly nodded toward Red. "He does. What are we going to do with him?"

"There's only one thing we can do."

I turned with the knife in my hand. It would be quieter than shooting him. Behind me, Annice had circled around to stand over Red. Every few seconds he spit more blood, which ran down his cheek and clotted in his light beard. She stood just out of his reach, while his good arm flailed toward her feet, trying to reach out to grab hold. Then she raised her hand. She had retrieved Red's pistol where it landed after the shotgun blast. Before I could stop her, she cocked the weapon and pulled the trigger. The report of the pistol startled through the grove of trees. She cocked it again. Another shot filled the night. I didn't reach her until after the second shot. Red was gone. Two holes punched in his forehead, a dumb look fixed to his open eyes.

As I gripped Annice and pulled the weapon free, her weight gave way. She folded to the ground and sobbed. The little girl wanted to run to her mother, but stood frozen in place. Her mother had just killed a man as she watched. If Red knew the Old Man had a daughter, I couldn't imagine what he had done to them.

I scanned the night before us, looking north to the tip of the island and then back south behind us. No one was coming, but every second counted as precious. Those extra shots would bring a response. We had to leave.

I gathered Molly up, holding her by the arm. A flash of anger crossed her face when I pulled too tight. I was holding her like Red. I eased up and spoke soft. The urgency overtook my voice as I fought to keep calm.

"We have to go, Molly. They'll hear the shots and come. Can you help me with the girl?" Molly nodded, but she felt distant. "I need you, Molly, I really need you right now. Do you hear me?"

Something snapped in her, like she had been underwater and just surfaced. Her eyes met mine, a cold hard look fixed upon them. "Yes, Joseph, I hear you."

She started toward the child and grabbed the little girl by the hand. I went to Annice and gathered her up, carrying her like a child in front of me. She was motionless, in shock. I tucked the pistol into the small of my back, where the derringer normally fit, and holstered my knife.

"Where are we going?" Molly asked.

I nodded toward the shore. The sound of water wasn't far away, bordered by the marshland that lead out into the causeway between the island and the mainland. We didn't have a lantern to signal William, but even with it, we wouldn't have the time to stop and try. I hoped he had ventured out, waiting for us. After we cleared the tall marsh grass we would be able to see a boat on the water and signal him.

Molly stood fast and glared at me.

"We don't have a choice, Molly. When they find us, they'll kill us. All of us."

I had given my word we wouldn't swim, but I had lied. There are only so many ways off an island, and there was no way to guarantee that promise.

Molly looked back toward the guesthouse. Far off, the horses were coming back. We had minutes at most. It was the dress. After everything that night, a wet dress would be our undoing.

Molly stood for another moment, further signaling her displeasure. Then she grabbed the little girl's hand and dragged her past where I stood holding Annice. She said nothing as she walked past.

Even before we hit the water the deep mud pulled at my boots. The smell of the marsh overpowered the rancid stink of my clothes. I was relieved for some mask of my own odor. Twice I nearly lost a boot until I stopped and removed them. I stood Annice in the mud and she appeared to recover enough when her bare feet eased into the muck. Molly transferred the girl to me, and we waded out into the tall marsh grass. Before we disappeared I looked behind us, our trails blazed through the vegetation. We would be easy to follow, especially as the moon strengthened by the minute.

We struggled through the mud until we hit the stream that flowed through the marsh. The water appeared deep, certainly over my head. I started to lead our way across when Molly grabbed my arm.

"Look," she whispered.

A boat bobbed in the creek to the south. A lantern hung on a post in the bow, illuminating the old rowboat and the figure in it. When Annice splashed into the water behind me, the person in the boat sat down and began rowing in our direction. It was much earlier than I had asked William to be ready, but if it wasn't him, we had nowhere to go. I stood the girl behind me and removed the Bowie from its sheath. I had left the shotgun back on the island, and Annice had spent two cartridges from the pistol. Molly handed me the derringer. She had saved it.

"I thought you was going to use a lantern, sir?" It was William. "I was getting the boat ready when I heard all that shooting and thought it might be you."

As he pulled the boat next to us, I handed him the child. He grabbed her and put her in the stern before turning to help Annice. Molly followed, and William pulled me aboard. We turned the boat around and rowed south down the creek, out of the marsh and into the causeway.

Annice and the little girl sat in the back of the boat, with Molly behind us in the bow. Both William and I took an oar. After a few pulls, we gained a rhythm that plodded us forward and through the dark water. I scanned the island in either direction—nothing. The sun would rise in a few short hours and we needed as much distance as we could manage. The *Drinking Gourd* peered through the heavens, calling me north.

William steered the boat north of the dock along the mainland. We landed by the rustic cabins he had pointed out earlier that day, unloading on a small rocky beach.

"Sir, I had your carriage readied case you came, but I don't think you can fit 'em all." He looked over the small crowd we had assembled. The carriage could take three at the limit—a cabriolet, not meant to haul more.

"Do you have a wagon?"

"There's an old one we could hitch up, sir. It won't get far. The axle is going bad."

"It'll do."

"A man came looking for you, too." Fear touched his words.

"What man?" I asked. I looked around to make sure we weren't prey to a trap.

"No, no, sir. He ain't here. He went to town at a boarding house for the night. He was asking if I seen you. Definitely was asking about you. I ain't seen too many Indians pass this way. No offense, sir."

"What did he look like?"

"A white man, younger than you. He was all beat up and had on a shiny suit. It made my eyes hurt to look at it in the sun."

Baxter. I should have killed him.

"He gave me this." William held a roll of bills in his hand. "I don't want it none, sir. You can have it."

I shook my head. "Keep it, William. What was it for? What did he say?"

"He said to come get him when I saw you. I won't tell him nothing."

"Help me hitch up the horses, William. Wait till first light, then tell them we passed through. Tell him we headed west." Maybe it would draw Baxter in the wrong direction.

"I don't have to say a thing, sir."

"He'll kill you if you don't. He'll find out we left the island and he'll come for you. I can handle him. Just give me a head start."

"Sir, my wife? Will you still ask on her?"

I had forgotten about it. "I'll do what I can."

"Can you give her this?" William handed me a medal, bronze and small like a quarter. Medals like this were popular in the War years for celebrating battles won or successful campaigns. On the front side it had a forged image of the Old Man with the word "FREEDOM" stamped above his likeness. Below his image "EMANCIPATION PROCLAMATION." I flipped it over. The date read "Jan 1, 1863."

"They was selling 'em a few years after the War, celebrating what the President gone and done for us. My wife called it a silly waste. She'll know I'm still thinking on her if she sees it. Tell me you'll give it to her."

The medal was tarnished and well carried. My hand closed around it. I placed it in my pocket with the black velvet bag, which had escaped the scrutiny of the island jailer.

They had killed his wife—no doubt in my mind. But I couldn't tell him. Norris would hold the hope of her release over William's head, but keeping her would be too much trouble. Exactly what Norris was doing to me, holding out hope to leverage me to his purposes. If I was honest with myself, I had likely lost Aurora like William lost his wife. It wouldn't make sense for Norris to keep her alive all these years. Despair rose in the pit of my stomach. William and I were prisoners of hope.

"I'll try."

CHAPTER TWELVE

Savannah was a ghost town—not a federal troop in sight. Night held too many dangers for them, even in the city proper. Our wagon wheels made a low, grinding noise against the cobblestones, which were poorly leveled, causing the wagon to rock even at low speed. I began to believe the rebellion had gained the upper hand and Norris might prevail if the rebels were united. Most of the buildings were in bad repair, with windows boarded shut and chimneys half-fallen. It was as if the city population had packed what they needed and started west.

We headed unmolested toward a safe house from years ago—the First African Baptist Church in Franklin Square. I hoped it remained, even if it sheltered children traveling in the opposite direction. When we arrived, it stood untouched from the only time my mother and I had passed through Savannah. Slaves built the brick building after ending their shifts in the fields. Its imposing steeple stood high above the city, yearning for freedom in a way its creators could only dream. But the steeple also served as a beacon, signaling a stop for runaways escaping up the eastern seaboard.

I knocked on the back door and waited. It was a makeshift door, the wood splintered and cracked, held together by a cobbled collection of timber and nails.

Nothing.

I pounded again and glanced back at the wagon. Emeline peered out. She stared at the commotion I made. After a few moments, a shuffling noise came from within. Light sneaked through the loose joints in the door.

"Who is it?" a voice called out—an older man. We had woken him.

"Travelers in search of shelter. Just for the night."

"There are boarding houses, seek those. We open in the morning if you need guidance of the spirit. Till then, we are closed."

"Please, sir," I said. "We need more sanctuary than a boarding house...like the space below the altar. Just one night, then we follow the North Star."

The light between the cracks became more intense as he lifted a lantern to peer out the thin slots into the darkness beyond.

"I don't know what you're talking about."

"I was here as a boy, guiding runaways. We stayed a night below the sanctuary. I can guess it might be filled with other passengers, but I have no care of it. I seek protection until I can get my cargo north."

"How do I know you're not—"

"A tracker? If I was, we wouldn't be talking. I would have broken down this door."

"I have a gun."

"And you may well use it if I am out of line." A few moments passed and the silence pressed in. "Please, sir. We are pursued and in need of help."

"How many?"

"Myself...two women and a child."

The light shone bright again through the cracks.

"Molly, Annice, come here. He needs to see you."

Both women dismounted from the wagon and came to the door.

"And the child?"

I motioned for the girl. She watched from the back of the wagon. Slowly she stepped down, her legs wobbly as she landed on the ground. The four of us stood in front of the door for his inspection.

The light dimmed from the cracks, replaced with the sound of metal scraping in a lock. When the door opened, a wedge of light spilled forth and reached in the direction of the wagon. Before us stood an older man, a colored man with gray streaking his tight curly hair. He had small spectacles, which caught the light. In one hand he held an oil lamp, in the other, a double-barrel shotgun—neither hammer cocked. He grasped the weapon awkwardly, like one not used to firearms.

"We're well past curfew," he said. "Sometimes the federals still patrol and arrest anyone they find."

I let the women enter first. The man escorted them down a short hall. The darkness of the church wrapped around us, with only the oil lamp guiding our path forward. The air was musty and stale. I pulled the door shut, ensuring the latch caught to secure the door, then rushed to catch up. He led us into the sanctuary, toward the front of the pews by the altar. Small holes in the floorboards almost blended in with the wood planks in the dim light. They were air holes drilled into the floor in ancient African tribal patterns, a means to disguise their purpose—ventilation for the chambers beneath.

The man opened an entrance to the hiding place below the floor.

"It might be tight for all of you down there."

"I'll stay above to keep watch," I said. "If you don't mind me sleeping on the floor."

The man shook his head as he showed the women down the steep ladder. "There's a bed with blankets down there, but I don't hold it much for comfort."

Molly smiled, the first I had seen since we left the island. She placed a hand on his arm, her voice soft. "Thank you, we'll make do."

The pastor replaced the floor as the women disappeared below. Then he turned to me. "Come with me, son. I have clothes, and judging from the smell, you need a fresh set."

My stench had become a constant background that I no longer noticed. He led me to a small room and dug through a dresser drawer until he found a pair of trousers, a shirt and vest, and a well-worn jacket.

"These look like they'll fit. They're not Sunday best, but they should work to get you out of the city."

"Thank you. We'll pay you for your trouble and the clothes." I started to unload my pockets, placing the items on the small bed in the room.

"I'm the pastor. I don't always stay here." The man nodded toward the bed. "Recently there have been lootings and robberies in town. Times are getting worse. Even the soldiers go hungry when the trains don't arrive. I expected visitors earlier, but it looks like they won't be coming tonight."

"Children?" I asked.

His posture changed—a slight shift in his weight as an uneasy silence settled in the room.

"Yes. We hide them from the federals when they get off the trains, then help them along. I never know if they find their parents." He got up to leave, but stopped. "You were here as a child?"

"Once. My mother and I came east as a favor to get someone, a daughter separated by a bill of sale."

"You were a conductor?"

"More a scout. My mother was the conductor." I placed my flask on the bed. Empty as it was, his eyes darted toward it. "I'd share, but I'm afraid it's empty," I said as I shook it to prove I wasn't holding out.

"I'll go see to your horses, and then maybe I can find us something."

He left me in the room with two candles fighting against the darkness. But they were enough by which to change and transfer my belongings. I repocketed the medal from William. The Bowie and the derringer fit in their usual locations, and I pulled on the fresh jacket to conceal both weapons.

I left the velvet bag out. Slowly I pulled out the silver necklace. Sitting on the bed, I rotated the delicate eagle's feather between the tips of my fingers. When I pictured Aurora's face, I only saw Emeline. She had the Old Man's eyes. I found it hard to look at her, like having the Old Man watch me. I worried that others would see it. But the color of her skin made the association unlikely—invisible, like I had been.

"Must be important by the way you stare at it." The pastor had returned and stood at the door.

"Reminds me of someone I lost."

"And you can't find them?" he asked as he handed me a bottle. "I don't have any glasses, so we'll have to settle for drinking straight from the bottle."

I pulled out the cork. The smell of whiskey wafted up from the open top. I breathed deep for a moment, savoring the flavor. For a second I almost passed it up, but then I took a long pull from the bottle—terrible whiskey, but perfect all the same. I handed it back.

The pastor took a swig. "You didn't answer. You going to find them?"

"I've tried a few times. Maybe I'm not meant to."

I put the necklace back in the bag and then in my pocket as he offered the bottle again.

"I never used to drink. But lately, things don't seem to leave me. If I don't have a little whiskey they find me at night." He went quiet for a moment. "Were you in the War?"

"In a manner. I didn't do well in uniform."

"The Army of Northern Virginia." He took another drink from the bottle.

"You were with General Lee?" I asked. It seemed impossible. "You're colored."

"There weren't many of us. We raised us two Negro regiments from Virginia late in the fight. Mine was hospital workers in Richmond. I never touched a musket—don't know if I could. They set us free if we enlisted. We didn't know how the War would sort out. We regarded Lee as a good general, the South believed in him. It could have gone either way."

"You could have traveled north."

He shook his head. "It's not that easy if you're caught in it. When I enlisted, my master freed my wife and son too. I couldn't leave without them. They were proud of that uniform—gray though it was. Our freedom."

I found it hard to think of a colored man seeing the Confederacy as freedom. The Old Man had been troubled by rumors of colored soldiers in Lee's Army. He worried that the Confederacy might free their slaves before the North delivered emancipation. It might have changed the nature of the War, especially if Europe sided with the South.

"You ever in Richmond?" he asked.

"A few times."

"The President came. I saw him myself after Lee fled the city. We took off our uniforms and followed a crowd to greet him. Don't get me wrong. I wore that gray uniform, but I would follow Father Abraham anywhere. Imagine...these eyes have seen the President."

The Old Man had insisted on seeing Richmond just hours after the city fell. I stayed at his side as he wandered the streets. The city burned, fires set by Confederate troops to destroy stores of tobacco left in the warehouses. The buildings were carved into rubble, and the President walked unmolested where hours earlier the seeds of dissent had reigned supreme. I thought it a grave risk, but the Old Man insisted. As we walked farther into the heart of Richmond, the city's slaves poured from everywhere. They knew the Old Man and flocked to him, calling out as they would to the messiah.

"He was a sight. But even he couldn't erase the horrors of that city. The hospital was terrible. I might have done better in the trenches. The men with arms or legs torn off, half a head missing, they all come to the ward. Artillery is godless. I hear those screams still...doctors sawing on limbs, men crying till they fainted. They put me on grave detail for weeks. I smell it sometimes." He took another drink.

"There's a reason for everything," he continued. He waved his hand while holding the bottle, indicating the church around us. "I found my ministry—taught myself to read so I could discover *His* word myself. Everyone has their purpose. It led me to this magnificent place where most every night we help little ones get home. I found my path clear through the suffering of Richmond. You'll find your way, too."

"I'm not sure that's true."

I had hurt everyone I loved—my wife, Molly, Aurora, the Old Man.

"I don't believe that," he answered. "That little girl out there, she's counting on you. So is her mama, and that other woman. I saw how they looked at you. I don't know your business, and I won't ask, but *He* brought you together for a reason. You're looking over that which is sleeping under my altar."

Shame came in a wave, overtaking me as I stared into my hands. This man was wrong. I did this for myself. I agreed to help the Old Man so he would forgive me. And then I agreed to help Norris because he would lead me to Aurora. None of it meant for the little girl in the other room. Everyone used her. I was using her.

"The two wolves," I said.

"How's that now?"

"My mother once told me there's a battle between two wolves inside each of us. One is evil—anger, greed, lies. The other is peace and hope."

"Which one wins?"

"The one you feed." I looked into my hands. Something had to change. "What's the best way out of the city?"

"Depends on where you head. You going north?"

I shook my head. For a moment, I paused. I didn't want to say too much, to even reveal a direction in case this man would compromise our flight. But that felt too cautious. I had been to Savannah only twice, and it might be better to ask for help in our escape, rather than risk wandering the city searching for the best route.

"West. What's the best way?"

"My guess would be through Atlanta. Then to Chattanooga. From there, the railroad heads west. Bound to be roads along the rails, though I've never been that way."

"When do the trains leave for Atlanta?"

"There's two passenger trains each morning, and a freight line that leaves before noon."

"What time in the morning—for the first train?"

"Eight-fifteen. You can set your timepiece to it. We'll hear it from here. The next leaves at ten."

"The first is best. Can you take us in the morning? I'd have to leave the horses and wagon with you."

"I couldn't pay you for the horses."

"There's no need. I don't plan on being back. You can have them."

The pastor nodded. "Well, then, I'll wake you plenty early."

I took another drink from the bottle and handed it to him. "Thank you."

"From the look of it, I think you found your way?"

"No. But I know where we're not going."

The pastor laughed. "Sometimes, that's the same thing."

CHAPTER THIRTEEN

West. During the fading days of the War, the Old Man feared the West most of all. He feared Lee's army would disappear into the wilderness, dissolve, and emerge as a guerilla force that would never cease the fight. The War would linger forever, the Union shattered by constant strife and death.

I cracked the hidden door below the altar and woke Molly early. She climbed the ladder slowly, and I showed her to the small room where she could clean up.

"We can't head directly to Washington. Baxter will be following us the whole way and Lamon will be waiting."

"Then what do we do?" She poured cold water into a washbasin and began to splash it on her face.

"We head west. Find somewhere we can stay for a time, and send word to Norris' journalists. That way, *we* control the situation."

Molly dried her face, standing in front of me when she was done. I expected some argument on her part, especially as I was dragging out the whole ordeal. Instead, she nodded.

"You're all right with that? I know you want to get back."

She nodded again.

"You don't have to come, I can take—"

She interrupted me. "Joseph, if you say that's best, I trust you. I'll get the girls up and ready."

Memphis was our new goal. In the days with my mother, we had made friends with plenty of riverboat captains. Even if none of them still plied their trade on the river, other boats would run up the Mississippi—an ideal way to escape, and one that Baxter might overlook. He'd head to Washington, and we'd be long gone and safe.

The train rolled straight through Macon, Georgia, on our way north, stopping in the city for only an hour to take on new passengers. It set me further on edge. Peering through the windows, Macon showed the potential of what the South could be. There were no signs of the War here, no burnt buildings, no wrecked roads and shuttered windows. It was thriving—a main hub for the Barons to extract their cotton and textiles. General Sherman had spared this city on his march to the sea, burning Savannah and the rest of Georgia, but skipping Macon altogether.

On our way to Atlanta a rebel unit barricaded the tracks, and the train glided to a long slow stop in time to meet the rebels— likely prearranged. A pair of men walked the train taking money from the passengers, an extra tax to fuel the rebellion. I worried we would be singled out for our pairing alone, but they were only interested in the money.

In Atlanta we transferred trains and made Chattanooga by first light—the rail gateway to the West. A thin ribbon of track connected it to Memphis and the mighty Mississippi River. We were stiff and weary as we walked to the station at Memphis and I gained my bearings. It was bustling with activity—trains changing tracks, people gathering their bags, wagons and horses dragging goods across the city.

"I'll rent us horses," I told Molly. "We can maybe get a wagon and use the roads from here."

"Won't we take the train?"

"Not from here. It's best to get off the rails. The trains from Memphis are a constant target, with supplies coming in from the west. We're better off making our own time along the road. And if Baxter's behind us, he'll expect us on the trains. That would be easier." I couldn't wait to be free of this place, to take the horses west over the mountains and across the state.

"Do you think he followed us?"

I made certain that Annice and Emeline could not hear as I drew Molly close.

"I hope not. We'll be harder to find if we abandon the trains, though. Pinkerton told me that Baxter had a network of informants, so we need to keep moving. From here, horses would be best—slower but safer."

"Why don't you let me rent the horses? A white woman will have better luck, and if I leave it up to you, we'll be riding a small buggy behind a pair of donkeys."

She was right. We were still too far south and my skin was too dark.

"Well, then, make sure you find us good horses, and check their shoes. No need throwing a shoe along the road. And the wagon, if you can—"

"Stop, Joseph. I know how to shop for horses." She was full of sass. I relented.

Molly left as I took Annice and Emeline to the nearest general store. In some ways, the three of us fit better without Molly. We bought cornmeal, salt pork, and coffee. Even with it, the trip would be difficult. I estimated ten days through the mountains. We would have to rely on the kindness of strangers, which I knew possible. The route I planned contained a fiercely independent people, who even during the War sometimes backed the Union. We would seek those enclaves, and with them, shelter at least for an overnight.

Molly returned with two horses and a wagon, though they appeared more suited for the plough than either the saddle or hitch. She watched me look them over.

"I thought you were bringing back horses."

Molly looked away. "The best I could do."

"But you were worried I could only find donkeys."

Molly glared. "Joseph, I am in no mood to be trifled with. I have no credit here. I told them I was newly arrived and required horses to pull my belongings from the rail yard. They would only allow me to rent two plough horses and a wagon."

Emeline watched the exchange and smiled. She knew I teased. I motioned her forward and held her up to the horses so she could stroke their noses and look into their eyes. They were old. I wondered what it would add to the journey. But they appeared well shod, and we could start with the wagon, abandoning it if we needed to take to the smaller paths through the foothills. I could walk the horses as the women rode. If we were slow enough, saddles weren't crucial.

Annice and Emeline rode in the back, while Molly sat with me. I steered us toward the passenger terminal of the railway, a quick stop, but one born of necessity. With little money left, we had no other way to secure the change of clothes we all so desperately needed. There would be plenty of baggage on the terminal, and it would be a simple matter to steal a few bags as if we were delivering them to the nearest boarding houses. Hopefully, they would contain clothing. A jacket for the child, or a trunk with blankets and bedding would greatly improve our lot, especially if greeted by any spring storms.

At the terminal, a porter approached and asked where we would deliver. I told him it mattered not to me—I would deliver to any locale in the city. I nodded to Molly and told him I had one passenger to drop off. Molly knew what I wanted, and played the role to perfection. She pointed to several bags and a steamer trunk to put on the wagon. The porter loaded extra bags and provided the name of a boarding house.

As a matter of habit I scanned the crowd as we pulled away. My eyes sorted through the suits and dresses, looking for anything out of place—nothing. I started us toward the road, when something at the far end of the platform drew my attention. In an instant, my heart rushed in my chest and my face flushed. I had caught a fleeting glimpse, a glimmer in the sun. I strained to get a better look.

"What is it?" Molly leaned in. She sensed the change in my posture.

I handed her the reins and pointed to the end of the rail yard.

"Take the wagon up there and wait for me."

"How long?"

"Not long. It's likely nothing, but I have to be sure. Go up there and wait."

I hopped off the wagon. I was out of sight of Annice and Emeline when I slipped the Bowie from its sheath. I carried it blade pointed up, pressed against my forearm, and concealed against my side. Up close it would be faster than a pistol, and the swarm of people provided the type of concealment needed to get that close.

I searched the crowd, moving no faster than those around me. At times I looked down to keep my gaze from revealing my true intent. His back faced me, but I had no doubt—Baxter. I was thankful for his hubris, the fault in him that demanded such attire.

I closed in slow. With luck, I could take him here in the platform, drag him out of sight and be gone. Perfect placement of the blade would make it silent. A risky proposition, but if accomplished, we would no longer fear what followed at our backs. I let him live once, a mistake I intended not to repeat.

He headed toward the end of the train, where the crowd thinned and cover became scarce. I mounted the next passenger car and exited on the far side. From there I mirrored his passage, keeping the train between us. As we walked, I checked between the wheels, tracking his progress, his suit perfect for stalking.

When I reached the caboose I flipped the Bowie in my hand. I waited for him to round the corner, but the footsteps stopped. I listened—nothing. *Had he seen me?* I dropped to my stomach to look under the train, but the large wheels of the car blocked my view. I slid under the caboose to look out the back end. Two sets of legs stood at the end of the caboose—one shiny, one in pressed black cloth.

I strained trying to hear what they were saying. Murmurs were all I made out. Slowly I crawled forward, taking care to keep the gravel between the rail ties quiet as I shifted my weight between my hands and feet. I squeezed close enough where I could reach out and drag either man under the caboose with me. Without a firearm it would be futile. They would both be armed, and I could only take down one at a time. So I listened.

Baxter's voice held a swagger, a maniacal intonation that spoke of some depravity, like how he had laughed when Norris' men brought him in—beaten and broken. He enjoyed it.

"A porter saw them a few minutes ago. He was sure it was them. I'll check the boarding houses and livery."

The other man spoke. I didn't recognize his voice—controlled and monotone, the southern accent impeccable.

"Don't kill him."

"All I want is the whore. She can be trained. Either way, you can have the Indian. But he's handy with that knife, and I won't be cut to save your revenge."

Baxter started walking away. Then he turned. "And Mr. Lamon sent a telegram. He wants you in Richmond."

He started walking again. I waited for a moment, but the car above me clanked as the wheels on either side started to rock. My cover was about to move. As the train started, I rolled out from under the caboose. Baxter would be too close still. I bounded to my feet and ran along the train toward the engine, grabbing the ladder at the head of the caboose. I swung up so neither Baxter nor his friend would be able to see me as the train pulled out. At the end of the rail yard I jumped off, landing near where Molly waited with the wagon.

I scanned the end of the tracks back toward the passenger terminal. The crowd had disappeared, and only the porters searched through the luggage and loaded the carts that delivered to the boarding houses. Baxter's accomplice had disappeared. The black pants were all I saw—and the southern accent. I couldn't place the voice, but my mind raced. *The Black Fox?*

I sheathed the Bowie and then mounted the wagon. Annice stared at me, clutching Emeline.

"We're fine. It was nothing."

Molly drove the wagon out and headed for the road. After Annice and Emeline settled in the back, and the rough roads hid our voices, Molly leaned close. She gripped my arm, holding it like she had done so long ago.

"How did he find us?"

"I don't know. But Baxter's not alone. We need to ride hard. They're sure to follow."

CHAPTER FOURTEEN

I drove the wagon through that afternoon and well into the night. Molly slept a spell and then took over. The road west and over the first ridgeline was the toughest. But once on top, the going became easier and we made better time. We were in the foothills now, the terrain rolling. The road followed an old trading route that had been widened and trampled over for decades as an important connection across the state. If Baxter discovered we rented horses, there would be only one route of pursuit. We were caught in a delicate balance. I wanted to use the road to put as much time and distance between us, but it could also be our undoing. At times like these I longed for a rifle, or even a shotgun.

I constantly scanned the road behind. My nerves jumped with every rider. Several times, I pulled the wagon to the side of the road and readied the pistol. Twice Molly dismounted and went into the woods with her revolver, a means to get a jump on anyone who might ambush us. But both times the riders passed without incident.

As the sun fell we needed to stop. I feared the moon wouldn't be bright enough to travel by, and what little strength I had drained fast. Molly looked similar. A few hours of sleep would improve our lot. We rode by several small villages or towns, but they all felt exposed with too many people who would tell of our passing. I wanted a place out of the way, off the road if possible.

Outside one small settlement, we found our best option. A worn cabin sat perched on a ridge above the road, barely visible through the trees. The roof sagged in the middle, and the siding was hobbled together with long boards patched by smaller sections. After the lamps were turned out it would be hard to find. It would also give us a good vantage of the road and plenty of escape into the ridgeline behind. I directed the wagon up the dirt path, holding onto the wood seat to keep my balance. As we pulled up my mood buoyed. A quilt hung over the railing of the porch, old and tattered, like the building—the shoofly pattern—a symbol I searched for when scouting routes in my youth. It signaled safety, or a person inside who could guide escapees to freedom.

I stopped the wagon and dismounted. The porch needed repair, but warmth emanated from the structure. The smell of dinner lofted outside, causing my stomach to tug. I had forgotten when last I ate, some salt pork along the road as we drove. Molly covered me from the wagon as I knocked on the door, her pistol at the ready under a small blanket we had found in the stolen luggage.

Feet shuffled toward the door. It swung open, revealing a large colored woman who filled the doorframe.

"Can I help you, sir?" She backed away slightly as she spoke.

"My name's Joseph, ma'am. We're traveling the road and can't make it much farther in this dark. We just need a place to stay overnight, and if you have extra food, we'd be willing to pay for a meal. The little one's in need of some time off the wagon." I pointed back toward Annice and Emeline.

The woman stared at us, examining me and then switching her attention to the wagon. We were an odd sight—a colored woman and her child, an Indian, and a white woman.

"I noticed your quilt. I used to look for these when I showed runaways north."

"You were a conductor?" She opened the door wider, her expression softened.

"In a fashion, more a scout for the next stop."

"Well, come on in." She opened the door. "When we was up in Ohio, I used to shelter them that made it that far. There weren't many, but enough passed my door...and none went for hungry. We escaped the whip ourselves, we did."

She ushered us inside, and I waited for Molly and Annice to dismount the wagon.

"I'm not set much for company, but my son will be home for dinner and I have plenty of stew cooking. He rode himself to town a while back for work. You can take the horses to the barn if you like. There's feed a plenty in there."

I unhitched the horses and walked them to the barn. It dwarfed the cabin in size, and from the outside, it looked better cared for. Three horses whinnied when I opened the door. They were muscular and well looked after. A pair of saddles hung along the first stall, and I stopped to examine them closer. They held fine leatherwork, expensive and lush with carved detail. It felt out of place. Normally I would have moved on, but hunger and weariness overcame me. There could be an easy explanation. I tied our horses outside and brought a tray of feed to where they stood.

Inside the cabin, Molly busied herself helping with the food, while Annice sat at the table holding Emeline. They were both quiet and subdued. Annice appeared to tire more each day, but slowly she had emerged from the shock and attended to Emeline. The girl tolerated the travel well, never fussing too much about the long days and stretches of boredom. She had never left Jekyll Island before, and took the whole thing as a grand adventure. Annice knew the danger, but she made a game of it to shelter the little girl from fear.

The woman accepted Molly's help over the stove despite an awkwardness about the interaction. I caught her staring at Molly. Likely, there had never been a white woman in this cabin.

"Can I ask where you's off to?"

"Toward Memphis," Molly answered instinctively. She shot me a glance, horror on her face. She had revealed our destination.

"Why, you have days left. And with this one so worn out?" The woman wandered over to Annice and held her face in a motherly show of affection. "How far along are you, child?"

Annice looked up, almost puzzled by the question. "Four months." Her voice cracked a bit as she answered.

"And you are just beautiful, little child. Are you her father?"

"No, I'm just working on getting them north."

"But her father is a white man?"

I nodded, but I didn't want to continue the line of conversation, her question more probing than I liked. Annice shot me a look across the table. It was a secret we need not have out.

"There's been many a white man who had their way with our Negro women." The woman rested her hand on Annice's head. "Not much to do 'bout it, I guess."

"Your husband's not here?" I asked. I wanted to change the subject.

"No, he done left during the War to enlist for Father Abraham. Went to Massachusetts to muster into the Fifty-fourth. Died near Charleston at Fort Wagner. They had themselves a battle there. I got a letter that came near a year after that did call him a brave man and gave me some back pay. Don't even have no likeness of him like those white boys send home to their mamas. Sure wish I did sometimes. I miss him, and growing up, my boy did too. But we was might proud he done fought well. He didn't have to go, you know. We was already free. I raised my boy myself, never let him forget his father and how that man did live."

"I'm sorry to hear it. The Fifty-fourth is famous."

"Is it, now? I never knew that. Did you fight in the War?" She scooped stew into bowls to place on the table.

"In a way, they stationed me in Washington, along the defenses. Not like your husband."

"So you done defended Father Abraham then. That's about the same of it to me."

She finished putting stew into bowls, carting them one at a time to the large wooden table in the center of the room. The kitchen served double duty as a dining room. A doorway at the back led to the bedrooms.

"Well, I don't know where my boy is. We may as well start without him. At times his work goes late, never can tell."

"What does he do?" I thought about the horses in the barn and the saddles I had seen hanging.

"Why, he heads south from here and looks for them escaped children from up north. Brings them back to the factories."

For a moment I stared at the table. *A tracker? A colored tracker?*

A chill took hold of me. Across the table, Molly felt it too. Annice met my stare. The horses and their saddles made sense. He would need them to drag children back north to get paid. Still, even up north they would never permit a colored man to rough handle white children. He had partners. This was not a good place for us.

I sat at the table and started into my bowl of stew. It had cooled to lukewarm, but I ate anyway, forcing myself to hide my concern. We hadn't had a hot meal since before Jekyll Island. Emeline finished her bowl and looked for more. At least the girl would get some food, and her mother needed more than we had brought with us from Chattanooga. The baby she carried surely did. We could gain something from this stop, even if we immediately pushed on.

The woman watched Emeline with attention, about to ladle another spoon into her bowl, when the cabin door opened. A young colored man stepped in, a shotgun in one hand and a gun belt slung around his waist. I counted him five years my junior, shy of thirty at best. He wore a long dark jacket with a weathered leather hat.

"Mama, what's with them horses at the...," his voice trailed off when he noticed us. "Who are you?" His tone was ice.

"They stopped for dinner is all, Douglas," she replied. "Come sit and have some stew."

The man looked around the table, examining each of us in turn. I nodded toward him when our eyes met. He didn't acknowledge the greeting. He placed the shotgun in the corner of the room, pulled off his jacket, then took the seat nearest to his gun.

"Where are you off to?" He stared at Molly. She looked away, uncomfortable under his gaze.

"Memphis." There was no use concealing it from him and arousing the suspicions of his mother. We already had told her we were headed that way.

"And then where?" He gave me the same cold look he had leveled at Molly.

Before I answered, his mother spoke up. "Douglas, this man was a conductor on the railroad. You remember those that brought us north?"

"That so?" He maintained his dismissive tone.

"Your mother told me about your father."

"I wouldn't know. He left when we was up in Ohio. I stood 'bout the size of that one." He pointed toward Emeline. "My mother and I disagree on such things. You wouldn't find me dying for the white man or his Union. A whole lot of nonsense for nothing."

He leaned forward, resting both forearms on the table. He glared at Molly.

"And now look here—a white woman in my house. Maybe you and your man here helped some runaways? That seems to make everyone up north believe they liberated us poor Negro folk." He held his spoon up, shaking it as he made a point. "We was liberating ourselves long before your armies came to deal with old Jeff Davis. I was eight when I walked all the way across the Ohio River myself, running from slave catchers. Colored people didn't need no help to be free, we already was, and proved it with our feet. Didn't need the likes of you—" he pointed at Molly, and then swung the spoon in my direction "—or you."

Molly's face was flushed. "And now you hunt innocent children that liberated themselves. How is it any different than was done to you? Because they're white?"

"Molly—" I reached across the table and grabbed her arm. We didn't need a fight.

Douglas leaned forward with both arms on the table, staring at Molly. "You ought to bridle your woman, especially in my house."

A bitter taste rose in my mouth. I pulled away from Molly's arm, readying myself for the fight. I had to get to my knife before he turned to his shotgun. Molly stared into her bowl. Across the table, Annice watched everything, clutching Emeline close. The girl looked to me and then at the older woman by the stove.

"Douglas, they are guests." But her voice went flat. Her son ruled the house.

"I suppose they'll be looking for a place to pass the night." He pointed his spoon at Molly. "She can sleep in my bed. I'll show her my appreciation." A smile spread across his face. He turned, letting me see the lustful gleam.

"We've intruded enough," Annice spoke up.

She pulled back from the table with Emeline in her arms. I nodded and started to stand, but the young man grabbed my arm. A twinge of anger surged through me, then faded. I could finish him before he made it to the shotgun.

"There's no hurry," he said. "After all, you are guiding my sisters here to freedom, ain't you?" He nodded across the table to Annice and Emeline. Then he turned and smiled at Emeline.

"Want to see something?" He reached in his pocket and took out a small leather pouch. He opened it and poured the contents onto the wood table. Several small thumbs fell out, blood clotted where they were severed—children's thumbs, all white.

"Oh God..." Annice stepped back, knocking over her chair.

"What are you so afraid of? Think of it as liberation. One less white planter, a child at a time."

He was a killer. This house and this man were so different than the place we left in Savannah with the pastor—a colored man who served in the Confederate Army, guiding white children home against the tide of the Draft. Before us sat another colored man whose father had enlisted in the Union cause. But this man hunted those same escaped children. The simmering aftermath of the War gave birth to such ugly contrast.

"Bastard!" Molly's face turned flush.

"Molly—" I wanted to calm her before it broke bad.

"Watch your tone in my house. If you were a man, I would kill you for less."

"Douglas, I done told you not to bring those things around my kitchen."

He laughed. It was awkward, and he still watched Molly and me. He scooped up the tiny shriveled thumbs and placed them back in his leather sack.

"We're going now." I motioned to Annice and Molly.

"I won't bother you none." He turned to his mother. "I'm going back out."

"So late?" she asked.

"Some men came in from Chattanooga looking for a guide west. They were back down the road at the Landry place. I told them I'd gather my bedroll and see them on their way."

A chill passed through me. *Could Baxter have followed us already?* They would be moving lighter and able to overtake us, though they would have to stop and question everyone along the way. It could be easy to pass us by and never know.

"You're going that way too, ain't you?" he asked.

I nodded, not wanting to say anything.

"We'll be by later if you want to follow. Though I expect it to be before dawn, and these men are in a hurry. You won't keep pace with that wagon or those tired horses."

"We'll make do without, start out at first light."

He stood, gathered his shotgun, and headed to the back room beyond the doorframe. A moment later he returned with a bedroll and a saddlebag. He walked to his mother, kissed her on the cheek, and headed to the door.

"We might stop by on our way back through, Mama. If we don't stay, I'll check on you all the same in a few hours." He closed the door behind him, and a few moments later his horse trotted off in the distance, down the steep slope toward the road.

"I hope he didn't bother you none." The woman looked concerned.

Molly shook her head, obviously shaken. We all were. Emeline clutched her mother. We needed to leave this place, especially if Baxter might draw near.

"He had it rough down south. His baby sister done died before we left the plantation. I'm afraid it filled him with the hate."

"How old was she?" Annice asked. She tried to break the awkward tension as Molly picked up her chair.

"I don't know I rightly remember. I tried not thinking on it much, though that little girl was also our savior. My husband decided to flee north after we lost her. He sent for us to follow once he found his way north."

"I was the master's nanny," the woman continued. "I could bring my girl to the big house until she was walking. Then it was too much to keep up with, and the lady of the house told me I had to leave her home. I had to leave my little girl to watch over another little girl. Where's the sense in that?"

Molly reached out to touch the woman's arm.

"You see, there weren't no one else to watch her. My husband was in the fields, and so was most other womenfolk. So I put Douglas to watching over her. I come home one day to find him in an awful way. He went out and played while she was napping. But she woke up, you see, wandered into the cotton field. Best we know she got lost, a little one like that could barely see over the cotton when it's all up in bloom. My husband did whip that boy good. We spent all night looking for her. It wasn't till three days on that a crew doing the picking found her. They wouldn't let me see her none. Buzzards had pecked at her awful, even eaten my baby's eyes."

Molly covered her mouth. The woman stared toward the stove for a long time, still remembering.

"My boy ain't bad. He just had to live with losing his baby sister on his own fault and all. Then his papa left for Ohio without us. The man blamed him for losing our angel."

I pitied any children who came across her son. His eyes had told me all I needed to know. And there was something in the woman's voice when she talked about her daughter. She didn't believe her own story, but it was easier than the truth. I pictured her son leading his little sister into the fields, finding a stone to bash her head with. He was a killer long before hunting white children.

"There ain't much room to stay in here, but the barn has a

loft with plenty of hay." The woman sounded distant, her voice heavy.

"I'll help with the dishes," Molly said.

"No, leave 'em for the morning. I'll take care of 'em then."

She wanted to be alone. We picked up and gathered our belongings, what little we had brought inside with us. We were quiet as the woman stared at her stove. She didn't move as we left.

Outside, the night held calm and the air crisp. I breathed deep, relieved to leave that small cabin. I looked in all directions, venturing to the edge of the drive, searching the road below. Pausing, I strained my hearing, listening among all the night noises for any sign that the son and his charges headed this direction. There was nothing.

Annice brought Emeline into the barn, holding a small oil lamp. I met Molly back by our horses.

"I'm sorry I snapped," she said.

"He realized he'd have to deal with the both of us."

"Do we leave right away?"

I looked to our horses. They were old, and weary. The other horses inside the barn stirred with our voices. They were fresh and rested.

"Not yet. Let the girl sleep an hour. When the old woman has gone to bed, we'll leave. We'll take the horses from inside and make our way."

"He'll pursue us."

"That will happen anyway."

"Do you think he's fetching Baxter?"

"It's possible. Baxter may know we left Chattanooga by horse. We need to stay ahead of him."

I waited outside while Molly readied the horses in the barn. She handed me the pistol. I stood overlooking the road, still straining to hear through the night. Clouds obscured the stars. It disoriented me, like we were adrift and unable to fix our direction of travel—in some ways that worked in our favor. They would beckon me north, like they had always done. For now, I had to ignore them as we headed west. Perhaps in Memphis I could find the *Drinking Gourd* again and follow it home.

After an hour or more the lights in the cabin went dark. Molly woke Annice and Emeline. The little girl cried at first, and we struggled to keep her quiet. She looked drained, and a good night of sleep would have done so much for her.

We opened the barn door and walked briskly back to the road with the new horses, trying to keep them quiet. A little ways up the road we came upon a path that branched off and traveled uphill. I wanted to be off the road, especially after stealing horses and knowing at least three men would be riding behind us. I led them up the small footpath, which wandered above the cabin and into the foothills. Certain we were alone, I stopped the horses and we finished strapping the saddles. Molly hadn't been able to tighten them enough by herself in the dark of the barn.

We were about to mount up when the sound of horses came from the road below. They trotted at a steady clip. Their hoof falls reflected off the bare trees.

"Stay here," I told Molly.

I made my way down the path to a point in the bushes close to the cabin. Three riders had ridden up from the road and were just outside the barn, Douglas among them. He clutched his shotgun. As for the other two, even in the darkness the faint moonlight reflected on Baxter's suit. Like he told me, he would keep coming, haunting our every step. He wanted to catch us exhausted and weary beyond fight. And Pinkerton was right—he was good at tracking. The third rider dressed all in black—Baxter's accomplice from the rail yard. At least we knew the odds.

The three approached the barn. Baxter dismounted after he pulled a pistol, while the man in black still sat atop his horse, motionless a few feet behind them. Douglas opened the barn door and both he and Baxter rushed inside. We had so narrowly escaped.

A few moments later they emerged. Baxter dragged Douglas out by the scruff of his jacket, as if punishing a school child.

When he let go he hit the younger man about the head several times. Douglas still clutched his shotgun. Baxter ripped it from his hands and then shoved the young black man to his knees, facing away from the cabin. The other rider dismounted and stood in front of the young man.

I crept closer, keeping the underbrush as concealment from the cabin. Even though there were two of them, I might be able to ambush them here. I pulled the hammer back on the pistol, ratcheting the cylinder to the first loaded chamber. My hands shook a little as the alcohol wore thin again.

But I couldn't do it. Not with only a pistol. My aim was unpracticed over these last years. Even if I were lucky, or good enough to take Baxter and his friend, Douglas would surely turn on me. The odds would be three to one. I de-cocked the weapon, riding the hammer forward with my thumb.

Baxter entered the cabin. He dragged out the mother, placing her next to her son. Baxter turned to his companion. Their voices were distant, but the cold night air carried the sound to where I hid.

"There's only the two of them," Baxter said.

"They were here," Douglas pleaded. "Their horses are still here." He pointed toward our old, worn plough horses. "I'll help you track them."

Baxter's companion said nothing. He turned and walked my direction, slow and deliberate, while he stared into the hill looming behind me. In the dim moonlight, he worked something in his hands, like he was rolling a cigarette. He walked to the edge of the brush, a stone's throw from where I crouched. The bushes in front of me suddenly seemed a scant cover, and I worried he would see me through the moonlight. I contemplated pulling the hammer back on the pistol again, but worried the sound would give me away. I left my thumb on it, just in case. He stood still, like he could sense my presence. I held my breath.

Then a shot rang out. I startled. Baxter had shot the young man in the back of the head. His body fell forward on the ground.

The mother wailed for a moment as Baxter placed his pistol against her head and fired. She fell forward and joined her son.

"You coming in?" Baxter called out. "She made dinner."

The other man stood for a moment. It felt an eternity. Then he turned and walked toward the cabin. When he reached the bodies he stopped and knelt, leaving something on the back of the dead tracker. I couldn't see it, especially with the pale moonlight. But I didn't have to. It was a little paper fox.

CHAPTER FIFTEEN

Our flight turned frantic. At first I tried hard to suppress any noise that might escape and reveal our position. But once out of range we fled as fast as we dared on the small path. Branches and thorns tore at our clothes, they scratched my face, but still we pressed on. Sleep wasn't possible, and with the adrenaline, I needed none of it. We rode to first light, then an hour more for good measure. When we stopped the horses were sweaty and in bad need of water. I tied them near a creek as Molly unwrapped the salt pork.

We still had food, even if only cornmeal and dried meat. It would last a few days if we were careful. Water turned into our largest worry. In our haste we left the canteens back on the wagon. We would have to stop and drink what we found along the trail. But I had another worry. My liquor had run out, and it was only a matter of time before my body became unsteady. I wanted off my crutch, but now was not the time. We needed Memphis.

As we pushed forward along the trail, questions wracked my thoughts. *If the Black Fox worked for Norris, why would he pursue us now? Why would he still be in league with Baxter?* The Black Fox had a different master, or a different motive. That was the only answer. It might explain why he tried to kill me in Ford's Theatre.

The next two days were a blur. The trail snaked and twisted, first up one small foothill, then another. It never branched, never offered another path. It doubled back upon itself, and at times I figured we spent half a day in the same mile radius. But we plodded ever onward, sleeping in bursts, resting the horses, and watching our backs. Even Emeline ceased whining about the pace. I put her on top of one of the horses with Molly, as Annice sat on the other. I was grateful we needed to travel slower for Annice as it kept me upright even when the terrain turned rough. We kept our followers at bay by moving, but it only bought us time. The horses cut deep footprints in the mud, making our trail easy to follow.

By the third day, we were near exhaustion. Baxter liked to work his prey into a frenzy, to catch them when they were most tired. We were falling into that trap. Our food ran low, and the morning meal saw the last of the salt pork. I gave my portion to Annice. Hunger had visited me many times, and I knew the rumbling in the pit of my stomach to be temporary, no matter how distracting.

Late in the afternoon the trail split—a single branch snaked to the right and through dense forest. It lay nearly invisible in the shadows, a deer path, not made by the hands of men. I pushed through the narrow passage amongst the branches, hoping for a place we could stop and rest, if only for a few hours. This would be a chance to break the cycle, to rest and gain strength.

I dismounted and led the horses along this new path. After a short stint it spilled into a beautiful clearing. For the first time in days the full force of the late-day sun fell upon us, its warmth glorious. Low grass filled the clearing—a soft green carpet spread over the land. At the far end of the meadow a single white oak tree stood in the sea of grass. The hand of the Great Spirit had guided us here. Instinctively, I headed for the tree. It provided the only cover, and its large trunk represented strength. It drew us near.

Molly and Annice collapsed to the ground. Emeline lay between them. The grass formed a soft bed, and the afternoon sun broke through the canopy of the oak in bursts. It was peaceful, secluded, and majestic. I walked the horses to a small stream not far away, and tied them to a weathered log lying along the creek bed. They could drink as much as they needed and feed on the sweet grass. I doubled back to the tree and sat with Molly.

"Can we stay? At least a while? I can't ride another mile." She reached out and let me hold her hand, smiling when I grasped it.

The weariness in my back begged me to lay with them, but I wasn't convinced of our safety. "I'll be back. I want to clear out the horse prints and hide our path."

The dense woods tugged at my jacket as I found the trail again. Baxter and the Black Fox would be coming. Perhaps they had taken the road at the cabin and not noticed that we branched off. I held my breath and listened, straining for any sound. Birds chirped and whistled in the trees, the wind blew through the branches. We were alone.

I cleared the deep ruts of the hoof prints from the small game path leading back to the women. Walking the trail, I obscured our passage along the thin tread of dirt snaking through the forest. I used the lessons my mother had taught, passed on to her through the generations—how to walk without leaving a trace, how to remove any trace once left. I even moved the brush enough to block the entrance to the path. We could gain one night of sleep and make a final push toward Memphis. The city must be close—another day, two at the most.

I walked back to the tree where the women rested. Emeline had grown close with Molly during the ride. The little girl clutched Molly's hand as they slept. My mother would like that we were here together. She used to say that our stories were already written. We had yet to act them out.

Annice sat at the base of the tree. Sleep had not found her.

"Are you all right?" I wanted to reach out, but I resisted.

She nodded. "He said he would send you when he could."

"He said he would send *me*?" I had assumed the Old Man promised he would get her out, though I never counted to be in his plans. He led the nation but couldn't rescue one girl from the South—both powerful and impotent.

"He talked of you. I knew when I saw you. He said you were part Indian."

"My mother is from the Miami people." It surprised me that the Old Man had spoken of me at all. He met this girl many years after I had left. "What else did he say?"

"You were the only one he trusted." She looked toward her daughter.

We were quiet for a few moments. She stared at her hands, then back to her little girl. Trying to judge her age, I would have said Annice was five years my junior, though old for a woman months away from a second child, at least compared to most new mothers. But she was beautiful, and likely a generation apart from the Old Man. I couldn't picture them together, couldn't place her skin with his. Not the contrast of color, but the perfection of it next to the Old Man. Flawless, an even light cocoa peered everywhere from her clothing. The Old Man had such deep wrinkles carved into his leathery complexion.

"It hurt him when you left. He said that once. You were family...like a son. Especially after his little one died."

Her words pulled me back to the White House, standing along the back wall in the Old Man's study. Memory can trigger such strong reaction—a distinct smell, of wood and polish, of power and loss. I stood with him through the dark spell after the passing of his Willie, the Old Man's joy. I alone remained the silent presence as those lonely days turned to months. A bond formed in misery can be stronger than any other.

"What else?"

She thought a moment. "He told me what you did for him and how you lost your little girl. You saved people. He said you could save me even when he couldn't."

For a moment I couldn't breathe. I stared at her. He didn't blame me for saving him from Booth's revenge—he blamed me for leaving. *How could I have been so wrong?* All this time I fretted over what had passed, that I made the wrong decision, that I cheated the Old Man from the ending he so sought—none of it true. Desperate to change the subject, I turned from Annice and watched Molly and the little girl.

"He doesn't know?"

Annice shook her head. "When I first found I was with child, I thought it best not to trouble him. I had no way to send word. When he came back a year later, I was scared. I didn't know what he would say." She stopped and stared at the ground between us.

When she looked up, her eyes watered. "What if he didn't want her?" Annice reached over and gripped my hands. "Promise you will keep her safe—even if he doesn't." She squeezed tight.

I nodded. She turned from me and grabbed Emeline, burying her head in the little girl as she slept.

"Get some rest," I said. "I'll stand watch."

I waited until dusk crept into the sky above us. Nothing emerged from the path, and no sound came from the forest. I wasn't sure we would hear passing horses on the trail, but the dark would add security to our position. When the moon emerged it would allow us to see anyone approaching the open ground to our tree.

Molly stirred and sat up. "Did you get any sleep?" she asked.

"Not yet. I'm waiting for dark." I scanned the forest. All around us the sounds of the coming night descended. They gave me comfort. "I'll go set a snare for a rabbit or the like. Overnight, we might catch something for breakfast." I handed Molly the pistol.

I headed toward the stream, stopping to loosen the saddles on the horses. I would take them off in a while, but for the moment we needed them ready. Upstream the forest appeared less dense, so I followed the creek through the meadow and into the woods. Tension left my body as my instincts took over. I looked for small paths through the underbrush, places to set snares. There were days my rope work had netted entire meals for five or six runaways as we moved through the southern countryside. My fingers remembered how to tie the knots, though I struggled to hold them still while working the twine.

Not far into the woods a distinct muffled sound reached me—water, cascading down rocks and landing in a pool. I walked toward it, following the creek until it opened into a small pool with a waterfall. Iron in the water stained the rock orange. The cliff and the drop of the water were not much taller than two men, but it would be an ideal place for a small water wheel. I closed my eyes and listened. I could stay here, keep Molly, Annice, and Emeline safe for a time, wait for the baby to be born. If we had more food, or tools to build a cabin, it might be possible.

The Old Man would love this place. Relieved of my guilt, I yearned to talk to him again. A weight had lifted. I could bring him his woman and daughter, and that would surely heal all there was between us. When he saw Emeline he would understand why I had left him. There is nothing like the joy of a daughter.

I set the last snares, gathered wood enough for a small fire, and headed to the meadow. Dark lurked all around now with the last of the daylight teasing above the treetops. I barely saw myself clear of the woods. At last I broke free and headed to the horses. I intended to take off their saddles and brush them down by hand, but when I arrived the lot of them appeared spooked. As I touched the first one along his muzzle he whined and shook his head. I turned toward the tree. Molly sat under the trunk. She faced my direction but remained still. The failing light made it too dark to seek out her face. I knelt down to drop the firewood.

Quietly I pulled my Bowie and treaded softly toward the massive oak tree. Molly stared at me. Fear held her perfectly still.

I peered around the great tree, angling as I approached. Annice and Emeline were out of sight. Whatever terrorized Molly, stood behind that tree. With no firearm other than the derringer, I needed to get close.

I placed each foot with purpose, straining to hear. Molly sat rigid. As I neared she caught my eye. She tried to tell me something. It distracted me. Stepping out from behind the tree, he caught me watching her. He held Annice around the throat, a pistol jammed into her jaw.

"Drop the knife."

CHAPTER SIXTEEN

Baxter.

I stared at him—my Bowie the only weapon I could use. I rocked my weight forward to charge, thinking I might cover the last ten or so paces and run him through. But it would kill Annice, and he would likely still turn the weapon on me.

"Drop it!"

He jerked the barrel of his pistol higher into Annice's jaw. She moaned and extended her body, standing on her toes to relieve the pressure from the gun. His eyes were wild—a grin consumed his face. Slowly I knelt to place the Bowie on the ground. The other weapons were out of reach behind the tree. Emeline lay on her back. A thin trickle of blood ran down her forehead.

"She's alive," Baxter said, "for now. Step back."

I took short steps, not wanting too much distance. I still had the derringer, but I would have to get it out and be as close as possible, and I needed to know if the Black Fox lurked nearby. My arms dropped a little as I scanned behind me.

"Don't bother. Lamon ordered him to Richmond."

"Why?" I stalled for time.

Baxter smiled but didn't answer.

"Why would he take orders from Lamon? He's Norris' man."

"Is he?" Baxter teased. "He *was* Norris' man. A twisted, sick, bastard." As if that provided contrast to himself.

"Was?"

Baxter laughed. "We *killed* Norris."

"You lie. Norris isn't dead. I saw you at the cabin. And I saw him with you. He's not in Richmond. You killed that woman and her son."

"You don't believe me?"

With his free hand he reached into his inner jacket pocket and took out a small bag. He tossed it to me. It landed at my feet.

Bending down, I opened the bag. In it were the severed fingers of a man—Baxter, ever the tracker.

One of the small fingers in the bag had a ring, a woman's wedding band. My stomach tightened—at once sick and angry. Norris was dead. I leaned forward and caught myself with one hand. My last connection to Aurora was gone, if she lived. My hands shook, and I clenched my jaw. Dry heaves worked their way from my gut. The lack of liquor was catching up with me.

"Lamon wanted Norris brought in," I said. "Why kill him?"

"That's what Lamon told you. But killing Norris was always the plan—right after we killed you. The Black Fox was supposed to dispose of you in Ford's Theatre, but he let you slip away. Arrogant bastard. I should have done it myself, but he was so insistent on his revenge. Though, we should be grateful that he failed. How else would we have found out about this nigger whore, or that one?" He waved his pistol toward Emeline. "Mr. Lamon will be most appreciative."

Baxter gripped Annice tight, holding her about the chest. He tugged her to keep her off balance. Terror gripped her. She kept glancing toward Emeline lying in the grass.

"Who is he?" I asked.

"You should know. Seems you killed his kin back when you went tearing through the South, mauling every Confederate in your path—someone important to him. I'm surprised there aren't more looking for you."

I had killed so many. I peered through the dark. He had to be in the shadows—waiting.

"I told you, he's not here. He turned around at that cabin, after your trail went cold. He has more important business to attend to."

"Like what? Why would he let you kill Norris?"

Baxter acted giddy, like a child with too much dime-store candy. He could barely get the words out. "Because he commands the entire rebellion now."

Pinkerton had been right. Lamon would continue the fight, and he found the best way to manage it to his benefit—control it with his own man.

"And he let you go on alone?" I asked.

"I wasn't supposed to catch you, just push you to Washington. That was *his* idea, not mine. He still thinks I will save you so he can kill you himself. I was glad to be rid of him. He has such little faith in my skills—another from your generation always thinking my youth a hindrance. But I knew I could handle you— one old man, two women and a child. Tracking through these woods is easy. With the path you left, I would have thought there was no Indian in you."

"You have it all figured...except..." I stopped, leaving him wanting.

"Except what?"

I played on his insecurity—his youth. I wanted him upset. "Lamon knows me, and I figure he counted on me doing you in. He no longer has need of you."

"You don't understand."

"I think I do," I answered. "How many people know about the Black Fox replacing Norris? I bet there's only a few, and the less the better. Lamon knows I'll kill you."

Baxter turned his pistol from Annice, first pointing it right at me before aiming over my shoulder to where the horses stood. He pulled the trigger and a shot ripped into the night. It dulled my hearing. In the dim light an orange flash consumed the barrel. Behind me a horse crumpled to the ground in a thud.

"Too bad you won't be there when I deliver a full bag of thumbs to Mr. Lamon." He pushed the pistol into Annice's jaw again, causing her to draw a short, sharp breath. Then he lowered his voice, as if letting me in on a secret. "I always liked you. I heard the stories long before I worked for Mr. Lamon. They wrote a dime-store novel about the great Joseph Foster. Did you know?"

I shook my head, shifting my weight and trying to lower my

right hand enough that it wouldn't be suspicious. The derringer was close to my fingertips. He needed to keep talking.

"But do you know why I really liked you?" He didn't wait for me to answer. "It's the knife. You have to get close, to watch that light flicker as they die. I'm not so good like that. I'm better at tracking, waiting for them to fall apart. The pressure kills most before I get there, and then I shoot them. They're not alive when I find them. I put them from their misery. But you—you take people who don't want to die.

"I tried your way," he continued. "I'm afraid I haven't the stomach for it."

"You used a knife?"

His eyes wandered when he spoke. Perhaps he did it on purpose, luring me to attack.

"Bloodied a suit. I killed that man in the church, the preacher in Savannah. He told me all sorts of things before he died—about Richmond, the bodies in the hospital. Talked about anything but you. In the end, he told us about Chattanooga."

The pastor. My stomach turned again, and my hands shook. I had brought this pestilence straight to his doorstep, leaving the trail of breadcrumbs Baxter followed. It was sloppy.

Baxter tossed Annice aside. She sprawled on the ground near her daughter. He took a step forward, still out of my reach, and raised his weapon.

"What's wrong, Joseph? How many times did you try to kill Norris? And now the War will end. I will deliver your death to Mr. Lamon, and these women. *I* will be the *hero*. Do you think they will write my story?" He reached into his breast pocket and produced a small book. He threw it on the ground in front of me—a dime-store novel with a poor drawing of me on the front. The pages had their corners turned down, the binding bent from repeated opening.

"Lamon doesn't want the fighting to end," I muttered. "You ended nothing."

Baxter laughed. "I will keep your whore." He waved the

pistol toward Molly. "And Mr. Lamon knew nothing about the little girl. Imagine his surprise when I tell him. But you, I'll kill last. Out of respect."

His face contorted into what might pass for a smile. He was making a critical mistake. I would kill my greatest enemy first, not save him for the end.

Baxter swung his gun toward Emeline, still lying in the grass. She stirred, holding her head. As he cocked his pistol, Annice sprang from where she sat—a reaction that I had never seen the likes of. I would never have closed that distance, never had covered Emeline in time. Baxter pulled the trigger and the shot cracked sharp and intense. The bullet struck Annice in the chest.

I dove forward and grabbed the handle of my Bowie. Baxter managed to cock the hammer and fire. The blast and heat from the muzzle went over my shoulder, and the muzzle flash left me groping. My hand closed on the barrel of his pistol as I brought up the Bowie. He grabbed my wrist and threw me past him. I landed hard on the ground and, when I flipped to my back, he flung himself on top of me. His fist fell heavily on my face—then another. My knife slipped from my grasp. I covered my face with both hands and tried to kick him off. He didn't budge.

He reared up with my Bowie in his hand and plunged it down. I twisted enough that it missed my chest but tore into my left arm and into the dirt. He pulled it out and drew back. This time I caught his wrists with both hands. He collapsed all his weight on the butt of the knife, trying to force it into my chest. He began to laugh.

"No...no...no," I screamed.

My left arm quivered, it would give out. I grabbed the blade with the other hand and tried to turn it. The edge sliced my palm, making the steel slippery with blood. The tip of the knife pressed into my chest as my left arm buckled. The steel pierced my jacket, slowly ripping the cloth. The individual threads let loose. My ears filled with a tearing sound. I stared at the blade, willing it to stop, pushing against it with all my might as it slipped through my drenched grip.

And then there was a sound like a ripe watermelon thrown against a tree. Baxter slumped forward. His head landed on my chest. Molly stood over us. She gripped a field rock the size of her fist. She reared back and brought the rock down on Baxter's head as she screamed. The thump sounded in my chest. She hit again, striking harder. Blood splattered my face, the taste of iron on my tongue. It was warm and squirted into my eyes. She hit him again, and his body went fully limp. Her screams turned to sobs. She grunted as she hit him—and hit him.

I pushed Baxter off, rolling him to one side. Molly was on her knees, and she reached out with the rock to hit Baxter a final time. I caught her hand and gripped the rock.

"Molly, stop."

She pulled her arm back, fighting to keep hold of the rock. I pried it from her hand.

"Stop...he's gone."

"No...," she answered. Her eyes were wild. Molly was transformed.

She pulled the knife from where it had fallen to the ground, and stepped over me. Rolling Baxter onto his back, she drove the blade deep into his throat, pushing it to one side and severing the artery in his neck. Blood spurted, covering her hands and face, turning the grass around us crimson. He gurgled through the blood. It remained trapped in his mangled throat.

I leaned up on one side and forced my way to my knees. I grabbed Molly. She shook me off and stepped away from Baxter, my knife still in her hand.

"Don't...," she said.

Emeline sat upright, the carnage all around her. Baxter's feet kicked for a moment and then they stopped. He went limp, the life pulled from his body as his maker took possession of what soul he had.

Molly dropped the knife and sat next to Annice. She picked

up the other woman's head and placed it in her lap. She stroked Annice's hair while one hand tried to stem the bleeding from her chest. It was futile. The smooth cocoa of Annice's face was replaced by an ashen foreboding—there was no staying the hand of death. I crawled toward the women. Emeline sat still, unable to move. I clutched Annice's hand. She pulled me near.

"You promised," she whispered.

Then she was gone.

CHAPTER SEVENTEEN

Molly pulled Emeline away and took her down to the creek. The blood trickling down her cheek made her head wounds look worse than they were. But this little girl would be scarred for all time—scars invisible to all but those of us who had been there. Molly felt it too. Her maternal instincts took over.

I sat for a while longer, and then began to function. Binding my arm and hand, I tore cloth from my shirt to stem the bleeding. The gash to my arm was nasty, but the pressure of the bandage took out some of the sting. My right hand swelled, and I cleaned it in the stream.

Finally, I turned to Annice. I closed her eyelids, letting her lie at peace under the stars. I searched Baxter's pockets for anything of use. His billfold contained a large sum of money—several thousand dollars, more than enough to reach safety. He also had a stack of telegrams from Washington and the notes to the telegram operator for the messages he sent. I didn't have the time or light to study them, so I tucked them into a pocket to examine later. Most important to me, he had a flask. I fumbled at the lid, and once opened, downed half of the sweet liquor. The rest I saved for later.

I dragged Baxter's body, but struggled with my injured arm. Molly came back from the stream and sat Emeline on the far side of the tree where she could not see her mother. Then she joined me, grabbing one of Baxter's legs. We pulled him to the edge of the woods and unceremoniously dumped him into the brush. We would bury Annice under the tree, but Baxter's remains would not desecrate her resting place.

I had no tools to dig except my Bowie. So I went about cutting into the earth. Molly watched for a time as she helped Emeline. The little girl sobbed uncontrollably. When she stopped, Molly fell to her knees next to me and began to dig with her hands. The dirt combined with the dried blood under her nails. We were silent as we worked; neither of us wished to talk. I stabbed through the sod with the Bowie. With each thrust the anger lifted. I wanted to punish something, anything, or anyone for this night. But the person most in need of it remained out of reach in Washington. With each blow to the earth, I vowed Lamon would pay.

We hollowed out a shallow grave under the tree and placed Annice in it. I went to the creek to retrieve river rocks. We couldn't dig deep enough for a proper burial, but we took the best care of her given the situation. Emeline and Molly watched from a distance; the little girl wept and clutched Molly.

At first light we placed the final rocks. Annice would forever lie under this tree, in this beautiful clearing with a bubbling brook in the background and a waterfall not far off—her unborn child still with her. At night they would have the stars for company. I knew no prayers, not even ones from my ancestors. So I begged the Great Spirit to take her, to ease her passage, and watch over her spirit. I placed a hand on the grave.

"I promise," I whispered to her.

We left her there, under that magnificent tree. We all found it hard to leave, but none of us could stay, not even for a bit more rest. Emeline said good-bye, the sobbing turned into dry wailing. Molly pulled her away.

The trail out was rough. I found it hard to hold the reins with my torn palm, and my left arm ached when I switched hands. At least Baxter's liquor had eased my shakes, though a dull headache remained. After less than an hour on the trail we emerged at a little town. A sign hung uneasily in the wind, one of the letters missing. The sun had tanned the wood around it, making the name still visible—Essary Springs. My stomach turned. If we hadn't stopped next to that great oak tree, Baxter wouldn't have caught us out in the open. There was no way of telling how close we had been to town, but that did little to ease my mind.

Essary Springs had a general store, but not much else. The

people here were rough mountain folk, the kind who never declared any allegiance during the War. They didn't seem to notice our odd assortment, or perhaps they didn't care. With Baxter's money we bought breakfast and some food for the road. I made sure to get extra whiskey, then we found the railway. By late the next day we arrived at the outskirts of Memphis. The Black Fox never emerged.

Memphis surrounded us with a different world—alive and pulsating. It felt more like an outpost than a city, transformed by the stalemate between the Union and rebels farther east. A nervous edge permeated the place, not how I recalled it. I had been to Memphis often with my mother, using the city as refuge, a place to get lost with our charges before taking the river as a means north.

The dirt streets were clogged with traffic. Dust rose until it obscured the view just a few blocks away. The buildings were mostly wood, with a few permanent edifices crafted from brick. It was a far cry from Savannah, a much older city brought to ruin through the war. Memphis had seen battle, a naval fight along the river. The city had fallen, and what portion burned during the fighting had been quickly replaced. Our misery imposed little desire for conversation, and the noise of Memphis was deafening after the silence of the woods.

"Where are we going?" Molly asked.

"We'll rent a room at the best boarding house in the city. Just let me do something first."

I longed to change my bandages and let my arm soak. But I had read the telegraphs from Baxter. To my amazement, they were in plain speak, not a cipher among them. Pinkerton would have insisted all correspondence be encrypted. Baxter had been lazy, stupid, or arrogant. I suspected a combination.

The telegraphs came from an address on Madison Place, near Lafayette Park in Washington, all unsigned. I knew the area, in a neighborhood where all the officials lived—like Lamon. But that mattered little. The messages showed a growing frustration with

Baxter, who deliberately stalled his progress. He provided scant details about our location or the chase. It must have enraged Lamon.

The telegrams did report that Colonel Norris was dead. Through the clipped writing Lamon appeared pleased with Norris' demise—his intent all along. Another message requested the Black Fox meet Lamon in Richmond to plot the course of the rebellion. And Lamon wanted us corralled toward Washington, just as Baxter had claimed. The telegrams did not mention Emeline. Baxter never wrote anything about her. She might be safe. It gave me an idea, a ruse to keep Lamon at arm's length until I could be sure, or fix it until we found her lasting safety. I would lure out the truth, and I would use Baxter to help.

"Are we still followed?" Molly asked. She reached out to hold my arm. Since killing Baxter she had clung closer, nursing Emeline while keeping me near. I liked the feeling. I needed her.

I shook my head. But in truth, I didn't know. The Black Fox was out there, likely headed east to Richmond. We didn't even have a name to call him by, or know why he was obsessed with me. I had killed so many in search of Aurora that there was no telling who still desired revenge in that wake.

We stopped at the telegraph office near the rail station. It was a simple wooden building, like all those that surrounded it. Several operators worked the lines, the tapping of Morse code a constant drone. Dust had worked its way inside, and a broom propped in a corner was ready to continue its losing war against the onslaught. I stood on the far side of the desk and crafted my message. I handed the note to the operator, including the address on Madison Place from which Baxter received his telegrams.

Foster and woman dead. Ambushed, no choice. Will stay in Memphis. Excellent food. Advise next.

The operator took the note and transcribed it into code for sending over the lines. He seemed to care little of the content, and asked not for a delivery name. Telegraph operators were accustomed to sensitive messages, and the best among them held confidential the secrets they transmitted.

We left the office and started to look for the boarding houses. A telegram back would take more than an hour by the time the runner made it to Lamon's house and returned with a message. Emeline clung to Molly, holding one hand while clutching Molly's dress with the other. Molly reached out and took my arm. Taking care of Emeline had softened her.

We wandered down the side streets, some of which I still recognized. The city was busier—everything had grown larger and more hurried. Goods flowed from the large western expanses across the river. We walked past wagons loaded with furs and pelts. Some still smelled as they had been dried and tanned in a hurried manner. Other wagons carted lumber to the mills and barrels of liquor to the saloons.

Molly caught me staring at one of the wagons loaded with barrels. "We'll stop and get more for the road," she said.

We tried to make our way to a general store, but found ourselves clogged in a crowd outside a city building. They had gathered to listen to a street corner speech, swelling until the street permitted no traffic. People were agitated, and more poured in by the minute to see the commotion. A man stood on a makeshift stage, made from the bed of a wagon, and held a newspaper high. He pointed to the headline and shook the paper, making it impossible to read.

"Damn them both," he yelled. "We need neither the North and its laws nor the South and its cotton!"

People in the front cheered, clapping at inopportune moments so as to obscure the speaker's words. Some around me muttered. Others tried to figure out what was happening.

"And now our children? Who among you fought for the Confederacy?" he yelled over the swell of voices. People shook their heads. Not a soul present admitted taking up arms against the Union during the War.

"Then why do they want our children, too? They can come, but I will meet them gun in hand! I'll let my powder do my talking." The crowd cheered. Men pumped fists high into the air.

Even the women, who up north would have refrained from such raucous occasion, joined the fray.

Someone yelled from the crowd. "Let 'em come, we'll move across the Mississippi."

The man up front held a hand to the crowd, and silence fell in a wave. "It won't matter where we go. They'll keep coming. When General Bell arrives, I'll let him know. We don't need any of them. Let the Union fight the rebels. It's time for us to be free of their affairs. Starting here, we make our own country. Now is the time. If they try to stop us, then I aim to finish what Booth started!"

The reference to Booth brought me chills. As the crowd exploded in applause and stamping feet, my anonymity melted away. What had started as a street corner gathering turned into a sea of people, swarming and pushing. Molly sensed the change in my demeanor. She gripped my hand and pulled me through the crowd, still clinging to Emeline. We brushed past arms and elbows as I held my head low. We pushed through to the general store a block from the street corner speech. Once there, I grabbed the nearest newspaper.

INVASION.

The headline made dramatic the claim. The city had been free of military influence after the cease-fire with the rebels in the West, allowing it to prosper and grow independent of Washington's influence. That appeared about to change. The Old Man— or someone in the White House—had ordered troops to Memphis. General Bell headed this way, and occupation lay in the city's future. If people resisted, as futile as that stand might be, it would open new conflict. The country would tear not only into northern and southern parts, but a western third as well. This had the feel of Lamon to it, forever advancing the interests of the industrial Barons. They stood the most to gain by bringing the West under control. The wealth of the frontier would further line their pockets.

"What do we do?" Molly asked.

"We can't stay." I flipped the paper to the back sections. It listed the riverboats, their cargo, and if they accepted goods to transport. I pointed one out to Molly, handing her the paper. The *Isaiah White* docked along the river.

"What is it?" Molly asked.

"Isaiah White's boat," I said. "He named it after himself. It's a gaming boat, but he docks at Memphis most of the year. It's got every sin you can imagine—money, booze, girls. He'll leave before this invasion. It won't be good for business."

"You know him?" Molly asked.

"An old friend. We should check on the telegraph."

Before we left for the docks, we made our way back to the rail station and the telegraph office. I wanted to see if we had a response yet. More people were out now. The streets filled, newspapers in hand. Word spread like fire in a dry brush, the smoke visible long before the flame.

Panic reigned inside the telegraph office—the smell of it distinct, a mix of body odor and whiskey. Men gathered waiting for news, the operators tapped out messages, while an assistant took notes. Another operator worked the receiving lines, transcribing the incoming telegrams. We had to get out of the city. There was no knowing what the Union forces would do. Martial law would be the first order of the day, only lifting months after they established security.

One of the operators looked up and recognized me. He nodded in my direction and held up a folded piece of paper. I had my reply.

Understood. Return soonest. Change started. Your skills critical. Repeat. Return soonest.

I couldn't get another message out, even if it would complete the ruse. The sense of pursuit returned. A tsunami headed our direction. *What did Lamon mean by "change started?"* It felt sinister, and large, as if the wave sweeping this way had already crashed over the country. The Old Man may have outlived his usefulness to Lamon and the Barons.

As I made my way out of the telegraph office to where Molly

and Emeline waited, a runner on horseback charged up to the office and jumped off his horse. He rushed inside.

"Blue jackets arriving on the rails. The first train is here." He rushed out of the office as the operators began tapping out their Morse code.

"We've got to go." I tugged on Molly. "They'll close the city. Even if we can't find a boat heading north, we at least need to find a way to cross the river."

I put Molly and Emeline into an empty wagon left unattended. As I pulled away, someone yelled after us, but it didn't matter. We only needed to make it to the docks. Any sheriff or marshal in the city had bigger worries than a stolen rig. I directed the horses down the familiar streets until we saw the smokestacks of the riverboats peering over the roofs.

Isaiah's boat was easy to find—not the typical working Mississippi boat. It exuded extravagance, a rear-paddle design with four decks and two smokestacks. Crowns decorated the tops of the stacks, painted gold in an ostentatious show to flaunt the boat's purpose.

Several men stood guard along the docks. Each carried a Spencer carbine and dressed identical in laundered black suits with bowler hats. The situation fast deteriorated, and the rifles were all that kept a crowd from stampeding. Memphis converged on its escape routes, the river principal among them. Other boats stocked supplies, while a steady flow of refugees headed toward the river, wagons overloaded with household heirlooms. People searched out the ferries, hoping for a shot across the river to avoid the impending devastation. They would try to ride out the occupation with the river as barrier. It hadn't reached the level of panic, but the grip on order was a single shot from chaos. The first sight of federal troops would incite the stampede.

I pushed Molly and Emeline through the swarm toward the boat.

"Back...back." One of the guards blocked our approach to the boat.

"I need to speak to Mr. White."

"I'm sure. Get back." He pointed for us to leave.

"I'm an old friend."

"Everyone's an old friend right now," he replied.

There was truth in that. I peeled off several bills from the wad of cash I had taken from Baxter's pocket. I handed it to him.

"Just call him, please."

The guard looked at the money. He took it and placed it in his pocket. Turning around, he signaled another man at the gangplank. That man walked back onboard the riverboat and disappeared. We waited a few minutes, while the crowd at our backs grew more unruly. The guards pushed them toward the city, but they would listen only a few moments before surging forward again.

Finally, Isaiah emerged along the lower deck of the boat—the only colored riverboat pilot. He wore a uniform modeled after a Union admiral, though more elaborately decorated. He walked to the gangplank and summoned us forward. A smile emerged.

"Joseph Foster. Does your mother still ask about me?" His voice boomed deep and commanding.

I dragged Emeline and Molly to the base of the gangplank.

"Whenever I see her."

"You're a terrible liar, Joseph."

Isaiah looked behind us to the crowd. Boats were setting sail into the river, the noise from the docks swelled to a dull roar.

"Please, we need to get north."

"Everyone has that idea," he said.

"We're happy to pay."

Isaiah looked at me for a moment, then turned his attention to both Molly and Emeline. His eyes lingered on Emeline.

"You still working for the President?"

"Not for a long time," I lied. "You haven't kept up with the papers much."

Isaiah stared at Emeline. I didn't like how he looked at her. Then he examined Molly. Emeline clung to Molly's dress.

"What's with the girl?" Isaiah tried to figure out our odd assortment.

"It's a long story, Mr. White. I'll tell you all I can. But right now, we need to get north." I removed a large sum of cash from my pocket. "We'll pay our way."

Behind us the sound of sporadic gunfire broke through the buildings. It remained far away, but echoed off the brick façades. Isaiah waved us forward.

"Put your money away. We'll talk about that later. Get them on board."

I lifted Emeline across the gangplank before helping Molly across. Isaiah gave her a hand getting on the boat. As soon as we made it over the walkway he signaled to his men.

"I guess it's time," he said. "Gunshots mean we're here too late."

The crew loosened the moorings. The giant paddle in the rear started, and the *Isaiah White* drifted into the current. To the south, steam filled the horizon. It rose as a wall of white, more than a simple boat or two making its way toward the city—an armada. Isaiah pointed downriver.

"I reckon that's the navy. Rumors made them out to be coming, though we didn't expect this for a week. I'm a betting they block the port and don't chase us north."

Isaiah left us and rushed up several flights of stairs. A few moments later, the giant wheel at the back of the boat churned the water at full fury—no simple cruise north.

It was escape.

CHAPTER EIGHTEEN

I took Molly's hand and guided her and Emeline to the hurricane deck—the largest uncovered deck on the ship. A crowd had gathered on the starboard side facing the city. Molly clutched Emeline, and helped the girl up the stairs. The passengers stared at us. We were still dirty from the trail, our clothes torn and stained. Their eyes fell upon Molly and then shifted to Emeline. We would need a good place for the girl on the journey, someplace with less scrutiny.

Thankfully, most of the crowd fixated on the city. The far eastern edge must have encountered the advancing federal force. The army broke over the buildings and the clogged dirt streets like a river through a splintered levee. Distant cracks from rifles forced everyone to strain their hearing. The shots weren't the organized sound of battle. They were sporadic and fleeting.

Smoke billowed from the east, near the rail station. If General Bell had adopted the methods of Sherman, then Memphis would know *"total war."* Only the brick chimneys would be left when the fires smoldered and faltered.

Isaiah proved right. The navy didn't pursue north of the city. He kept the ship at full steam for almost two hours until certain, often coming to the back of the boat to scan downriver. Slowly, we outran a flotilla of smaller vessels, all escaping before the city closed.

When we were safely north, Isaiah ordered the game tables opened. Just like Jekyll Island, the passengers here were the elite crust of society. Not as high as the industrial Barons that Lamon dealt with, but a close second if one existed. And their motives were no different. These men booked passage to see the West, for a taste of excitement as they gambled away their fortunes, and looked onto the danger past the river's shoreline. They hoped they were safe, but that nagging doubt fueled their journey and instilled a belief in courage. Everyone wanted to believe themselves courageous—the genius of Isaiah. He robbed them blind while they loved every minute of it.

Isaiah provided us with a stateroom on the third deck. Molly helped me strip my bandages, and applied an ointment from the ship's supplies. At first it stung, but she bandaged my arm tight, dulling the pain. After Molly and Emeline were settled, I left them to explore. I wanted to believe we were free, but I had to be certain. The Black Fox haunted my thoughts. Likely, we had made it to Memphis free of his shadow, but I searched anyway. The saloon served as the largest central room of the ship, with a second-floor balcony wrapping around three sides of the inner galley. The walls were ornate, painted white with gold trim. Wood pillars were carved to look like ancient Greek architecture, and glass chandeliers hung from the ceiling. Patrons played poker, smoked cigars, sipped on their expensive Kentucky bourbon, and enjoyed the company of the barmaids. I recognized no one.

When I left the smoke to get some air, I found Isaiah at the back of the boat, still scanning the river to our south. I stood next to him on the railing, breathing deep and enjoying the scent of the water. I had loved standing in this very place as a boy.

"What will you take for our passage?" I knew him well, and he would charge. He never took money from my mother, but everyone else paid—somehow.

"I don't need your money, Joseph." His attention didn't leave the water. "There's enough in the saloon that will soon be mine." He nodded his head toward the sound of piano music behind us.

"What do you need, then?" We had little else we could give him.

"There is one thing you could do. This time last year I was robbed, right here on my boat. The guests minded it as character to their journey, which I counted as lucky. I'm partial not to be taken again."

"How many men?" The riverboat was little more than a floating bank.

"Six. They were my security. Two were left behind. I let them swim off."

By the look in his eye and the upturned smile, he lied. He let them swim as far as they might, with a section of iron chain tied between them. They were dead.

"So what do you need from me?"

"I got new men. The ones you met on the dock. Four—big and strong. They was dockworkers with no skill in the killing business. I hired them for their size. Watch them. I don't trust no one no more."

"That's it? Just watch them?"

"Teach them, and watch them," he answered. "Watch everything."

It was an easy job—exactly what Pinkerton had trained me for. And it provided ample opportunity to prowl the boat while Molly and Emeline rested in the stateroom or toured the decks together. It also allowed me as much whiskey, or bourbon, as I preferred. I filled my flask as I walked about.

Isaiah gave me a pistol, a Colt revolver—an old 1851 Navy model. The weight of it felt odd on my belt. He also introduced me to his men, who gave me little regard. Both dwarfed me in size. On our first day together, as I taught them how to disarm a man, I made sure to bring the largest one to his knees. They hadn't expected the knife, and when I slashed him across the throat with the dull side of the blade, their demeanor changed. I held more years, but judging me too soon would have cost at least one his life—had I chosen to use the knife properly. Even wounded, I was more than their match. It gave me confidence, a good thing after the encounter with Baxter where Molly had saved me. But these men weren't warriors, not like the Black Fox.

I spent most of my days watching the gambling saloon—the central feature of the riverboat. Tables filled the room, and I stood on the second-floor balcony, watching it all. Behind me, the barmaids tended to their clients. They were whores, the nicety of Isaiah's label for them notwithstanding. They were all colored. Indeed, it seemed not to diminish their business, rather enhance it. Isaiah knew what his white patrons wanted on a trip like this. They left their wives at home to better network and gamble their money. And nothing spoke more to the cravings of danger and excitement than the allure of forbidden flesh on top of the other sins Isaiah offered. He was a dealer of debauchery, revenge on a society that had for so long kept him underfoot.

Our next stop lay in St. Louis, a natural place to make port and bring on supplies. It would take the better part of two days to reach port, and Isaiah slowed the boat to half-speed, allowing the poker tables to reap as much as they could. Our reduced pace relaxed my nerves—Molly, as well. We walked the upper decks and watched the river. Emeline followed us everywhere, slowly letting go of Molly's dress as she became more comfortable. The mighty river flowed underneath us, and with each mile north it washed away the stress.

On the first night, we let Emeline sleep and stood outside toward the balcony. Our room faced out along the river. The moon reflected bright against the water, not a cloud to obscure its brilliance. We could see the far shore, the tall grass along the edge and the rough country on the other side. Overhead, I searched out the familiar constellations—the *Drinking Gourd*. The North Star guided our path. It called me home.

"What will we do with her?" Molly asked.

"Isaiah promised to drop us in Ohio."

"Then what?"

"I know people there."

"Joseph, that doesn't tell me anything." Molly looped her arm through mine. "Will you raise her on your own?" She mocked me.

I hadn't considered it. Escape had so preoccupied my thoughts, but with Norris and Annice dead, there were few options. I couldn't turn Emeline over to Norris' newspapermen. And I couldn't see how she would be safe if I delivered her to the Old Man.

Molly pulled me tighter. "We could do it together." She was serious.

I pulled away from the rail to look at her. "You don't have to do that."

"What do I have to go back to? My brothel?"

"Pinkerton will expect it."

"I can't, Joseph. I just—" she stopped. She pulled her arm from mine and leaned against the railing. She picked under her nails where the blood and dirt had lodged. They were clean now, but still she pulled at them. "I keep thinking about that man, and the rock. I never—"

I pulled her close, and she placed her forehead against my chest. "You had to, Molly. You did the right thing."

"But I—" she stopped again. "I didn't do it to save you. I *wanted* to kill him."

"I wouldn't be here if you hadn't."

Molly nodded, though it brought her no comfort.

I turned and looked out over the river. "Before, when I left you," I continued, "I had a name of a man—John Everett. I'll never forget the name. He was there when my wife died, and he helped Norris bring Aurora south. I found him in Richmond, half-drunk in what passed for a brothel. The city still smoldered, and he was easy to find. I threw the woman out of the room. He tried fighting me, but the whiskey made him slow. He told me exactly what I needed to know, gave me a name of the next man to look for, the one who brought Aurora to Savannah. Everett didn't know anything else, but it didn't matter. I..."

I took a deep breath. Molly leaned close and looped her arm through mine.

"I did awful things to that man. I *wanted* him dead. He begged and screamed, but I didn't care. I finished him with Booth's derringer. I still see his face right before I shot. He had a crooked mustache and a scar on his cheek. When I left the room, the entire brothel stared. That was the worst part, how they looked at me. No one said anything—they gave me plenty of room to go on my way."

"Does it go away? Even a little?"

I took out my flask and unscrewed the top. I took a drink before I answered. "You learn to live with it."

Molly reached out for the flask. She took her own long drink before handing it back.

"How is your arm?" She tried to change the subject.

I nudged her chin up to look into her eyes.

"I meant it. You saved me."

Her hand reached up to hold mine, pressing it against her cheek.

* * *

The next day, Molly and I took turns watching Emeline, rarely leaving her alone for more than an hour or two. The girl started to trust me. I took her on walks along the decks. She held my hand, squeezing when frightened—like when we reached the hurricane deck and she peered over the edge toward the river. She bore a weight, a quietness that should never descend upon one so young.

I took her to the front of the boat. With a small piece of paper, I folded a paper ship. I handed it to her and showed her how to toss it off the bow into the water—a game my mother had played with me. We would race along the side of the boat until we reached the stern, to see if our little paper boats had made it past the wake off the bow and through the paddlewheel. We cheered when one sailed off behind us. Emeline loved it, and again and again that afternoon we ran along the boat to see if any of our paper vessels remained intact.

As evening fell, Molly came to fetch Emeline. Isaiah followed. Molly took the girl as Isaiah and I leaned against the railing watching the water. We were silent for a time, watching the muddy eddies unfold around the hull as the last of the sun disappeared over the horizon.

"St. Louis is an hour out," Isaiah said. "We'll take on liquor, but no passengers. Get the men ready. Rumors say the army marches north after Memphis. People will know what happened, so they may try to board. I don't want to stay long."

He started to walk away, but then turned around and joined me again. He watched the river for a few moments. He always wrung his hands when he had something to say.

"She looks like him. You know that, right?"

A cold rush passed through my body. *Had he put it together?* I focused on the water, not wanting to glance up. He might be probing for a reaction.

"How's that?"

"I think it's the eyes," he said. "I've been trying to figure out why you were back south again."

My hand dropped from the railing—slowly, not to cause alarm. It brushed back my jacket and rested on the butt of the Bowie.

"It's not surprising, I guess," Isaiah continued. "Look at these men here, falling all over our Negro women." His hand cast back toward the gambling area.

There seemed little point to deny it now. I drew the Bowie. When it freed the sheath, I angled my body toward Isaiah.

"No harm becomes that girl," I said. I stared through him.

"I mean her no harm. But you know what this means, what this could do for us?"

"Not at her expense. She's a little girl, nothing more."

"She's everything, Joseph. Think about it. If even the President would take a colored woman, then we're not just men. We're equals. It means everything."

I pulled back, giving me better access with the knife. Isaiah noticed the movement this time, looking down to my hand.

"I have killed too many to care about adding another," I said. "She is not a thing you can use. She's a little girl. I intend to keep it that way."

Isaiah stared at me for a time. It seemed forever. He shook his head. "I don't much feel like being run through by your knife.

I would summon my men, but I know you would dispatch them without effort."

"We'll leave in St. Louis."

Isaiah shook his head again. "I promised you Ohio. I keep my promises. But think of it, Joseph, please. She's not just a girl. She's not *your* daughter."

My hand clenched my knife hard; even without looking, I knew my knuckles to be white with the pressure. It took all I had to put the knife back and walk away from him. He was wrong. She *was* Aurora—innocent, and helpless to the forces around her. I left him standing along the rail.

Back inside the gambling proceeded in full swing. Music filled the galley, and the booze flowed. Liquor loosened the purse strings. I grabbed a shot glass from a passing barmaid. She smiled and tried to rub my arm when I took the drink from the tray. I shook her off and downed the shot.

I found Isaiah's men and passed the word to get ready. The lights of St. Louis reflected on the water up ahead. I positioned the men along the bow and stern, a rifle covering each gangplank. If there were crowds, we could push them back and get the boat into the river quickly. I spoke to the pilot, telling him to be ready for haste if I signaled.

The boat slowed as we eased into the city. Isaiah's men tied her to the dock, but I didn't let them lower the gangplanks. I left to find Molly. Isaiah may have promised Ohio, but it would be better to leave in Missouri. We could find our way from here. No one had followed us, so it would be easy to disappear and find a place to settle for a time—across the Mississippi or along the west coast of California. Not even Lamon could find us there. As much as I wanted to hunt Lamon and make him pay for Annice, I couldn't. The conversation with Isaiah had sharpened my resolve. We would protect Emeline. We'd leave in St. Louis, where I would signal the pilot from the docks. They'd be down the river before Isaiah discovered our departure.

I walked back through the saloon, taking to the balcony to watch over the floor below. Molly stood in a crowd of men. Emeline wasn't with her. We had been getting too relaxed in our posture. The boat felt safe, but Isaiah's words had proved that danger lurked even in the familiar. The girl likely slept, but I needed Molly ready, and someone should be with Emeline, especially with Isaiah and what designs he might have for her. I started toward the stairs but I couldn't take my eyes off her.

Molly held such grace, handling herself in these social settings with ease. The back of her neck turned me to memory—the nights spent together. The guilt wracked me still, but the power of Molly was undeniable. It reached through the years. She looked up, shaking me from my dream. Our eyes met, her smile natural, beautiful. There was something different in the smile she saved for me.

As I started down the stairs I searched the room, surveying the guests. Some were old, some young. They all dressed alike—different style suits and hats, but all alike. They were peacocks, dressed to impress, with false bravado behind the expensive foreign-made clothes.

Then a worn suit drew my attention. It was still fresh with the dust of the trail. He stood with his back toward me, and his hat shielded most of his face. The suit was all black, and he wore long riding boots. It didn't fit. His movements were slow and deliberate as he walked from table to table. He didn't place wagers on the games. The breath of pursuit teased the back of my neck again.

Molly stared up at me. Her lips moved, "What?"

I flung myself down the nearest stairs and out onto the gambling floor. I pushed through the people, trying to keep the worn black suit in sight. My hand reached for my Bowie. I unsheathed the knife and held it low and out of sight.

When I was directly behind the man, he still hadn't turned to face me. I didn't want to reach out and touch him. He might have been trying to lure me in. But I couldn't help it—I had to know. I grabbed his shoulder and spun him, bringing the blade up to eye level to strike.

He was older, much older than the Black Fox. His hair fell in streaks of white, not the blond locks of my adversary. I paused, frozen as we eyed each other. He shook free of my grip and backed away. I let the blade fall.

The startled faces around me peered to see what had happened. I followed the wrong man. I searched the crowd, looking for the Black Fox. From face to face my eyes darted. He wasn't there. I resheathed the knife as Molly pushed through the crowd.

"Are you all right?"

"Go get Emeline." My voice fell flat as I continued to search the faces.

"What? Joseph, why?"

"Just do as I ask and get the girl," I snapped. "Bring her here."

A flash of defiance crossed Molly's face, but it faded. She left, headed for the stairs that would lead to the stateroom. I melted back into the edge of the crowd. The music swallowed up the commotion, and the passengers seemed to enjoy what they saw. It put another twinge of danger into their night. I looked toward the balcony. Isaiah stood there. I couldn't say what he had seen, but if he had taken witness of it, he would know it only enhanced the gambling.

It took a few minutes before Molly arrived. She dragged Emeline behind her. The girl should have been asleep, but she remained in her dress.

"I found her on the lower deck, trying to throw those boats of yours in the river." Molly turned to the girl. "You should have been sleeping like I told you."

I reached out and put a hand on Emeline's head. I breathed deep.

"Sorry." Her voice was small.

"It's all right." I took Molly's hand. "I'm sorry. Something happened, we'll talk later. We need to get our things and be ready to leave. And we can't leave her alone anymore, not even here on the boat."

Molly forced a smile. I was scaring her.

Emeline looked at both of us, reading our faces and listening. "I just wanted to do the boats once more before bed. Then a man came and showed me how to fold an animal."

I knelt to be at her level. "What man?"

Emeline didn't answer. Instead, she held out her hand—a piece of folded paper.

A black fox.

CHAPTER NINETEEN

I grabbed the paper animal from Emeline's hand. The folds were meticulous, the same design and manner I had seen before. Molly's face went white with my reaction. I swung around, searching for the man himself. He was here, watching us.

I grabbed Molly's hand and backed toward the wall. Molly pulled Emeline in tight and stood behind me. I pulled my pistol.

"Is it *him*?" Molly asked.

"It has to be." I kept my voice low, concentrating on the faces around us. The music still played, the gambling in full swing. Raucous voices filled the saloon. Men laughed and cursed, depending on their luck. No one noticed us.

"I thought he was in Richmond." Molly leaned close—her breath caught my ear.

"I guess not."

"Joseph—" Molly looked past me at something along the balcony on the other side of the room.

He stood above us. His coat hung open, his blond hair pulled just under the hat—the stare piercing, his face gaunt and leathered. I went for my pistol, but he pulled faster. Molly pushed me to the ground and dragged Emeline with us as the first rounds landed against the wall. He shot on either side of us. He didn't try to kill us—yet.

The gambling hall fell into disarray. Men dove under the tables, a few pulled their own guns. One fired into the ceiling, obviously not trained with the weapon. I pushed Molly and Emeline into the center of the saloon where a table had tipped over, throwing them behind it. My thumb pulled at the hammer of my pistol, and I managed a shot—then another. They hit the pillar next to the Black Fox. He never flinched.

He fired until his first pistol went dry, then pulled his second gun. He stayed calm and methodical. I managed another shot as he drew, my aim no better. I was unpracticed with a gun, and the deep gashes in my palm from the fight with Baxter were no help.

A staccato rhythm of gunfire filled the saloon—slow and purposeful. He didn't aim to hit. This was terror. With his last shot of his second pistol he dropped a man to my right. The body landed on top of me. Pushing the fat corpse off, I struggled to my knees. I fought to hold the gun steady when another man nearby pulled a small pepperbox derringer. He leveled the weapon in my direction, though he had little gun skill. One of Isaiah's rich patrons trying to get in on the action for the stories he could tell later. Molly reached up and grabbed the man's arm, causing the weapon to discharge. The blast sent little lead balls ricocheting into the floor at our feet. I thrust my pistol under his jaw and pulled the trigger. His blood showered my shirt and Molly's dress.

I pulled his limp body in front of me, holding it as a shield. The Black Fox reloaded a pistol while walking toward the top of the stairs with a measured stride. He held no hurry. Pinkerton was right—more beast than man.

One of Isaiah's men ran up the stairs with a shotgun in hand. The Black Fox dropped the last cartridge into his pistol and clicked the cylinder shut. He lifted the pistol effortlessly and fired. Isaiah's man fell backward down the stairs.

Then he turned on me again. A bullet struck the dead man I held. I dropped the weight as I ducked behind the table. Three or four more shots ripped through the room, then it went quiet. Peering out, I scanned the balcony. I couldn't see him.

The saloon fell into full panic. Men picked themselves up and ran for the exits. Molly stood behind me and yanked the nearest oil lamp off the wall. She hurled it toward the staircase. It landed on the rug, sending out orange tongues of flame that took hold on the stairs. It would slow his progress. I looked to the stairs and started to advance into the chaos when Molly screamed.

"Joseph! Joseph!" Her voice shrieked in pure despair.

She held Emeline. Blood soaked the front of the little dress. I rushed to Molly. The girl was still alive.

"We need a doctor," Molly pleaded.

I picked up Emeline and draped her over my shoulder. With my pistol in the other hand, I pushed through the rich men around us. I shoved them aside, struck a few with the pistol, and even threw one over the railing in my rush to the main gang-plank. Every face that turned our direction was the Black Fox. I leveled my pistol at everyone.

Rushing down the gangplank, I yelled at one of Isaiah's men. "Pull the walkway, get the boat out of here."

I dragged Molly behind me. We ran across the dock and huddled behind the first crates we found. Men ran off the boat. A few jumped after the gangplank was pulled in. One missed and landed in the river. I searched their faces, but none matched. I swung my arms wildly for the pilot to see. Then I fired my remaining shots skyward. The riverboat throttled forward, the great paddlewheel thrashed the water.

With my back to the crates, I desperately reloaded. My fingers fumbled at the percussion caps in my pocket. I dropped one or two. Molly picked them up and handed them to me as I managed to load six onto the new cylinder. I searched the dock. People peered from behind crates and lampposts, using them as cover from the boat as it floated into the middle of the river, catching the current. Sporadic gunfire crackled.

Molly had torn open Emeline's dress and tried to stem the bleeding—her right shoulder or chest. Torches and gas lamps lit the dock area, though the poor light flickered and barely pushed away the shadows. I stood, still trying to find the Black Fox.

From the direction of the boat we heard a splash. Onlookers at the dock pointed and ran to the edge. Someone had jumped. I leaned down and picked up Emeline. Molly took the pistol as I hoisted the little girl with both arms. She moaned. Her hand flailed against my back. We ran toward the nearest wagon. A man sat on the front bench, and I shoved him over while Molly held him at gunpoint.

"Where's the nearest surgeon?"

He stared. I handed Emeline to Molly, who had settled in the bed of the wagon.

"Take us to a surgeon!" I pulled out my knife.

The man regained his senses and started the horses. As we pulled away, I strained to see behind us. *Had anyone come out of the river?*

We drove the wagon down small side roads. They were dark and dusty, with only a few drunks stumbling in the poor light. Finally, we pulled onto a long main street deep in the city. Molly sobbed behind us as Emeline continued to moan. The man didn't drive fast enough, so I pulled the reins from his hands. He directed us to a Queen Anne-style house with a large bay window. There were no lights, but a sign hung near the door—a medical symbol. I thrust the man onto to the porch. He knocked while I held Emeline. With no response, I pushed the door open and barged into the house.

We found an office immediately inside the threshold, filled with cabinets and medical supplies. I brought Emeline in and laid her on a wooden table. Molly rushed to her head and stroked her hair. The girl drifted in and out.

An older man came down the stairs, a coal oil lamp in his hand.

"What's this about?"

"They said they needed a surgeon."

"Then why'd you bring them here?" The older man pulled up suspenders while trying to adjust his small spectacles.

"It's a colored girl. I wasn't bringing her to no real doctor."

I looked to the cabinets filled with bowls and vials. "What kind of doctor are you?"

"Mostly horses, but cows and swine when I'm out in the country." He walked past me and started to examine Emeline. His hair was disheveled. We had caught him asleep.

I approached the other man. He stepped back.

"Not to a real doctor?" I raised my fist and struck him across the head. As he slumped down I beat him again, and again. I kicked with all my might. Molly caught my shoulder and pulled me away.

"Don't, Joseph. Please."

I took the pistol from her, pointing it at the older man.

"Where's the nearest surgeon?"

"You don't have time," he replied. He walked past me, as if he didn't see the gun. He pulled a bowl off a shelf. "No need for that, son. I started in this business by working on people. Patching up soldiers during the War. I'll get my kit, and we'll take a better look. Fetch me those bandages over yonder." He pointed to a desk near the window.

Then he turned to Molly. His voice turned soft as he pulled one of her hands from Emeline's forehead. "I need help, dear. The kitchen is through the back. Get me some more water boiling, there's a wood stove should still be lit. Put a pot on for me."

I stood in the foyer and watched. I couldn't walk into the office and see Emeline on that table. Molly was stronger than I. Instead, I made myself busy checking from the windows. I bound the hands of the man who had brought us here. We would free him when we left, but for now, he didn't need to raise any alarms. The older man worked for an hour, maybe two. I brought in several lamps to increase the light. But I never stayed. Emeline looked chalky and gray in the lighting—like her mother before she passed.

When they were done, Molly and the doctor stepped out of the office. I searched both faces for the prognosis. The man carried Emeline and laid her out on a couch in the next room. He propped her head slightly with a pillow. Molly smiled weakly.

"She'll make it." The man handed me a small lead ball, fired from that pepperbox derringer. "I stopped the bleeding. The ball was high in her chest, and it took some work to get out. But young ones heal fast. You'll have to get those stitches pulled in a few weeks." He stopped to look at me before rubbing his hands with a cloth, ensuring all the blood was off them. "I'm not one to pry into the affairs of others, especially a man with a gun, but she's not fit to travel, at least not over rough roads. I'm assuming you'll be pressing on."

"We'll leave you be as soon as we can," I answered.

"I'll go see to that other man you brought in. You knocked him around something good. When I'm done, I'll look at that arm of yours." My bandages had bled through, and my jacket held a dark stain along my shoulder. The older man started to walk away.

"Sir—" I stopped him. He turned. "Thank you."

He nodded and left Molly and me alone to talk.

Molly waited until the doctor walked out of earshot. "What will we do, Joseph?"

"If we run, this will never end."

"Then what will we do?"

I looked out the window.

"He wants me, Molly. We split up. You take Emeline to safety, and I'll finish this thing. That's the only way she'll ever be safe."

"But where do I go?"

There was only one place. "To Ohio. There's a town along the rails north of Cincinnati called Yellow Springs. It's got a small college. We used to guide runaways to the town. Find the Methodist church and ask for Flora. They'll know how to find her, and you'll recognize her. I have her eyes."

"Flora? Your mother?"

"Give her this."

From my vest pocket, I produced the velvet bag. I opened it and handed Molly the necklace, complete with the silver eagle's feather—so delicate, so clean, despite the journey.

Molly took it, holding it in her hand. "It's beautiful, Joseph."

I nodded. "Tell her I will come—after I fix this."

"Where will you go?"

I took out the roll of cash I recovered from Baxter. I kept a few bills for myself before I handed the rest to Molly.

"Lamon wanted us back in Washington, so that's where I'll head. And this other man, I'll let him track me. I'll draw him off you." I held the little black fox from Emeline in my hand.

"Who is he?"

"I can't say as I've ever seen him before. I killed a lot of Norris' men trying to get Aurora back. Chances are that Baxter was right. I wronged him at some point."

"But you will come back to me?"

I nodded.

"Promise me, Joseph. You will come back to me?"

I squeezed her hands. "I promise. And you...," I paused, seeing the image of Annice pass before me. "You'll watch over her?" I didn't have to ask.

"Like she was our own."

CHAPTER TWENTY

It took three full days to get east on the trains, never once catching sight of the Black Fox. I slept little. The tracks were rough and jolted me awake whenever sleep found me. The wooden bench held nothing in the way of comfort, and I walked the passenger cars often searching among the faces. I felt him—watching, waiting. I arrived in Washington late, a few hours before curfew fell. Pinkerton's house was dark, with no guards. I made my way to his study, where an oil lamp burned on a far table. In the flickering light I made out his form as he lay on a couch—either asleep or dead.

I crossed the room, easing each foot down. Once at his side, his breath sounded deep and rough. The smell of whiskey permeated the area, his beard a sharp stubble. He hadn't shaved in days. I shook his shoulder trying to rouse him. He didn't stir, his slumber too deep, enhanced by the liquor.

I shook harder. Finally, I slapped him on both cheeks. He startled, bolting upright. The sudden movement caught me by surprise. The hand that had been pinned against the side of the couch rushed forward with a small double-shot derringer. I barely grabbed it in time, deflecting the muzzle as I held his wrist. He pulled the trigger and the report of the gun flooded my hearing. I jerked the weapon from his hand and struck him hard in the face. Pain seared through my arm. I feared I had ripped out the stitches the surgeon in Memphis had sewn in. I laid the Bowie across his neck. His eyes were wild. He stared at me as his body tensed and bucked, threatening to push against my blade.

"It's Joseph," I hissed. "It's me. Easy."

For a moment, his face held no recognition, then he eased with relief.

"I thought you were *him*."

I pulled the Bowie away and let him sit upright.

"Who?"

"That interminable ghost." His eyes darted around the room.

"Lamon?" I asked.

"No. His man. The Black Fox."

"Why would he be after you?"

Pinkerton shook his head. I sat next to him on the couch, taking the time to put the Bowie away.

"Look at me, Joseph. When I said my sun was setting, I meant it. Lamon forced me out. He'll send his man for me eventually. But he wants me to suffer first, to hear every creak in the night and cower in fear. He's doing a damn fine job of it, too."

"Where are your men? I didn't see anyone downstairs."

"They're gone. Everything's gone."

"What do you mean? What happened?" I had seen him drunk, but never despondent.

"Lamon happened. His final plan is in motion, a massive power grab."

It had to be what Lamon alluded to in the telegram he had sent back to Memphis.

"And the President? What about him?"

"It won't be long," Pinkerton answered. "He's safe, maybe until September, before the election. After that, there's no telling."

"I thought they needed him."

Pinkerton tried to stand. I rose to steady him, grabbing hold of one arm.

"There was always going to come a time when they would move against him. You watch, Joseph, Lamon himself will run for president. But they can't let it happen much before the election. Vice President Johnson doesn't fancy himself an industry man. He wouldn't go along with them and he hates Lamon."

"So we have time."

"No," Pinkerton answered. "We have nothing."

We were quiet for a moment. When he spoke again his voice was lower, more resigned.

"I know about the President's woman, Joseph. If you had managed to bring her back it would have forced the President out. He would have left to protect her. We would have had a chance against Lamon."

I stayed quiet for a moment, picturing Annice lying in the grass, the blood pooling from the wound in her chest—the promise I had made to her. But I never told Pinkerton about the Old Man's request.

"How did you know about her?"

"Do you take me for a fool, boy? I have some tricks left." He struggled across the room to the bookshelf near the door. A bottle of whiskey sat on the lowest shelf at waist level. The top lay beside the bottle. He poured us both a drink—the expensive stuff. It burned all the way down. Pinkerton watched me drink the first glass, then poured me another.

"It's been a while?" he asked.

I nodded. I took off my jacket and examined my arm. It bled, but the surgeon's work held.

"Looks like you had your wear, but I'm glad you're not dead," he said. "That telegram from Memphis bought you time. Lamon believed it, certain you had failed."

"I sent it."

"I figured as much. But the Black Fox sent word from St. Louis."

"Did he say anything else?"

Pinkerton shook his head. "That's when Lamon threw me out, claimed I conspired with you to kill the President. He's got the city on alert looking for you."

"The Black Fox didn't mention the girl?" I asked.

"He said she died, as well as Baxter."

"No, not her. There's another." I paused. I didn't know if I should tell him. But if he knew, he might find a way out for us. Pinkerton could see the politics—where the pieces fit. "The President has a daughter."

Pinkerton steadied himself. He hadn't known.

"How old?"

"I'd say five."

"Like Aurora?"

"Close. Aurora was a couple years younger when they took her."

"I didn't know." He took another drink. "It would have been at the first peace conference then. Where is she?"

"I have her. She's safe."

"Who would have thought? Help me to my desk."

When he sat I went back for the bottle of whiskey and placed it between us. I eased into the chair across from him, the same seat I had used so many weeks earlier.

"Does she look like him?"

"Mostly it's the eyes. But she's tall, too. If you know it, you can see him in her."

"Does the President know?"

"I don't think so."

Pinkerton rubbed his beard and then pinched his nose between his eyes. He stayed like that for several moments, before sitting upright and taking another drink.

"I don't think it would make a difference. He covets that office. There is no way to separate him from it. He needs to resign and let Johnson take over. If he waits until the election, Lamon will move against him. And I don't see him resigning for a little girl, not when he's sacrificed so much already. He wants to be immortal like Jefferson."

"We can try," I urged. "Let me talk to him."

"You'll never get close. Lamon has him locked tight, under guard all the time. Even those escape tunnels of ours are closed now."

"Then it'll have to be outside the White House. When does he leave?"

"Never," Pinkerton barked. He took another sip of his whiskey.

We sat quiet for a minute. I swirled my drink, letting the fumes of the good liquor reach my nose when I bent toward the glass. Pinkerton spared nothing on his whiskey.

"Unless—"

"What is it?" I asked.

"Tomorrow's Thursday."

"What of it?"

"It's theatre night. The President still insists on his plays. He's like clockwork—I set the day of the week by his schedule."

"That'll work," I said. "I can meet him at the theatre, especially if we know which one he'll use."

Pinkerton sat straighter in the chair and furled his brow. "There's only two playhouses open tomorrow. There's a new comedy at Grover's Theatre, and some foreign play at Ford's. He'll choose the comedy. And ever since that night with you, he only goes to Ford's if there's nothing else."

"Perfect," I said. "I'll meet him at Ford's."

"Didn't you hear me? He'll go to Grover's Theatre."

"Exactly. We need to cancel the play at Grover's. Once he's already out, he won't be keen to return to his cage, not if there's an alternative. You must know someone?"

Pinkerton looked annoyed. "You think I can do anything? There are limits to what I am capable of, especially now. How do you expect me to cancel a play?" But before he finished his sentence, his voice betrayed him—a subtle shift in inflection.

I waited for him to think it through.

"They can't have the play without the actors," he said.

"You're not going to kill the actors."

"Of course not. We're not going to kill anyone. We only need to remove the lead actor and his understudy. One is a notorious drunk, and the other has a terrible affliction for this redhead across the river in Virginia. She's in my employment."

My face must have betrayed me.

"Not *that* redhead," he said. "But he'll have security." Pinkerton became excited, the corners of his mouth turned up, and his finger thumped on the desk. "But there's no telling if just because we cancel one play then he will shift to the other."

"Then we do it as late as possible. He won't want to head back to the White House. The theatre was always his escape. And I'll arrange for the box at Ford's."

"They might search it," Pinkerton countered.

"I can get around that."

"You won't have much time with him. What exactly will you tell him?" The smile on Pinkerton's face grew. This was the man I knew. He saw a way out, a way back on top—a way to defeat Lamon.

"I'll handle that. I know exactly what will get to him," I lied. "I know him better than anyone."

"What if you can't?"

"I will."

"That's not good enough, Joseph. What if you can't? The nation may depend on this. He is the obstacle to ending this War. You have to make him see that, he has to know. One way or the other, he can't leave that theatre and still be the President."

"I'll think of something." Pinkerton annoyed me. But, in truth, I had no plan. Getting to see the Old Man would be hard enough.

Pinkerton shook his head.

"You don't understand. This is our one chance. If you can't talk him down, then you have to make sure that Johnson is the president tomorrow morning." Pinkerton paused. "He may only leave in a pine box. You have to be ready for that. Those dreams of his always had that damn wallpaper. Maybe he was right about them."

I shook my head. "You trained me to protect him."

"I trained you to protect the nation. At the time, he was the nation. Now the country needs him to step aside." He took a deep breath and another swig of whiskey. "I'm not saying that should be our first option, but it may come down to our last. We need to kill this War, or she will tear the nation apart."

I didn't say anything. Maybe the Old Man's dreams were right—he would be our last sacrifice so the nation could move forward. Even if he left willingly, it would be like death. He had become the office. Leaving it would kill him. *What else did he have? The daughter he didn't even know? How would I protect her?*

Pinkerton reached for the bottle. "I suppose I should stop

drinking. I have to get things ready for the theatre." He filled his glass, took another sip, then handed the glass to me. I finished it.

"If Lamon figures out what happened," I started, "he'll go after the Vice President. Can you get men to guard him?"

Pinkerton nodded. "I have little choice. I'll find someone. And you better leave that pistol of yours here. I hate to ask you to be unarmed, but the soldiers will be sure to stop you with a gun belt."

"I won't be unarmed." I took off the belt and pistol that Isaiah had provided. I placed it on Pinkerton's desk. I had my knife, and Booth's gun.

"What else do you need?" Pinkerton asked.

"Powder." I took the derringer out from where I had tucked it into the small of my back. I wanted to make sure it worked, especially if it all came down to this one small pistol.

Pinkerton opened his desk and handed me a powder flask. "In case you can't convince him? That might be best."

I didn't answer. I unloaded the derringer as he watched, removing the ball and cleaning out the bore from the old packed powder. I worked the mechanism, letting the gun dry fire several times. Then I reloaded the ball after I placed fresh powder behind it. I handed the flask back to Pinkerton.

He held up his hand and refused to take it. "Keep it, you may want more."

I shook my head. "No. If I have to use it, I'll only need one shot."

CHAPTER TWENTY-ONE

Ford's Theatre sat silent, not another soul in the place. It proved an easy matter to have the theatre manager relinquish the State Box for me. Hope overwhelmed him, that the Old Man might grace his establishment, even though Grover's Theatre had already printed handbills announcing the President as its guest.

Once inside the State Box, I walked behind the Old Man's chair and placed my hand on the top. The country would be very different if I hadn't been there that night, or if I had heeded the Old Man's dreams and remained silent against the wallpaper.

Out of habit I searched the box, looking for anything out of place. I glanced over the edge of the balcony to the stage. Booth had landed below. At the time, it left a bloodstain upon the wood. It had been scrubbed clean, the floor refinished. Not surprising. No one here wanted reminders of that night.

Behind the inner door I found a broom, and it gave me an idea. Booth had tried something similar that night, using a piece of a music stand as a means to blockade the outer door. I broke a length of the broom, and fashioned it into a bar, a near perfect fit. I felt along the wallpaper. The mortise that Booth created years earlier remained carved in the wall. They hadn't fixed it. I fit one end of the broomstick into it, and let the other end fall across the door, blockading it like Booth had done. Then I took the bar out and put it along the wall inside the box. I might need it later.

Within the hour people arrived. The audience filled slowly. Their voices lofted into the box. They seemed a poorer folk, not the top crust of the gentry that used to habit this theatre. Another consequence of the curse I had cast upon the place.

It didn't feel good to have so many details out of my control. I hated trusting to others in this manner. My fate was in Pinkerton's hands, if he could fix the other play. And Molly—so much pinned on her getting Emeline safely north. I closed my eyes and smelled her perfume, the scent of her deep rich hair, the softness of the skin along her neck.

The dimming of the house lights shook me from my daydream. I stood to inspect the stage below, the curtain poised to open—no sign of the Old Man. If the play made it past the first act there would be little hope of his arrival. I stayed along the back wall as my fingers traced out the leaves on the wallpaper, recalling what Pinkerton had told me about it. Without watching, I listened to the actors below, but didn't follow the plot or care about the action. I waited.

With each minute, hope slipped through my fingers. *How else could I get to the Old Man? Where else could I arrange a meeting?* It might be best to sneak out of the city undetected, stay with Molly and Emeline. We could head west, get lost in the sea of humanity filling out the frontier. It would mean running, and we would be hunted.

As I sat pondering my options, the audience shifted, something more than the play. I dared not step to the edge to look. Instead, I held my breath and listened. The play stopped and chairs turned, their wooden legs creaking. People stood, small gasps replaced the dialogue from the actors. Someone clapped—then another. The entire audience erupted. The orchestra tuned and belted out the first measures of *Hail to the Chief.*

The plan had worked.

I stayed against the back wall, venturing only to the gas lamp to turn down the light. The Old Man would come this way, but who would be with him?

I took the Bowie from its sheath and stood in the same location where Booth had passed me by, in the corner behind where the inner door entered the room. It was easy to overlook someone standing there. I liked the wallpaper. The dark color further buried me into the shadows. The clapping grew louder on the second floor—along the dress circle in back of the seating. An entourage came down the steps, not just the stride of a lone man. His guards were many.

The outside door opened—the yellow one. I had left the inner door open, and the applause reached into the box. A guard made his way into the State Box, scanning the area in a haphazard manner, never looking over his shoulder to see me standing behind him. The angle of the wall hid my presence, just as it had blinded Booth so many years earlier. The Old Man followed him in.

"It is empty. You may leave, I wish to be alone." The Old Man stood by the inner door, his back to me. I remained undiscovered as the guard left.

The orchestra finished their tribute, and the Old Man leaned over the railing, holding out one hand, waving. The applause intensified for a moment, but he held his hand up, motioning for it to stop. It died as he took his seat. We were alone.

I waited for the play to resume—the actors once again worked through their dialogue. But they injected new life in it, more energy. They played to the Old Man, knowing the opportunity before them. The President once again graced Ford's Theatre.

I stepped forward and stood behind him, near to where Booth had paused before drawing his weapons. I had my knife in one hand, and I pulled the derringer in the other—just in case. I stood like Booth had, behind the Old Man watching the play below.

Could I convince him?

All would be lost without that. We needed him to leave the Presidency. Pinkerton's words ran through my thoughts—*the only way out might be in a pine box*. I shook them from my head. Pinkerton couldn't be right.

Without making a noise, I knelt behind him to where the audience couldn't see me. I reached out and put a hand to his shoulder.

"Sir, it's me, Joseph."

"I know." His eyes never shifted from the play.

It caught me off guard. "You knew I was here?"

"Of course. I've never heard of a lead actor forgetting a performance, and the understudy too drunk to perform. The manager brought me whiskey while we waited. Pinkerton's brand." He turned to see me. "Did you find her?" Desperation seeped into his voice.

I ignored his question. I didn't want to deal with it yet, and I feared how the Old Man saw through the ploy. Lamon might as well. My time was short.

"Does—" I began to ask. The Old Man interrupted me.

"No," he said. "They know nothing. It was my idea to come here. After seeing the whiskey I knew what had happened. You're not the only one Pinkerton trained." He smiled slightly. Something in his voice reminded me of the Old Man I used to know. "Lamon told me you died, but I knew it couldn't be," he paused. "Did you find her?"

I pictured Annice's face as she lay dying on the grass, her hand clutching mine.

"I couldn't save her," I offered—little consolation. I reached for his arm, holding it softly. To my surprise, his other hand reached over and clutched mine. He began to weep. His shoulders slouched forward and his body rocked.

"How?" he asked.

"Baxter. He found us outside Memphis."

The Old Man turned abruptly—anger furled his brow. "Why would Baxter pursue you?"

"Lamon sent him. He was to kill me, then Norris. When he found out about Annice, Lamon told him to track us." I hadn't thought about how to broach the subject of Lamon. I had not intended to do it so bluntly.

The Old Man sat quiet. I reached into my suit jacket and produced the telegrams. I leafed through them in the dim light, finding the most damming among them. I handed them to him.

"I took these from Baxter."

I gave him a few moments. They stretched into minutes as he read, flipping through one at a time. His eyes fell upon the address—his shoulders slouched further.

"He never wanted Colonel Norris alive. It would dismantle the fight," I said.

The Old Man crushed the papers in his closed fist as he faced the play.

"Why would he take her from me?" I barely heard him through his clenched teeth. "She was innocent of all this. She had nothing to do with Norris." He glanced in my direction.

"Sir, if anyone found out about Annice, then not even the Barons would keep you in office. They need you, until right before the election this fall. Lamon plans to take your place. They can't risk the Vice President mounting a campaign and getting elected."

"No one will take my office. It is the only way I can fight back against the cancer of their consortium. I will find a way to stop them."

"No, sir. It's time to leave. That's how you thwart their plans. You make them scramble, and let the Vice President have the office. Let him fight."

He shook his head. "He doesn't have my experience. I won't step down until the Union is preserved. No one can do that except me. It is my job, and I will see it done." He was defiant. I had challenged the one thing he had left—the Presidency.

My stomach ached. Pinkerton was right. The Old Man couldn't separate himself from the office. Too long at the seat of power, it had warped his perception.

"If the Barons are a cancer, then *you* let them grow!" Anger touched me, and I fought to control it. I had to make him see. "They didn't take over in a day, and if you couldn't stop them then, you can't defeat them now. Let someone else take hold of the fight. If you step down, there might be enough of Congress not on the Baron's payroll who will see that the system crumbles. They won't be afraid to speak out."

"I will not leave *my* office until I see the last impediments to reunification lifted." He raised his voice as he shifted in his chair to see me.

"The time is here," I said. "*You* are the last barrier."

He turned sharply. Anger held his face. We sat still for a moment as the play filled the box. My fingers gripped the derringer and my thumb ran over the wood. I felt the hammer, instinctively pulling it back until the weapon was primed. When intermission came, I would be out of time—I had to convince him.

"Did you know about Memphis?" I asked.

"What about it?" His voice fell short.

"General Bell marched on it."

"I never gave that order," he said. "Are you sure?"

"I was there. We barely escaped. They use you as a puppet to project power. They need you, but only until the election. Then, even I won't be able to protect you."

I reached in my pocket and brought out the medal that William had handed me. I had carried it since Jekyll Island. "People believed in you—they still believe in you. You did everything you could for the nation, but now it's time to let others finish it." I handed him the medal.

He stared at the worn bronze, flipping it in his hand, reading the words.

"Sir, don't let them tarnish what you did for us. Lamon and his Barons are pulling this nation apart. The rebellion strengthens by the day, the West threatens to secede, and the Barons only care about their profits. If you want the country to be whole, you need to step aside."

He held William's medal and stared at the side that read "EMANCIPATION"; his thumb stroked the engraved word.

"What would I do?"

"Find that cabin you wanted."

He shook his head. "I am not a young man, and I have nowhere to go. There is no life for me outside the White House." He sat still for a moment, still holding William's medal. "Maybe it is best if you do what you came for, Joseph. We both know why Pinkerton sent you. I always knew it would be here, in this place. You gave me seven extra years, and Annice. Without her, I have no reason to leave. There is nothing." He looked around the room, then closed his eyes while resting his head back—waiting.

The derringer was heavy in my hand, such a crude weapon at this range. Pinkerton would tell me to use it, and the Old Man was resigned to it. But it couldn't end this way.

"You have a daughter."

His hands stopped moving along William's medal.

"Did you hear me, sir?"

He turned. "I don't understand."

"Annice had a daughter. She's yours. By her age, I would say from the first peace accord."

"How do you know?"

"The eyes. She has your eyes. But she's tall, too."

"How old?"

"Four," I answered. "Maybe five."

"She never told me. Why would she not tell me?"

"She didn't want to harm you. And she didn't want the girl put in danger."

"What is her name?" The Old Man spoke softly. He believed me.

"Emeline. And she's beautiful, like her mother. If you saw her, you would know."

"Emeline," he repeated. "Emeline." He shifted so he could see me. "She carries her mother's beauty?"

I nodded.

"It is a blessing, for look what she might have taken after." He smiled as he clutched my hand. This was the Old Man I knew.

"She's not safe if you stay in the White House," I said.

He clasped the medal in his hand, enclosing it in his fist. His other hand clutched over top. "I am the very thing I struggled against. How did I become this?"

"Slowly, sir. They took it from you slowly. This War is harsh. She'll take all she can, like how she turned Mr. Lamon. But you're not him. You can still help us end it. Come with me and meet your daughter. It's a chance at something new. There's no reason to die here."

"They will use the Vice President in a similar manner."

"That's why I will handle Lamon," I answered. "With him gone, the Vice President has a chance."

The Old Man shook his head. "You'll never get to him. He's guarded. Good men, too."

"Who can get close?"

"No one other than me," he said.

We were quiet for a moment. I handed the Old Man the derringer.

"Do you know how to use it?"

He took it from my hand but said nothing.

"He killed her," I said. "He killed Annice. Baxter pulled the trigger, but Lamon ordered it. And he...," I paused, "...he killed your child."

He wept again as he held the gun, running his thumbs over it.

"Where is she?" he asked.

"Annice?"

He nodded.

"I buried her."

"But where? I need to know."

"A beautiful place—under a great oak tree in a clearing. There's a stream nearby and a large meadow. The nearest town is called Essary Springs. At night the stars are clear and perfect, a little waterfall back in the woods, and not far along the path, *Big Hill Pond*. I think that's what the locals called it. Everything you could ask for, secluded and perfect."

The Old Man nodded. "Thank you."

He fingered the gun some more, holding it in his hands. He sat undecided. The sounds of the play filled the box. The Old Man continued to massage the gun. I wondered what else to say, what else would convince him. The house lights turned on for intermission. He would have to stand to greet the crowd again, but, instead, he just sat.

"Sir?" I tried to gauge his mood.

But he didn't have time to answer. Behind us, the door opened. I rushed to my feet and then to the back wall, seeking security along the wallpaper. A man walked into the box, one of Lamon's security men. He came up behind the President, reaching for the Old Man. He stopped, sensing something. Turning, he looked straight at me.

A moment passed, a second where we stared at one another. He pulled back his jacket and reached for his pistol. I rushed forward, trapping his hand in the holster. With my other hand still clutching my Bowie, I struck him across the face. He staggered as I spun him until I had his back. My arm throbbed and my stitches tore. But still I clutched him about the neck, squeezing until he went limp. I let him down on the floor so as not to make a sound.

I had to go. The Old Man stood with the commotion, still clutching the derringer. He knew what to do. I headed to the door but stopped frozen in the doorway.

At the top of the dress circle two guards descended the stairs toward me, led by a single man in black. The brim of his hat obscured his face. Behind him, the guards flanked another man—Lamon.

For a moment, our eyes locked. We stared, neither of us moving. Wide eyed, Lamon pointed and yelled at the top of his voice.

"Assassin!"

CHAPTER TWENTY-TWO

My first instinct told me to charge. I would run him through with the Bowie—watch the blood drain from his body, his eyes drift toward gray. But I stood hopelessly outnumbered. As I stepped forward, they rushed in my direction. I had no choice.

Reaching the outer yellow door, I slammed it shut. Then I propped it closed with the broomstick I had fashioned earlier. It would buy time, mere seconds, but it all counted. I bolted back through the box. The Old Man watched me, the derringer still in his hand. I had only one way out.

"Stop, Joseph. Stop." The Old Man grabbed my arm. "We'll do this together." He held out a hand. "Give me the knife."

I was puzzled. We both turned toward the door as someone began kicking it in.

"Now," the Old Man said. "Give me the knife. They'll shoot if you have a weapon. I'll handle this."

He took my Bowie from my hand. "It will be okay. Trust me."

He stepped in front of me as the splintering of wood signaled the last resistance of the door. The Black Fox rushed in followed by two other men. They had pistols drawn.

The Old Man held out his hands. "Lower your weapons."

Lamon entered the room behind them. "Take him," he ordered.

The men stepped forward, but the Old Man countered. "Enough, Ward. Stop! All of you."

Lamon looked out the window of the balcony and stepped around the presidential chair to close the curtains.

"He came to kill you, let us take him," Lamon said.

"He came for no such thing," the Old Man answered. "I know about everything, Ward." He leaned down and picked up the telegrams from his chair. Then he threw the stack of folded papers at Lamon. They hit his chest and fell to the floor. "I know it all. There's a saying about a fox in the henhouse. It seems that's what we have."

"I don't know what he has told you, but it is nothing more than Pinkerton lies. Everything we have done has been for the nation."

"Everything *I* did was for the nation," the Old Man said. He tossed William's medal. Lamon caught it and rolled it over in his hand.

I turned my attention to the Black Fox. His skin was bleached white, thin as paper stretched over bone. There was something about his face, but I couldn't place it anywhere. He knew me. The hatred that rose to the surface revealed as much. His eyes deep set, his blond hair wispy and graying. A demonic smile spread across his face until the joy filled his entire being. I stared at *Death*.

"Was killing Norris necessary?" the Old Man asked.

"Yes. It cripples the rebellion!" Lamon yelled. He glanced to the Black Fox. "We are on the verge of winning."

"It changes nothing." The Old Man rose to his former self. "It keeps this strife eternal. You were to bring Colonel Norris in, to disable the rebels. Killing him only encourages the resistance."

"Then we will expand the Draft and crush the rebellion." Lamon's voice became heated. "It is working."

"The Draft must end," the Old Man answered. "And it is time for the South to vote. That is the only path to make this nation whole again. Our government must be restored to represent *all* the people."

"We will have another war unless the South is equal and rebuilt before they vote." Lamon waved his hands about as he spoke, inching closer to the Old Man. "To hand it over now means Congress will become logjammed like the pre-war years. You know this. Do not waver from our course because Pinkerton feeds you lies."

"Do you mean another war like Memphis? Who gave that order?"

Lamon turned on me. If fire could have poured from his eyes, he would have burned me alive where I stood.

"Memphis—they were lawless and needed to heel like disobedient dogs!"

"And how about Annice? Another dog to be tamed?"

"Yes!" Lamon yelled. "If her existence had become known, if your bastard child had been born, you would have ruined all we built!" He stepped forward to grab the President.

But the Old Man raised the derringer. "I will be a party to this no more."

Lamon stopped. The two men with the Black Fox raised their pistols, not knowing whom to focus on. The Black Fox stepped slightly to his side, as if he would rush and flank the Old Man. I angled myself to match him.

"Kill him!" Lamon pointed at me. His men hesitated, looking at the Old Man and then back to Lamon. "Now. Kill him!"

The Black Fox stepped toward me, and I turned to anticipate the attack. I wasn't watching the Old Man, and the shot that ripped through the State Box startled me—Booth's derringer. Lamon collapsed to the floor like several bags of potatoes. As he fell, his head bounced off the presidential chair. From the other side of the curtain, the crowd gasped.

Lamon's men hesitated. They stared at the Old Man. Then the Black Fox raised his pistol and shot the first man. The second realized what had happened and began to react—too late. The Black Fox shot him as well. I stood frozen—it made no sense. Then he turned the gun on the Old Man. He wanted no witnesses.

I dove forward and grabbed the muzzle. He pushed me to one side, striking my arm, and sending me sprawling along the floor. The gun ripped from his grip and landed hard against the far wall. I struggled to stand, but the pain from my arm delivered me into dry heaves, forcing my feet from underneath me. The Black Fox reached the President. He grabbed the Bowie from the Old Man's hand and plunged the blade into his chest.

I pounced from behind, stumbling as I grabbed the Black Fox by a shoulder. What muscle he had felt lean and hard. My fingers dug with all their strength as I pulled him from the Old Man. I gouged him from his eye to his upper lip, digging with my fingers until they dripped blood.

He reared up and struck me across the face. My head slammed into the floor. The room faded, and when I came to, he straddled my chest, pinning my good arm to the floor as I fought against his weight. I struggled to breathe. My Bowie was in his hand, the tip pushed up and under my chin.

"You don't know me? Do you?"

I didn't answer. His voice held a refined and deep southern accent.

"Don't you want to know?" He pressed the blade upward. "But you remember my sister."

I struggled to talk. "I've never killed a woman." My mind raced over the faces I had silenced. The men who had come after me, the ones I had sought out on my desperate rampage to seek Aurora—not a woman among them.

"Didn't you now? You didn't drive the knife into her yourself, but you killed her all the same—the moment you took her from our family, the moment you cast a spell of revenge upon yourself. You killed her."

"I don't know what you're talking about." The Bowie cut into my chin as I spoke.

"You never met me because our family shunned your wedding. But I should have come if only to have killed you then. My sister would be home, where she belonged—with *our* people."

"Sara?" My wife had died in my arms that terrible night. Her brother had been a cavalry officer, a man riding with Nathan Forrest during the War and with Bloody Bill Anderson before that. I never met him, but the stories made him into a Confederate hero—the men he killed, the fearless charges into the thick of battle. The soldiers called him the *Gray Devil,* a warrior who killed without mercy, and escaped every battle without a scratch. He had sold his soul. I was nothing compared to him. The fear seeped in like a cold chill pouring from his body. It paralyzed me.

"My father would have loved to see you die."

The Black Fox rose up with the knife. Behind him, the Old Man struggled to his knees. He wasn't gone yet. Holding his chest, he pulled the Black Fox backward, grabbing the arm holding the knife. My hands shot out, searching for anything to use as a weapon. They fumbled at something hard on the body of one of the guards, and I pulled at it. A federal marshal's badge tore loose in my hands. As the Black Fox regained his balance, he struck the Old Man across the face. I lashed out with the badge. It tore him across the cheek with one edge. He let out a cry and covered his face with both hands as he dropped my knife.

I scrambled for the weapon but saw a pistol across the floor. Sprawling out, I managed to grab the gun and pulled the hammer back. The Black Fox fled toward the door. I fired once; the bullet kicked plaster off the wall from under the wallpaper. He disappeared down the vestibule.

Once in the theatre, he began yelling, "He killed the President! Get the soldiers on the street!"

I knelt by the Old Man. His breathing labored and his face had gone pale. He clutched my knife and handed it to me.

"It seems I am forced to retire." He tried smiling, but it faded. "Watch over her, Joseph."

I tore some cloth from one of the dead men's shirts, and I stuffed the Old Man's wound. There were footsteps nearing, men running. The Old Man squeezed my hands. "Go," he said. "It's all right, Joseph. Go."

I stood, then pulled back the curtain. The crowd below looked up anxiously. Actors stood on the stage. They stared toward the State Box. I placed one hand on the railing and vaulted myself over the balcony.

CHAPTER TWENTY-THREE

The horse dragged me through the night—its hooves echoed into the dark. With every jolt my leg begged to stop. Up ahead, I approached a small crossroads along the road south. There was a building, a rough box structure that served as both inn and post office for the county. I had been here once before on an outing with Molly.

I pulled up to the side entrance. It looked closed for the night, but when I tugged on the door it opened. The smell of whiskey and leather rushed out, filling my nostrils and creating a longing for drink. It would dull the pain, I told myself. The post-and-beam ceiling was low, and I stooped to enter, nearly stumbling on the rough wood floor. The lighting was poor, and behind me two other people sat at separate tables. An innkeeper nodded when I entered.

"You taking a room?" he asked.

"Dinner and some whiskey."

"Only if you're taking a room."

"Then I'll have a room." An hour or two of sleep would be useful before taking off again, especially with my leg. It was broken. The jump from the balcony should have been easy, but the theatre had hung extra banners. They caught my boot as I sailed over the railing, and I barely righted myself in time to land on the hard wood of the stage. I fell heavy and my left leg buckled. My only luck had been a horse tied up behind the theatre that got me over the Navy Yard Bridge and into Maryland.

The innkeeper brought a bowl of unrecognizable stew and a half-full bottle of whiskey. I handed a few dollars across the table.

"Is there a doctor in the county?" I asked.

"What's the trouble?"

"Horse threw me, hurt my leg." I kept it vague.

"I saw you was limping when you came in." He shook his head as he walked away. "Nearest doctor's about four miles south on a farm in Bryantown. He don't do house calls this late at night, you'd have to go to him. It's the Mudd farm you want. Samuel Mudd is the doctor."

"Thanks." I tasted the stew—truly wretched, but I was hungry. "How much to bed the horse down?"

"Another dollar for the night. You have to put her up."

I nodded and opened the whiskey. Despite the rough flavor, it felt good going down. I didn't want to drink too much, fearing I might not move. But I poured a second glass.

Maryland could not be counted as neutral ground, more like a hornets' nest of rebel dissent. During the War, it never brought arms against the Union, though it sent many of its sons to battle, flowing into the Army of Northern Virginia. I was far from safe and knew almost nothing of this state. All of Pinkerton's escape routes had been north, fleeing into friendly territory with the Old Man. I rarely ventured south, save a few occasions with Molly.

I finished my dinner, not wanting to move on my leg to go work the saddle off the horse. As I stared at my empty bowl, a rider arrived. The hoof falls were heavy as the rider pushed his beast to a steady run. Behind me, one of the other men sat with his head against the table—passed out under the whiskey. The other looked to be well on his way too.

The rider burst through the door so fast it startled me. My hand fell to my knife. The boy was young and agitated about something, barely glancing at us as he found the innkeeper.

"The President's dead!" he yelled.

I froze, the words crashed over me. The pain in my leg disappeared with the pitching of my stomach. The Old Man was gone—my knife had claimed another victim. I stared at the boy, waiting for more news.

"What?" the innkeeper came around the bar. "What's this?"

"Them Yanks are all riled up on the other side of the river, gettin' cavalry ready to come down here. The killer fled the city."

The innkeeper looked to me, then back at the boy. I drew my Bowie, keeping it out of sight and on my lap.

"What happened?" The innkeeper grabbed the boy. They knew one another.

"Don't know. But the man who killed the President hurt himself on fleeing. He's got a limp. I got to go spread the news."

I was mired deeper than ever. The entire Union would hunt me. The boy ran back out the door, leaving the innkeeper standing in the threshold. The excitement in the boy's voice affirmed that I sat not among friends. These people would celebrate the Old Man's death.

The innkeeper returned behind the bar. He glanced at me several times, then pulled a rifle from under the cabinets—a Spencer repeating rifle. My knife held nothing against him now.

He walked toward me, cocking the weapon to make certain it was loaded. The blood rushed to my face, my hands began to sweat. I had no way out, not with a broken leg and only a knife—even if I got him close.

The man stopped just short of my table and stared; he held the rifle across his chest, ready to use it any moment.

"I'm from Virginia," he said. "Two years ago, they came for my son, moved him north to the factories. I haven't seen him since."

"They took my daughter."

They weren't the same people he spoke of, but he wouldn't know that.

He looked at the rifle and then placed it on the table in front of me.

"God bless you, sir. You'll need this. I'll pack some food, provisions for the road, and draw you a map to the doctor's. Sounds like you need to get a move on—they'll be here before long."

I stared at the rifle. I would need it. In an instant I had become the darling of the South—an enemy of the state.

That night, I followed the map right to the doctor's house. He put me up, after setting my leg and fashioning a pair of wood crutches. Dr. Mudd asked no questions, but knew the situation, the chaos the nation faced. He patched my arm too. I slept a few hours, but my slumber was rough. The sound of horsemen on the road outside the farm stirred me often. At one point they came to the house, but the doctor talked them out of a search. I barely avoided capture.

Before leaving, he handed me another map, another safe house. I had stumbled onto a different kind of Underground Railroad, one of rebel devise. I was now a ward of the rebels, passed from one sympathizer to another—an unexpected consequence during my flight south. I had long considered these people as hostile, especially with a price on my head from Norris. In a bitter irony, my enemy had become my savior.

During the day I stayed off the road as much as possible, preferring to ride as evening fell. The darkness obscured my retreat. At the next farmstead, they put me up for a night after I used my map as a letter of introduction. They took it from me and provided another, farther south, away from Washington and deeper into rebel land. I traveled under the moniker *Smith,* not daring to reveal my name. If Norris were alive, he would have liked this turn of events. I wondered if Pinkerton still lived. I figured him caught for aiding in my plot.

At the final safe house in Maryland, they passed me to a rebel agent—an idealistic young man who kept an incessant conversation going. I sipped whiskey through my flask, hoping to dull the pain. The doctor had given me a vial of opium, but I was loath to use it, worried I would fall under too heavy a fog to defend myself. I kept it for later, in case I found a safe time and place.

That afternoon we crossed the Potomac River. At first we tried the ferry, but it was on the other side and not due back for a time. When I pressed on the urgency of not waiting for federal troops to arrive, the young agent bartered the use of a small fishing skiff. We paid for it, and the two of us battled against the current to make it across the river.

The atmosphere on the other side appeared more relaxed. We landed in Virginia, and news of the President's demise hadn't arrived this far south. No one spoke of it. No cavalry troops harassed the countryside. Since Virginia had long been a hot seat for the rebellion, the occupying federal authorities forced information to a crawl. They wanted to cripple the rebels by any means possible, so searching the mail and controlling the flow of news was critical.

The young man brought me to a farmstead, a tobacco farm south of Port Royal. The family there made no mention of the President. My companion left me with this family. They seemed none too happy to have me, providing a place in the barn to sleep and wait my new friend's return. I sent him into town for information, for anything that would aid our flight. I was thankful for the barn. Sleep would find me without any social obligation, and I wouldn't have to be guarded in my speech. It would clear my head and let me think about my next move.

At the top of the barn I fixed a bed of straw. It was an ideal place to watch for anyone who entered, and the Spencer rifle would make short work of them. My leg ached, more than the whiskey could dull. There would be no way to sleep through the throbbing pain. I took out the bottle of opiates. A small cork stoppered the bottle. I pulled it with my teeth and smelled the drink. No odor rose above that of my whiskey, so I pushed the bottle to my lips and drank. It held a mean, bitter aftertaste, and I forced a swig of whiskey to chase it down. As the drug took over, my body relaxed, a warm glow extended to my arms. My fingers went numb, a comfortable tingling the only sensation. I saw the Old Man, the look on his face as I left. And then Molly— as I closed my eyes I pressed my face into the small of her neck, breathing deep into her hair.

It seemed I had barely fallen asleep when the sound of horses jolted me awake. Night still reigned, and it took a moment to gain my bearings. I sat upright and limped to the window at the top of the barn facing the house. They had it surrounded— federal cavalry everywhere. The riders carried torches, circling the small farmhouse. It was stupid to take the opium, my sleep too deep when they approached. I rushed to the far side of the barn and looked out the back into the tree line. It wasn't that far.

I headed to the ladder when a voice broke through the noise of horses outside. It was directed at the barn.

"Joseph Foster!"

I recognized it—deep and commanding, back to its full vibrancy. It had me lost.

It was Pinkerton.

I froze, standing on the top floor of the barn, clutching the rifle. *Why was Pinkerton here?*

"Joseph, I'm coming in to talk."

I positioned myself where I had easy aim to the front of the barn. The door opened. Pinkerton stepped past the threshold with both hands held high.

"Where are you, Joseph?"

"What's going on?" I called back. I drew a bead with the rifle, placing the front sight on his chest. If he had double-crossed me, I would make certain he died before me.

"Come down from there, son. We have much to do before dawn." His voice lowered, more of a hiss, like he didn't want those outside to hear.

"I don't understand." I held my ground on the second floor. "I didn't kill the President."

"I know that," Pinkerton said. "He's alive! Tough old man. But, unfortunately, there's a hundred thousand dollars on your head—dead or alive. You can thank the Barons for that. They still control the newspapers and have called it an assassination attempt."

"It was the Black Fox."

"I know. The *Gray Devil.*" Pinkerton shook his head. "I knew of him during the War—merciless bastard. He would shoot his own men if they were too far gone, not wanting to be slowed by tending to the wounded."

"Do you have him?"

"Not yet. But I have everyone I can muster looking. He fled the city. We'll prove you had nothing to do with all this, and, when I can get the reporters in front of the President, we'll straighten out the papers. The Barons were hoping someone would get to you before I found you. Their power is crumbling. Using you as a scapegoat was their only option."

"But the President...won't they still use him?" I asked.

"He resigned two days ago. President Johnson was sworn into office in secrecy. We'll bring it all down, then announce the switch. But before the Old Man resigned, he issued several executive orders. The Draft lotteries are canceled—the children in the factories were all dismissed. They'll head home soon! He issued the vote for the South. The Barons will mount some challenge to it all, no doubt, but with no Lamon to control the new president, and elections only months away, this country will be very different. This bitch of a War is all but dead. She'll die with Lamon—fitting, if you ask me. He loved her so."

"So you're here to bring me in?" I asked.

"Hell no! That's the quickest way to get you dead. President Johnson knows the truth, but it will take some doing to get your name cleared. Come down, I don't want the world to hear everything."

I struggled down the ladder, keeping most of my weight on my right leg.

"You did hurt yourself," Pinkerton said.

"Broke it. A doctor set it a while back, but it's hurting."

Pinkerton motioned for me to follow as he crossed the barn to the far side, the one facing the tree line. He opened the door and gestured outside for someone to come in. A man stepped out of the woods, pulling a horse behind him. A canvas-covered lump straddled the beast—the shape of a man, or a body.

The man walked the horse into the barn, and he helped Pinkerton lay the body on the floor. Pinkerton motioned back to the woods.

"Wait for us out back," he told the man. He wore a gold badge—one of Pinkerton's detectives.

"You got your men back," I said.

Pinkerton smiled, in a fine mood. "I got everything back,

thanks to you. I'm alive again. And so is the nation. The yoke of War will lift, and it will set us all free!"

He knelt down and cut open the canvas bag. It was stitched across the face, a makeshift body bag. As it opened I recognized the dead man—Lamon. A hole centered in his forehead. The entrance wound from a .44-caliber ball. Powder burns smeared across his face.

"Everyone in Washington believes Lamon went missing. And that's perfect. It will keep the Barons off guard until they finally give him up as dead."

"So why'd you bring him here?"

"To protect you and the President at the same time, Joseph."

"I don't understand."

"In another minute, I'm going to leave. I'll tell the cavalry that you refuse to surrender, that you're crazed and won't trust me. We'll fire the barn to smoke you out, and by the time the fire has died, all we'll find is a body."

"We fake my death?"

"Exactly. You can go back to obscurity. No more running. Make a new life."

"Why don't we just lift the price on my head?"

"We will, but even after we clear your name, it wouldn't do much. The Barons want you dead. And when they figure out what happened they will settle for nothing less. Your only safety is in death. Embrace it."

"So I die here, and you take care of Lamon's body at the same time."

Pinkerton nodded. "And in so doing, we protect the President. The country heals. And you...," Pinkerton paused, "you take care of that little girl and go find Molly. Think you can do that? Your last act as a presidential bodyguard?"

"What will happen to the Old Man?"

"I thought leaving the office would kill him—that you might have to do it yourself. Whatever you told him, it worked. He wants to live. That wound from your knife lost him a lot of blood, but he's a fighter. The doctors say it will be a few weeks before he's up and moving again, but I haven't seen him like this in years. He's alive too. The entire nation will be born again, Joseph."

"Did he say anything about his plans?" I asked.

"Nothing, but he left this for you." Pinkerton took out an envelope.

I tore open the top and opened the note.

April 19, 1872

Joseph,

When you have a chance, I would like to meet Emeline. Please bring her at your convenience. I am forever in your debt.

—A. Lincoln

"There's one more thing," Pinkerton said. He removed a photograph from his suit pocket and handed it to me. It was of Norris, sitting next to a little boy—his missing grandson. They were seated in high-back cushioned chairs, with a younger man and young girl standing behind them.

"What's this?"

"Look at the photograph," Pinkerton said.

I studied it for a moment. "It's Norris' grandson. I wrote my mother to find him. That was Norris' idea. Did she?"

"I'm told she did. But look closer."

I turned back to the photograph. Norris didn't seem so evil in it—just a man sitting with his family. His hand extended to hold the little hand of his grandson. We all have a human side, even men like Norris.

I shrugged and handed it back to Pinkerton.

"Have you forgotten everything I taught you?" He pushed the photograph toward me. "Look again."

Pinkerton wanted to tell me something, but I had to see it first. I examined the man standing behind Norris. It must have been his son, the one killed in a raid on federal troops. They looked close enough to be kin. But the face of the girl standing with him was undeniable—like looking at my wife. She wore a silver chain around her neck, and, although the image wasn't in perfect focus, it looked like the chain held a silver eagle's feather. I turned to Pinkerton.

"We found Aurora. Norris had kept her. He treated her like a daughter," he paused. "He made her part of his family."

I stared at her, the little girl who had followed me all over Washington. I never believed I would see her again, even in a photograph. She'd grown, and she was beautiful. My eyes welled and my stomach turned. "Where is she?"

"She's still south. But I sent word to your mother. She's already left to get her. There is no better conductor than your mother. If anyone can find her, she will. I think it's time you went home. You've earned it."

I stared at the photograph.

"Come on," Pinkerton said. "Change your clothes. We're going to make this look good. I have another set for you."

I changed, placing my belongings in a neat pile—my flask, the marshal's star, and the Bowie—all I had left. I changed as Pinkerton struggled to dress Lamon in my clothes.

"You'll head out the back," Pinkerton said. "My detectives are covering the tree line. They'll take you to the nearest railroad, and from there, you disappear."

I looked down at the shoddily dressed Lamon. "Will they believe this? He doesn't much look like me. He's a bit taller."

"No one will question it. You can take your things, except...," Pinkerton paused.

"Except what?"

"Except that knife of yours. Everyone knows you have it—that you would die with it. When they find a burnt body with that knife, no one will question that you perished in the fire. That will be what the newspapers publish."

I picked up my Bowie. It had been with me so long. My fingers ran over the worn wood of the handle, the pitted and tarnished blade. I was naked without it.

"You have to leave it, Joseph. I have no others that could substitute. And it's best. You need to start fresh. Leave it."

I unsheathed it one last time—the knife that had killed Booth. It was so perfectly balanced—a tool of destruction that had no equal. My fingers traced the blade, the two wolves battling inside me. He was right. It represented the past, the conflict within that had started the moment of my conception as my mother plunged this very blade into the man that fathered me.

I tossed it onto Lamon's chest.

Pinkerton produced a small flask of liquid. It smelled like kerosene when he poured it onto Lamon's body.

"It'll burn fast. You better leave."

He held out his hand. I grasped it.

"I have to train your replacement. President Johnson will need protection, I suspect," he said.

"But you love it."

Pinkerton smiled. "I do. Now go, and give my regards to Molly."

He turned and walked to the front of the barn. I made my way to the back, but I paused to see him standing at the far door. He tipped his hat, then stepped out toward the cavalry. I waited until his door closed, glancing back at Lamon's body—my Bowie still lying on his chest.

Then I opened the door and stepped into the dawn.

CHAPTER TWENTY-FOUR

The sound from the iron rails slowed as the train approached Yellow Springs, the small town I knew so well. Molly would be there with Emeline at my mother's house. I wasn't sure how many years it had been since last I saw her. We had walked runaways along this very route north from Cincinnati, scurrying into the woods with the sound of an oncoming train. I was so close.

I stood in the place between the car and the caboose. My leg ached, the bracing of the splint dug into my calf. And my arm was still sore, though it was healing, and I would pull the stitches in another week. As I leaned on a makeshift cane, I pulled out my flask and unscrewed the lid. Lifting it to my lips, I thought better of it. I still needed it, but I didn't want to. Not now.

I held the opened flask over the rail and upended it, watching the liquid pour out into the blur of the ties and rail bed below. When the flask emptied, I dropped it. The pewter clanked as it hit the ground, skipping along as the train pulled away. It felt good to cast off such things. No longer did I want the flask. It was like my Bowie—lost.

Above me, a crow landed on the roof of the caboose. It cawed at the sound of the flask hitting the rails and stretched his neck to look at me. I startled, never having seen a bird on a moving train, let alone a crow so big. I leaned against the car as I gripped the rail. His wings were tattered, but his feathers were black as a starless night. I held the railing, transfixed on the bird.

He stretched his wings and then lifted into the air, soaring above us along the track. I craned around the caboose, my hands turning white-knuckled in their grip. I didn't want to believe the superstitions of my mother's legends, but, in truth, I had never entirely dismissed them. He flew off and to his left—*a herald of death*.

I shook the feeling from my head, but a general uneasiness took hold. We were only a few miles short of the station, and I yearned to see Molly, to make certain with my own eyes. The wait was torture.

I walked down the aisle and sat. Lying back in the seat, I looked down at the floor. The man across from me held a paper, the headlines filled with stories about me, the bodyguard turned would-be assassin. They used old photographs, which held little likeness to the man I had become. That was fortunate. I was a public fascination. The editorials were full of conspiracy theories, ranging my motives from complex to outright bizarre. In time it would fade as Pinkerton released the truth.

The man slowly turned the pages as I noticed his hands—thin skin, delicate fingers. He lowered the paper, revealing a face as white as his hands, a gash running from one eye to his lip, where I had gouged it with the marshal's star. I stared at the devil.

"You've been difficult to track, Joseph." His pronunciation was immaculate through his slow southern drawl. It betrayed his elevated upbringing.

"How...?" My voice trailed off.

"Finding people is my specialty. And when I am done with you, I will seek out your daughter."

His right hand dropped to the butt of his pistol. Fear trapped me—there was no escape from this seat. I sat paralyzed, powerless to save myself. Even in my prime, I was no match for this man.

"I didn't kill her," I said. "I loved her. I would never hurt her."

"That include the whore you kept? How about a child conceived before a wedding? Is that what you mean by love?"

A wave of shame washed over me. In a fashion, I had no argument. But even if my marriage had come as a necessity before Aurora arrived, I had loved my wife—long before the relationship fell apart, and before Molly. There would be no explaining it to this man.

"I followed those men." The anger rose, the bitter taste filled my mouth. My paralysis faded. "I killed every last one of them.

Colonel Norris ordered the mission that killed your sister. You worked for him."

"Colonel Norris apologized to my family and my father. For his mistake, he allowed the child of your marriage to live. He treated her as one of his family after we would not take her in."

My face flushed. They had rejected Aurora. Despite my sins, she was innocent. This man and his family hated me so much that they couldn't see their way to care for a three-year-old child—their own blood.

"Why kill Norris?" I asked.

His hand caressed his pistol. "There would always come a day when he would pay for his transgression, but he led our cause, and my father insisted he live until we no longer needed him. After losing his son he became soft, asking for peace from men like Mr. Lamon and Mr. Lincoln. His grip on the rebellion had slipped. It called for a new leader to cast out your armies of occupation and free our Southern nation."

"And you will take his place, appointed by Lamon himself?"

He paused, studying me. "I would never work for Lamon. I deceived him in that regard, to gain his confidence before invigorating our fight. Lamon wants the Draft to continue, to expand. That is exactly what the South needs, to see the oppression of the North and to rise up to cast it out. The tide of my Southern nation will turn with the right man at its helm. There are few as qualified. I believed I had even taken Mr. Lincoln to his grave, though the papers now report him to have survived." He paused as he shifted on the bench. "His time will come again, and you will not be here to see our glorious rise. My father wished nothing more than to see you dead. He didn't live to see this day, but he will know it as he looks down on us."

"If you shunned your sister, why would you care what became of her?"

The Black Fox reached into his jacket and produced a letter. He threw it at me. The paper landed in my lap.

"She was leaving. After you defended that abomination of a

president, she knew her duty was to return to her family. My father welcomed her back, but your actions killed her before she had the chance to make it to us."

I opened the letter. The paper contained my wife's handwriting, beautiful and flowing. Her upbringing impeccable, an education by the finest tutors the South had to offer. She had planned to leave—she should have.

"Get on with it," I muttered.

His smile dropped. He saw the change in my demeanor.

"Don't think about your knife. You will not steal my—"

I cut him off as I dropped my hand to where the Bowie should have been. This wasn't part of his plan. He pulled his pistol, and I lunged across the aisle, hoping to catch it in the holster. He was fast.

I didn't hear the shot. I felt it—a sledgehammer hit me in the side. The blast from the powder was so close it burned my skin. I sensed no pain, only pressure, immense pressure. My hand found the barrel of his gun and pushed it past my body. He fired again, the bullet slammed into the seat behind me. The barrel singed my palm, but I didn't let go. I collapsed upon him and dragged the barrel between us, angling it under his chin. My other hand fought for the trigger. I managed to force the hammer back and pull. Blood splattered across my face and in my eyes. But he had moved the gun. The bullet caught him somewhere in the shoulder. We wrestled for the weapon, flailing it back and forth. There were screams around us; passengers leapt from their seats. Our window broke as the pistol struck it. The gun flew from our grip and out the train.

My fist crashed down on his face, but a sharp pain surged through my body. I had little power. He countered and slammed my side with a knee. It almost blinded me. Fighting to breathe, my vision narrowed for a second. I grabbed his jacket and knocked our heads together. His hands grabbed his face. Blood from his nose gushed on both of us.

Scrambling on my hands and knees, I made it partway down

the aisle before attempting to stand. He still sat, wiping the blood from his vision. I limped in the direction of the caboose. A fire axe was bolted on the outside of the train where I had stood to empty my flask. It was the only weapon I remembered. I had left my cane behind, and my leg and side ached with each step. Scared faces looked at me as I passed—people cowered in their seats and gave me wide berth.

The noise of the rails flooded in as I opened the door. We were going much slower now, and if not for my leg, I could jump to safety. I stepped onto the ledge between the car and caboose to pull at the axe. It wouldn't budge. Leveraging it to the side, I freed the handle and tugged desperately. I didn't have my full strength.

He struggled down the aisle, holding his shoulder where he had been shot. I leaned with all my weight against the handle. The head of the axe dislodged, and I fell hard against the railing of the car. It buckled and broke free. For a moment, I held the rusted metal, feeling it tearing into my palm as my fingers slipped. It felt like forever as I fell backward off the train. I landed hard on my back and slid down the sides of the rails. My head barely missed being thrown under the caboose. The axe fell off the car and landed farther up the tracks. The train continued its journey north as I lay in the dirt breathless, watching the caboose pull away. Pain radiated from my side and my leg. I vomited. I wasn't sure what I had landed on, but my hands were torn and my back hurt.

He appeared at the back of the caboose. For a moment, he searched the rails. I froze, remaining as still as I could manage. Then, with a fluid motion, he jumped off the end of the car and landed perfectly on the wooden ties between the rails, kneeling to maintain his balance—the grace of a cat. This was a mythical beast, not a man. Slowly, he stood. He took a few steps, and bent to pick up the axe.

CHAPTER TWENTY-FIVE

I struggled to my feet as my stomach resisted. Dry heaves left me doubled over, but I managed to stumble along the rails. I checked over my shoulder. He was hurt but still coming, dragging the head of the axe along the steel rail. The grating reverberated up and down the tracks until it drowned my thoughts. He would torture me until he could kill me.

Looking around, there were no weapons—no loose branches, no large rocks. I was nothing against this man. Fleeing was my only option, but I had one advantage. I had been here before and knew the town well. I headed into the woods, east down the ravine toward the creek. A gristmill sat at the bottom, Moody's Mill, and a nearby colony founded by escaped slaves. When we lived here my mother would send me to the mill for flour. I would find people there, someone to help—or at least a weapon. I slipped and fell several times. I collided with trees and slid down the slope, leaving traces of blood on the bark, either from my side or from the hand I used to stem the bleeding. Every time I looked behind me, he had gained. I picked myself up and pressed on.

At the creek, I waded across and headed downstream. The mill perched on a giant limestone foundation with a large, under-shot waterwheel. The wheel turned, propelled by the current. At the front door I banged with my fist. It left flecks of red paint embedded in the side of my hand. No one answered. I tugged at the sliding door, and it opened. I pulled it enough to slip through.

"Help!" I yelled into the millworks.

The only reply came from the groaning of the large axle attached to the waterwheel. Machinery filled the lower floor of the building, turning gears and belts connected to the grist sifters. They made a musical sound as wood gears met under the force of the water. The millstones were pulled apart, and someone had started dressing the large stones with a mill pick—a small, hammer-like tool with a pointed end to strike the rock. I found no other weapon, so I hobbled toward the millstone.

Behind me, his footsteps fell heavy on the wood deck outside. I turned to the door. I hadn't pulled it closed or barricaded it shut. The axe head dropped against the wood in regular intervals, as if he used it as a walking stick. He meant it as torture, signaling he was coming. In a moment there would be no escape. I searched out a place to hide, but I saw no use staying among the turning gears and belts. I was barely steady on my feet, and I didn't fancy being crushed if I lost my footing.

I headed to the stairs. As a child, I had run up and down them, hiding in the office on the second floor. Leaning on the railing, I pulled myself up a stair at a time. My hands were wet and sticky from the blood loss, and several times they slipped. I didn't have much fight.

The second floor was mostly empty—storage, nothing of use. A few sacks of flour sat in the corner with a coil of rope. I could heft one and toss it down the stairs, but the pain in my shoulder made me think better of it. I hadn't the strength. Some heavy wood planks leaned against the wall behind me, but they were also far too heavy to lift, let alone use as a weapon. The office held a desk with a ledger and writing supplies, but nothing to fight with. The mill pick would have to suffice, even though it fell short against an axe.

In the main storage area, sunlight streamed through a doorway along the back wall. I struggled in that direction and pushed it open. It was a large utility door with a huge, overhead beam extending outside the building. A block and tackle hung from the far end of the beam, directly above the spinning waterwheel. It was used to maintain the wheel, to pull it out of the current for repairs. There were no stairs, but a rope hung from the beam. In the distance, I saw a few men up along the road. They carried lumber and a saw between them. If I swung down and made it to the road, my odds greatly increased. Molly was somewhere in the town. I could find her. I let the mill pick drop to the wood floor, and I pulled the rope in my hand to loop it around my grip.

Behind me, his feet fell heavy on the stairs, moving a step at a time. He walked slowly, stretching out the hunt. I looked to the ground below, planning on how I would lower myself down and where I would flee. I had to cross the creek and scramble up a small incline to the roadbed. With my weight on the rope, the rough twine cut into my skin and rubbed the cuts raw on my palm. The pain felt good.

I stopped. The other wolf inside me woke again.

There was no outrunning the devil. He would keep coming. And if he replaced Norris, then he held the last embers of the fight. He could revive the fire of conflict—resurrect the dying War. I had never been the warrior to match him, but, if I fled, it would never be over. He would hunt until he finished me, and he would find Aurora, and Molly. Running toward Molly and Emeline only put them in danger. If I wanted to be free, truly free, I had to finish it. I had run from everything too long—from Norris, from the Old Man, from Molly. That was my past, and it had to die like the War.

I stooped to pick up the small mill pick. Slowly, I shifted it back and forth in my grip, wiping one hand against my trousers, ridding it from the blood that robbed my grip. There was too much of it.

Halfway up the stairs, I saw the top of his head, then his upper body. He said nothing. Step by step, he inched closer. A pale façade gripped his face, worse than back in the train. His wounds drained him too.

"No more running." His words formed through a hissing sound as he gritted his teeth.

He stood on the top step and leaned on the axe. We stared at one another. The wolf begged me to lunge forward and tear this man apart, to pull him to pieces as my fingers dug into his flesh. But my side would explode, and my leg was too weak, sending pins through my back each time I bore full weight on it.

Taking the last step, he swung the axe onto his shoulder and began to circle toward me. My grip tightened. The mill pick compared in size to a small hatchet. I had my mother to thank for small lessons, like hunting rabbits in the bush.

As he rushed and swung the axe, I threw the pick. It sailed between us and hit him in the face. Unused to the balance of the weapon, I had timed the rotation wrong. Only the wood handle struck him, but it hit an eye. His swing died, and the axe landed in an arc between us. The blade embedded in the floor. When he covered his face, I pried him from the axe handle and threw him to the floor.

For a moment I found myself on top, then he rolled me. He was little more than a skeleton, and I managed to flip him back over, using my weight as leverage. The pain in my side over-whelmed me, and I vomited what I had in my stomach. It covered his face and shirt—he fought desperately to clear his vision. My hands found his neck, and I squeezed. Raising his head, I slammed it to the floor. A sick dull thud filled the room—like when Molly struck Baxter over the head. As I rode him forward, I used a knee to trap one of his arms. His other hand reached out to gouge my face.

But I didn't let up. I leaned with all my weight. His face turned red, a hideous sound came from his throat. His feet thrashed, his heels kicking against the wood floor underneath us. Still, I held on, crushing with every ounce I had. As his fight slowed, something came over me.

My mother would have called it a sign from the Great Spirit—the other wolf. I had killed so many, and the Spirit had for so long abandoned me. My hands let up. He writhed slowly underneath. As I sat up and released his neck, he gasped for air. Both of his hands reached for his neck as if they could open his throat wider.

I rolled off him and stood. Walking over to the axe, I pried it from the floor. With both hands on the weapon, I towered over him. His gasping slowed as he stared. The wolves tore inside me, locked in their own battle. If I didn't kill this man, he would hunt me. He had forsaken Aurora, and he would come again to kill. But I had so long fed that first wolf.

I raised the axe and swung it down on top of him with all my might. Pain surged through my body as the blade made contact, the steel buried into the floor right next to his head. It cut his blond hair and nicked his ear. He didn't move. Then he coughed again and clutched at his throat. I started toward the rope. I would drag him to the sheriff and send a telegram to Pinkerton. He needed to live, if only to expose him and crush the rebellion with his capture. They needed no other martyr after Norris—no other banner to rally behind.

I reached the rope, but behind me he struggled to his feet. When I turned, he was standing. His hatred burned as deep as ever. He pulled at the axe while watching me. It had buried deep in the wood flooring, but it broke free when he put all his weight against the handle. Stumbling backward, he caught himself in time. His back foot rested on the edge of the open utility door. A smile spread across his face as he looked over his shoulder to the waterwheel below. He turned to me, switching the axe between his hands.

As he stepped forward, something flashed across the doorway behind him—the crow. It flew back into sight and landed on top of the great beam. Its massive wings beat the air as it fought to keep its landing. A raspy cawing filled the room.

The great bird startled him. He swung the axe wildly, as if someone attacked from behind. The weight of the weapon pulled him off balance. There wasn't enough floor as he took a step to recover. His foot landed on air, and he plunged out the door. No sound came from below—no body hitting the ground, no scream of pain.

I stood. The great crow tilted its head and stared. The moments stretched on with the bird sizing me up. My heart beat in my side, and I clutched my wound with one hand. Without a sound, the crow dove off the beam and glided out of sight.

CHAPTER TWENTY-SIX

I woke in a bed. It was large and soft, a comforter spread from my feet to my lap. My leg ached and my side hurt. I didn't recognize the room. I shifted, taking stock of my surroundings. A night table stood next to me. It held the photograph of Aurora and the marshal's star I had used to gouge the Black Fox. From the window, the afternoon sun fell on the bed. When I turned to the other side, a little boy stood in the doorway. I knew him from the photograph—Norris' grandson.

He stared at me from a safe distance, watching my every move. I reached out for the night table and grabbed the marshal's star. I held it out for him. He walked into the room, just far enough that he could take it from my outstretched fingers.

"If you come here," I told him, "I can pin it on."

He remained motionless, studying me. He didn't know if he wanted to come too close.

Then a voice echoed through the door, as footsteps fell on stairs.

"Daniel, it's time for lunch."

It was Molly.

"I'm up here," I called out.

She rushed up the stairs and into the room, brushing past the little boy to the bedside.

"You're awake," she said. She clutched at my shirt with both hands as she sat on the side of the bed. "Damn you, Joseph. Don't you do this to me again. You hear me? I thought I would lose you!" Her face was flushed with her temper flared.

"I hurt everywhere, Molly."

Slowly, she let go of my shirt. I reached up and grabbed a hand. She pulled it away from me.

"The doctor left not too long ago. He bandaged your side and left medicine."

"Where are we?" I asked. "How'd I get here?"

"We're at your mother's, where you sent us. Emeline's downstairs." Her breathing slowed.

"How did I get here?"

"They found you in the mill, passed out upstairs. What happened, Joseph? The newspapers...," she couldn't finish her thought. "I thought you were dead when they brought you in."

"Molly, I didn't do it," I said. "The Old Man's alive." I wasn't sure what she had read, or if the papers had published the truth yet.

"We heard yesterday. But who was he? That man? The one they found at the mill?"

"Is he...," I stopped. "Is he dead?"

She nodded. "They had to take the wheel off to get him loose. Who was he?"

"It doesn't matter." I wanted it all behind us.

"The Black Fox?" She lowered her voice to a whisper.

I nodded. "He's gone. We're safe." I paused as I looked at her, reaching for the side of her face. "You'll stay?"

"Of course." She wiped her eyes.

"No, Molly. I mean it. You'll stay with me?"

She gripped the hand that held her face. "Yes, Joseph. I will. But what will we do?"

I shook my head. "We need a quiet place—somewhere to settle for a while. Pinkerton thinks people may still come, but I don't want to run anymore. I'm tired. Eventually, I have to find the Old Man."

"No more trips, Joseph. We need you here." Her tone became sharp again.

"We'll all go. He needs to meet her."

"Emeline?"

I nodded. "Where's my mother, is she here?"

Molly's eyes welled up. "No. She left a few days ago. Pinkerton sent a telegram. She went looking for Aurora. Daniel here knew enough to tell us where to find her, on a small farm in Georgia. Norris' place. Georgia's a big state, and we're not sure exactly where, but it's a start."

The little boy watched from a safe distance.

"He's been asking about her," Molly said. "He has no one else. They're all gone."

"I know." I took Molly's hand, thinking about how the Black Fox and his family had rejected Aurora. "He has us."

"Could we build a house?" she asked. "Somewhere where there are stars? I want to look at the stars at night."

From the corner of my eye, the little boy moved closer. He stared at the marshal's star in his hand. In a refined southern accent he spoke. "Aurora showed me the *Drinking Gourd*. It's in the stars. I can show you."

She remembered.

"I'd like that," I said. "Sometimes, I have trouble finding it."

CHAPTER TWENTY-SEVEN

The wagon jolted when it hit fresh ruts, bouncing Molly and Emeline in the back. The road was newly cut, winding up the slight grade from town toward Big Hill Pond. Much had changed in a year.

The last few miles were rougher still, and, at one point, we nearly dismounted to walk the horses in. But Molly protested, and would not leave her dress unattended. It was still wrapped in the packaging, and she wouldn't open it in front of me, citing bad luck. Her superstitions ran deep. When she was determined, I found it best not to fight her.

The great oak stood tall. It reached into the sky as it had the first day we laid eyes upon it. The small mound of stones had been replaced with a real grave, marked by a carved headstone. Farther along the creek a wretched cabin stood. It looked as if it might collapse in a strong wind, the sides made of scrap wood that were roughly cut. A trickle of smoke made its way from the chimney and into the sky. Even the stones of the chimney threatened to roll off the roof. At the side of the cabin, the Old Man stood with an axe in his hand. He had been chopping wood.

Emeline walked between Molly and me, holding each of our hands. The little boy walked on my far side, holding fast to my trousers. He had warmed to us, though he still asked about his mother. He had seen her shot before they seized him and brought him north to the factories. There was little we could do to heal that wound, other than to take him in.

Emeline skipped as we made our way across the meadow, bouncing and tugging at our arms. The Old Man buried his axe in an upright log and then wiped his brow with a cloth. From a distance, he looked years younger. When we came closer, Emeline let go and clutched Molly's dress. Maybe she recognized the place, or maybe it was the strange man.

"Miss Molly, is that my uncle?"

"It is, dear."

We hadn't told her the truth—not yet. The time would come for that, when she knew who to trust and how to keep it quiet otherwise. The Old Man stared at her as we walked up. His expression revealed none of what he was thinking. He met us along a narrow path in the tall grass, no cane in hand.

At first, he didn't say anything. He just stared at Emeline. Then, slowly, he knelt to her level. "My, you are tall. They must feed you too much, my child."

Emeline pulled at Molly's dress and looked to us. "Miss Molly said my father was tall."

The Old Man reached out and brushed her cheek. Emeline pulled closer to Molly. "Miss Molly is right."

He stood, pushing up on one knee to rise. "She is beautiful, Joseph—just as you described her." He still looked at Emeline while she played shy. "Thank you so much for bringing her. And it is so good to see you both. I have been practicing my part for Saturday, and I believe my memory is intact. I promise not to fumble over the words, and I will keep my remarks as short as Gettysburg, though a more joyous occasion it will be."

"You'll have another week to practice," I said. "We've met with a small delay."

"How's that, Joseph?"

"My mother will be a few more days."

"Oh, yes. I did forget to ask. Did she find her? Please tell me her search was not in vain."

"She telegrammed before she left Georgia. She found Aurora and will bring her straight here. It took us over a year—such is the state of the South. I nearly lost hope, but not my mother. She is tireless."

The little boy spoke, his voice faint. "That's my sister."

"How's that?" The Old Man asked.

"Aurora is my sister," the boy replied.

The Old Man looked to me, puzzled.

"This is Daniel," I said. "He's Colonel Norris' grandson."

"I see." The Old Man rubbed his chin. "Sister?"

"Norris took in Aurora. That was why it was so hard to find her. It's all the boy has known."

"Will you find his people?"

"No one is left. We are his people now."

The Old Man placed his hand on the boy's head and tousled his hair. "Well, that will be a joyous day to get your sister back." He spoke to me. "I know how long you have waited, and I dare say that I may know a little of how you feel."

"It will be as joyous as this day, Mr. *Mayor.*" Molly emphasized his new title while placing a hand on Emeline's head.

"Yes. Today is indeed incredible, Molly. So much so that I am a bit lost." He looked to Emeline. "And, as for my new job, it is surely a mistake that the good people of Essary Springs will undo at the next election," the Old Man said. "Politics was the last thing I planned. I intended to come see Annice, and then leave. But I found myself at a town council meeting, and they asked for a speech—they expected one. So I dredged up my old stories, the ones, Joseph, that you are most certainly sick of hearing. And they loved them! I did indeed bring down the house with laughter, and the lot of us stayed for several hours, discussing the state of the frontier. I am sure my fame will tarnish with time, but, until then, the politics of a little town are most refreshing. I hear complaints about chickens and cows, while back in Washington, President Johnson has barely escaped the impeachment vote. I am so relieved to be free of that burden."

"I told you, he would handle the fight well."

"Indeed. It was close. If the papers hold the account right, he kept the office by a single vote. It appears that, sometimes, one man's voice can be all that separates darkness from the light." The Old Man reached out to take hold of my shoulder. "But, as for more parochial matters, we are in need of a good sheriff in Essary Springs. I told the town council that I had a name in mind—someone perfect for us."

Molly reached out and took my hand, squeezing hard. "We're hoping for less adventure for a time."

"Well, that's a shame. This winter was most exciting. We had to find Mrs. Grayson's lost cow, and she turned up in her neighbor's barn. It was a long, mile walk to get her home. Identifying the branding marks was very stressful, Molly, so we may not want to put Joseph through all that."

"We can talk about it." I returned Molly's squeeze.

"Well, perhaps I can sweeten the deal, or so the saying around here goes. I happen to know the owner of this marvelous piece of land." He swung his hands out in all directions. "There is room aplenty for several houses. And you're in luck, because I also know something about building them."

I looked at the cabin behind him. "I'm sure we can manage something, sir."

Emeline tugged on Molly's hand. "Miss Molly, is this where we left Mommy?" She stared toward the great oak tree.

"Yes, dear." Emeline recognized the place.

The Old Man held out his hand. "Would you like to see her?"

Emeline looked to Molly.

"It's okay, you can go with your uncle," Molly coaxed.

The Old Man glanced between us. I shrugged. "Best we could come up with. We'll have time enough to discuss it all."

He nodded. Emeline reached for his open hand, and he grasped it like he would a flower, unsure of how to best hold something so delicate. If he had seen what the girl had been through, he would not have been so worried.

"There's a present from a mutual friend on the porch," he said over his shoulder.

Molly and I watched them walk toward the great oak tree. The past year had grown Emeline into a gregarious child. She warmed instantly, the earlier shy play I figured as a ruse for more attention.

"Did you know my mommy?"

"I did."

"And my father?"

"Yes."

"He was tall?"

"Yes. It is lucky you got her looks and his height, not the other way around."

Their chatter turned indiscernible in the wind.

"Complaints about chickens and cows. At least it's a change," Molly said.

"He loves it."

"No," Molly answered, "He *needs* it."

We made our way to the porch, the little boy at our heels. I wasn't sure the loose decking would hold my weight, and the whole structure groaned when I stepped onto it. An old table sat between two chairs, and on the table perched an expensive bottle of whiskey—Pinkerton's brand.

"I thought you didn't tell him," Molly said.

"I didn't. But he hears everything."

"Do you think he'll come?"

"Most likely," I muttered. A small tin sheriff's star next to the whiskey caught my attention. I picked it up. Molly watched as I ran my thumb over the surface of the star.

"I guess he figures we're staying," she said.

"Would you mind? From the looks of it, we need to stay long enough to rebuild this place." I reached out and held one of the porch supports. I dared not shake it. "And he needs some time with her."

"It seems a perfect place—quiet. I'll have my stars. But do you think anyone will come? Will the Barons send anyone?"

"They might. But no more running."

Molly leaned close. She placed a hand on my chest as she pulled me near. Taking the tin star from my hand, she pinned it to my jacket.

"They'd be fools to try. But if they do, we'll be fine," she said. "I know the sheriff."

AUTHOR'S NOTE

THE AMERICA THAT MIGHT HAVE BEEN

I read just about everything I can, but historical fiction holds a special place for me. A good historical is an antidote for the horrendously boring history texts I pored through in my youth. But until I tried my own hand at writing an historical novel, I never appreciated all the research that goes into even the smallest of details. It's not enough to have a great story, and to follow that up with good writing (hopefully), but you have to make the story fit into the context of the time period.

Anyone who has read *Lincoln's Bodyguard* will realize immediately that while it is a work of historical fiction, it's also a work of revisionist history. I've had the audacity to not only try to place my story in a unique time period in American history, but I've also taken the liberty of changing History herself. It comes from a simple question: *What would America have looked like if our greatest president had lived?*

To answer this, we need to look back on April 1865, one of the most pivotal months in American history. The Civil War had raged for four long years, and, slowly, the North had gained the upper hand through its sheer indomitable resources. Yet as April opened, Confederate forces led by General Lee were still firmly fixed in Richmond and Petersburg, Virginia, with General Grant leading the siege of the cities. Further South, Union General Tecumseh Sherman skirmished with Confederate General Joe Johnston. Knowing that the circumstances looked grim, Confederate President Jefferson Davis wrote to both Lee and Johnston, and instructed his generals to resort to guerilla warfare before surrender. It was President Lincoln's worst fear, that the Confederates would not surrender, but instead would melt back into the fabric of the South and never end the fighting. There was precedent in that fear.

The South had used small bands of partisans to hold back much larger advancing Union forces in the West, and Davis, Lee, and Johnston—all West Point graduates—had studied guerilla movements across the world that would be the basis for their plan.

Yet, as history would have it, General Lee became trapped near Appomattox Courthouse, Virginia. His army had tried to break out from Petersburg and Richmond in order to join forces with Johnston further south, but the better fed and equipped Union had cut off his retreat. He was faced with two options—surrender or disband his army into a guerilla force. Remembering the devastation that had been caused across Missouri by the bands of partisans, Lee chose surrender. It was April 9, 1865.

To President Lincoln, that was the first great sign that the War was coming to an end. But there were still almost 175,000 Confederate soldiers in three armies south of Virginia, and they were still at the fight. Even so, Lincoln allowed himself a night of distraction, to take his mind off the War. He headed to Ford's Theatre to catch a play with his wife. It was April 14, 1865, and, after that night, the nation would never again be the same.

After learning of Lee's surrender, General Johnston agreed to meet with Union General Sherman and negotiate terms for his own surrender. Johnston still had marching orders from Jefferson Davis to disband and fight on, and, indeed, he had nearly 90,000 men under his command, with a significant number of cavalry. It was a very real option. But on the first meeting with Sherman, the Union general handed Johnston a telegram from Washington, DC. President Lincoln had died. Johnston knew what it meant—the Union had a martyr, and Johnston and his army would be the focus of their revenge. The southern general disobeyed the orders of Jefferson Davis, surrendering his forces on April 26th. The last remaining Confederate generals followed suit, and the Great American Civil War came to an end.

So what would America have looked like if Lincoln had lived? It's an enticing question, and one that no one can answer with exact certainty. Lee surrendered before Lincoln's death, so the Army of Northern Virginia was already disbanded. But what about Johnston? Without that telegram from DC informing him of the president's death, he may well have followed Jefferson Davis' instructions. With 90,000 men at his disposal, he could have held up the Union indefinitely, retreating into expanses of mountains, forests, swamps, and rugged territory that littered the Confederacy. The Union would have been forced into an occupying role, needing many hundreds of thousands more soldiers to set up patrols and small bases to control the South. Even then, the attacks would be relentless. As a military officer who has spent three combat tours in Afghanistan, I have seen firsthand how a small insurgency can quagmire an entire army. General Grant sensed the potential strife to come, noting, "To overcome a truly popular, national resistance in a vast territory without the employment of truly overwhelming force is probably impossible." This is exactly the state of affairs we find in 1872 when *Lincoln's Bodyguard* opens. The South is still in rebellion, with a guerilla war embroiling the nation.

Faced with such a scenario, the reconstruction of the South would have been significantly delayed. Instead of setting up new state governments, and allowing southerners the vote after taking a loyalty pledge, the entire former Confederacy would have fallen under martial law. Without the southern vote, Lincoln would certainly have won a third term in office in 1868, as term limits were not established until the 22nd Amendment to the Constitution in 1947. This was also the time period of the Second Industrial Revolution, where the North was rapidly developing manufacturing capabilities to compete with England and other European industrial powers. So the rising industrial Barons would have directly competed for labor against the ever-increasing needs of the army in the South. The political power of the corporations and their influence would have been a strong force, like today. The Draft, where children of former Confederates were sent north to work the factories, would have been a horrible yet effective way to fill the factories and even punish the South, especially considering that throughout the 1800s child labor was commonplace. Again, the narrative of the novel imagines scenarios that could have been our history, considering the increasingly dire state of the nation.

Against this backdrop, Lincoln's bodyguard, Joseph Foster, returns to the White House at the request of his president. As he is sent south on his secret mission, he sees the effects of insurgent warfare, and the intolerant policies like the Draft that do more to fuel the fires of conflict rather than to douse the fight. He also finds the Underground Railroad active again, this time moving children south instead of sending escaped slaves north. The Quakers and other abolitionists who fought so hard against slavery would certainly have been opposed to the Draft, which, in a turn of fate, enslaved white children in northern factories. They would have fought back in the same manner, with the same techniques that had ferried thousands of enslaved Americans to freedom.

While we'll never know for sure what would have happened if Lincoln had lived, the reality certainly would have been much messier than the myth of a popular and forgiving Lincoln. Lincoln's reputation as our greatest president was not something shared in the 1860s, but has come from the lens of time and reflection. And he may have known, or at least suspected, that his own death was a necessary part of the healing of the nation. He told his confidant and friend, Ward Hill Lamon, about premonitions of his own death, just a mere ten days before his assassination. According to Lamon, Lincoln had a dream where he was killed by an assassin, and "although it was only a dream, I have been strangely annoyed by it ever since." Ultimately, John Wilkes Booth may have done more to hurt his Southern cause than anything that had come before him. Lincoln's death was a final act of revenge by the South, yet it ushered in the surrender of several southern armies and an end to hostilities.

While *Lincoln's Bodyguard* is a work of alternative fiction, it actually sets out to disturb history for only a short time period. By saving the President, Joseph derails the original timeline from the moment of the actual assassination. The rest of the novel shows how history rights herself seven years later and brings the nation back to the course we know. During the climactic scene where Lincoln confronts Lamon at Ford's Theatre, Joseph is left to escape after the struggle. In a tip of the hat to actual events, Joseph escapes along the exact route that Booth took in April 1865, jumping from the balcony, breaking his leg, fleeing on horseback, and escaping over the Navy Bridge into Maryland, rendezvousing at the roadside tavern to retrieve a weapon, traveling to Dr. Mudd's house to set his leg, and, ultimately, being captured at the same tobacco farm in Virginia.

Along the way, we see the raw realities that were part of life in the post-Civil War United States, particularly in the South. We remember just how close the nation came to fracturing, and yet Joseph's mission is one that will ultimately provide what Lincoln called for in his famous Gettysburg Address: "a new birth of freedom, and that government of the people by the people for the people, shall not perish from the earth."

My research drew from many writers and historians, but, for additional reading, I highly recommend the select few sources here. They are written in a manner accessible to the nonhistorian, and bring history alive in exciting narratives that will make you see the nation's greatest conflict through a new perspective.

Select Bibliography:

April 1865: The Month that Saved America by Jay Winik

Abraham Lincoln: The Man Behind the Myths by Stephen B. Oates

Manhunt: The 12-Day Chase for Lincoln's Killer by James L. Swanson

Lincoln As I Knew Him: Gossip, Tributes, and Revelations from His Best Friends and Worst Enemies by Harold Holzer